GU00862532

Rafael Sabatini, creator of some of
was born in Italy in 1875 and ed
Switzerland. He eventually settled ir
time he was fluent in a total of five languages. He chose to write in
English, claiming that 'all the best stories are written in English.'

His writing career was launched in the 1890s with a collection of
short stories, and it was not until 1902 that his first novel was
published. His fame, however, came with *Scaramouche*, the much-
loved story of the French Revolution, which became an international
bestseller. *Captain Blood* followed soon after which resulted in a
renewed enthusiasm for his earlier work.

For many years a prolific writer, he was forced to abandon writing
in the 1940s through illness and he eventually died in 1950.

Sabatini is best remembered for his heroic characters and high-
spirited novels, many of which have been adapted into classic films,
including *Scaramouche, Captain Blood* and *The Sea Hawk* starring
Errol Flynn.

The Banner of the Bull

Rafael Sabatini

HOUSE OF
STRATUS

Copyright © Rafael Sabatini

All rights reserved. No part of this publication may be reproduced, stored in a retrieval system, or transmitted, in any form, or by any means (electronic, mechanical, photocopying, recording, or otherwise), without the prior permission of the publisher. Any person who does any unauthorised act in relation to this publication may be liable to criminal prosecution and civil claims for damages.

The right of Rafael Sabatini to be identified as the author of this work has been asserted in accordance with sections 77 and 78 of the Copyright, Designs and Patents Act 1988.

This edition published in 2001 by House of Stratus, an imprint of Stratus Holdings plc, 24c Old Burlington Street, London, W1X 1RL, UK.

www.houseofstratus.com

Typeset, printed and bound by House of Stratus.

A catalogue record for this book is available from the British Library.

ISBN 1-84232-798-4

This book is sold subject to the condition that it shall not be lent, resold, hired out, or otherwise circulated without the publisher's express prior consent in any form of binding, or cover, other than the original as herein published and without a similar condition being imposed on any subsequent purchaser, or bona fide possessor.

This is a fictional work and all characters are drawn from the author's imagination. Any resemblances or similarities to persons either living or dead are entirely coincidental.

E per pigliare i suoi nemici al vischio
Fischió soavemente, e per ridurli
Nella sua tana, questo basalischio.

DECENNALI, I. MACCHIAVELLI

Contents

THE URBINIAN

In that shrewd chapter of his upon a prince's choice of ministers – of which I shall presently have more to say – Messer Niccoló Macchiavelli discovers three degrees in the intelligence of mankind. To the first belong those who understand things for themselves by virtue of their own natural endowments; to the second those who have at least the wit to discern what others understand; and to the third those who neither understand things for themselves nor yet through the demonstrations which others afford them. The first are rare and excellent, since they are the inventive and generative class; the second are of merit, since if not actually productive, they are at least reproductive; the third, being neither one nor the other, but mere parasites who prey for their existence – and often profitably – upon the other two, are entirely worthless.

There is yet a fourth class which the learned and subtle Florentine appears to have overlooked, a class which combines in itself the attributes of those other three. In this class I would place the famous Corvinus Trismegistus, who was the very oddest compound of inventiveness and stupidity, of duplicity and simplicity, of deceit and credulity, of guile and innocence, of ingenuity and ingenuousness, as you shall judge.

To begin with, Messer Corvinus Trismegistus had mastered – as his very name implies – all the secrets of Nature, of medicine, and of magic; so that the fame of him had gone out over the face of Italy like a ripple over water.

He knew, for instance, that the oil of scorpions captured in sunshine during the period of Sol in Scorpio – a most essential condition this – was an infallible cure for the plague. He knew that to correct an enlargement of the spleen, the certain way was to take the spleen of a goat, apply it for four-and-twenty hours to the affected part, and thereafter expose it to the sun; in a measure as the goat's spleen should desiccate and wither, in such measure should the patient's spleen be reduced and restored to health. He knew that the ashes of a wolf's skin never failed as a remedy for baldness, and that to arrest bleeding at the nose nothing could rival an infusion from the bark of an olive-tree, provided the bark were taken from a young tree in the case of a young patient, and from an old tree in the case of an old patient. He knew that serpents stewed in wine, and afterwards eaten, would make sound and whole a leper, by conferring upon him the serpent's faculty of changing its skin.

Deeply, too, was he versed in poisons and enchantments, and he made no secret – so frank and open was his nature – of his power to conjure spirits and, at need, to restore the dead to life. He had discovered an elixir vitae that preserved him still young and vigorous at the prodigious age of two thousand years, which he claimed to have attained; and another elixir, called Acqua Celeste – a very complex and subtle distillation this – that would reduce an old man's age by fifty years, and restore to him his lost youth.

All this and much more was known to Corvinus the Thrice-Mage, although certain folk of Sadducaic mind have sought to show that the sum of his knowledge concerned the extent to which he could abuse the credulity of his contemporaries and render them his dupes. Similarly it was alleged – although his adherents set it down to the spite and envy that the great must for ever be provoking in the mean – that his real name was just Pietro Corvo, a name he got from his mother, who kept a wine-shop in Forli, and who could not herself with any degree of precision have named his father. And these deriders added that his having lived two thousand years was an idle vaunt, since there were still many alive who remembered to have seen him as an ill-kempt, dirty urchin wallowing in the kennels of his native town.

Be all that as it may, there is no denying that he had achieved a great and well-deserved renown, and that he waxed rich in his mean dwelling in Urbino – that Itala Atene, the cradle of Italian art and learning. And to wax rich is, after all, considered by many to be the one outward sign of inward grace, the one indubitable proof of worth. To them, at least, it follows that Messer Corvinus was worthy.

This house of his stood in a narrow street behind the Oratory of San Giovanni, a street of crazy buildings that leaned across to each other until, had they been carried a little higher, they must have met in a Gothic arch, to exclude the slender strip of sky which, as it was, remained visible.

It was a quarter of the town admirably suited to a man of the magician's studious habits. The greater streets of Urbino might tremble under the tramp of armed multitudes in those days when the Lord Cesare Borgia, Duke of Valentinois and Romagna, was master of the city, and the peaceful, scholarly Duke Guidobaldo a fugitive outcast. Down that narrow, ill-paved gap of sordid dwellings came no disturbers of the peace. So that Corvinus Trismegistus was left to pursue his studies unmolested, to crush his powders, and distil his marvellous elixirs.

Thither to seek his help and his advice came folk from every quarter of Italy. Thither in the first hour of a fair June night, about a fortnight after Cesare Borgia's occupation of Urbino, came, attended by two grooms, the Lady Bianca de' Fioravanti. This Lady Bianca was the daughter of that famous Fioravanti who was Lord of San Leo, the only fortress in Guidobaldo's territory which, emboldened by its almost impregnable position, still held out in defiance of the irresistible Valentinois.

With much had heaven blessed Madonna Bianca. Wealth was hers and youth, and a great name; culture and a beauty that has been the subject of some songs. And yet, with all these gifts, there was still something that she lacked – something without which all else was vain; something that brought her by night, a little fearfully, to the grim house of Messer Corvinus as a suppliant. To attract the less attention she came on foot and masked, and with no more attendance than just that of her two grooms. As they entered the narrow street, she bade one of these extinguish the torch he carried. Thereafter, in the dark, they had come, almost groping, stumbling on the rough kidney stones, to the magician's door.

'Go knock, Taddeo,' she bade one of her servants.

And on her words there happened the first of those miracles by which Madonna Bianca was to be convinced beyond all doubting of the supernatural quality of the powers that Messer Corvinus wielded.

Even as the servant took his first step towards the door, this opened suddenly, apparently of itself, and in the passage appeared a stately, white-robed Nubian bearing a lanthorn. This he now raised, so that its yellow shafts showered their light upon Madonna and her followers. There was, of course, no miracle in that. The miracle lay in another apparition. In the porch itself, as if materialized suddenly out of the circumambient gloom, stood a tall, cloaked figure, black from head to foot, the face itself concealed under a black visor. This figure bowed, and waved Madonna onward into the house.

She drew back in fear; for, having come to a place of wonders, expecting wonders, she accounted it but natural that wonders she should find, and it never entered her mind to suppose that here was but another who sought Corvinus, one who had arrived ahead of her, and in response to whose earlier knock it was that the door had opened, just a courteous gentleman who stood now deferring to her sex and very obvious importance.

Devoutly she crossed herself, and observing that the act did not cause this black famulus – as she supposed him – to dissolve and vanish, she reflected that at least his origin could not be daemoniac, took courage and went in, for all that her knees shook under her as she passed him.

The supposed famulus followed close upon her heels, the grooms came last, together and something cowed, though they were men she had chosen for the stoutness of their courage. The gloom, the uncanny gentleman in black, the grinning Nubian, all teeth and eyeballs, affected them unpleasantly.

The Nubian closed the door and barred it, the metal ringing shrilly as it fell. Then he faced about to ask them formally what and whom they sought. It was the lady who answered, unmasking as she spoke.

'I am Bianca de' Fioravanti, and I seek the very learned Messer Corvinus Trismegistus.'

The Nubian bowed silently, bade her follow, and moved down the long stone passage, his lanthorn swinging as he went, and flinging its yellow disc of light to and fro upon the grimy walls. Thus they came to a stout oaken door studded with great nails of polished steel, and by this into a bare anteroom. There were dried rushes on the floor, a wooden bench was set against the wall, and upon a massive, four legged table stood an oil-lamp, whose ruddy, quivering flame, ending in a pennon of black smoke, shed a little light and a deal of smell.

Their guide waved a brown hand towards the bench.

'Your lackeys may await your excellency here,' said he.

She nodded, and briefly gave her order to the grooms. They obeyed her, though with visible reluctance. Then the Nubian opened a second door, at the chamber's farther end. He drew aside a heavy curtain, with a startling clash of metal rings, and disclosed what seemed at first no more than a black gap.

'The dread Corvinus Trismegistus bids you enter,' he announced.

For all the stoutness of her spirit the Lady Bianca now drew back. But as her eyes remained fixed upon the gap, she presently saw the gloom in part dispelled, and dimly she began to perceive some of the furnishings of that inner room. She took courage, bethought her of the great boon she sought at the magician's hands, and so crossed the dread threshold and passed into that mysterious chamber.

After her, in close attendance, ever silent, came the gentleman of the mask. Believing him to be of the household of the mage, and his attendance a necessary condition, she made no demur to it; whilst the Nubian, on the other hand, supposing him, from his mask and the richness of his cloak, to be her companion, made no attempt to check his ingress.

Thus, together, these two passed into the dim twilight of the room. The curtains rasped together again behind them, and the door clanged sepulchrally.

Madonna peered about her, her breath shortened, her heart beating unduly. A line of radiance along the ceiling, mysterious of source, very faintly revealed her surroundings to her: three or four chairs, capacious and fantastically carved, a table of plain wood against the wall immediately before her, crowded with strange vessels of glass and of metal that gleamed as they were smitten by rays of the faint light. No window showed. From ceiling to floor the chamber was hung with black draperies; it was cold and silent as the tomb, and of the magician there was no sign.

The eeriness of the place increased her awe, trammelled her reason, and loosed her imagination. She sat down to await the advent of the dread Corvinus. And then the second miracle took place. Chancing to look round in quest of that black famulus who had materialized to escort her, she discovered, to her infinite amazement, that he had vanished. As mysteriously as he had first taken shape in the porch before her eyes, had he now dissolved again and melted away into the all-encompassing gloom.

She caught her breath at this, and then, as if something had still been needed to scatter what remained of her wits, a great pillar of fire leapt suddenly into being in mid-chamber, momentarily to blind her and to wring from her a cry of fear. As suddenly it vanished, leaving a stench of sulphur in the air; and then a voice, deep, booming, and immensely calm, rang in her ears.

'Fear not, Bianca de' Fioravanti. I am here. What do you seek of me?'

The poor, overwrought lady looked before her in the direction of the voice, and witnessed the third miracle.

Gradually before her eyes, where there had been impenetrable gloom – where, indeed, it had seemed to her that the chamber ended in a wall – she saw a man, an entire scene, gradually assume shape and being as she watched. Nor did it occur to her that it might be her eyesight's slow recovery from the blinding flash of light that conveyed to her this impression of gradual materialization. Soon it was complete – in focus, as it were, and quite distinct.

She beheld a small table or pulpit upon which stood a gigantic open tome, its leaves yellow with a great age, its colossal silver clasps gleaming in the light from the three beaks of a tall-stemmed bronze lamp of ancient Greek design, in which some aromatic oil was being burned. At the lamp's foot a human skull grinned horribly. To the right of the table stood a tripod supporting a brazier in which a mass of charcoal was glowing ruddily. At the table itself, in a high-backed chair, sat a man in a scarlet gown, his head covered by a hat like an inverted saucepan. His face was lean and gaunt, the nose and cheek-bones very prominent; his forehead was high and narrow, his red beard bifurcate, and his eyes, which were turned full upon his visitor, reflecting the cunningly set light, gleamed with an uncanny penetration.

Behind him, in the background, stood crucible and alembic, and above these an array of shelves laden with phials, coffers, and retorts. But of all this she had the most fleeting and subconscious of impressions. All attention of which she was capable was focused upon the man himself. She was, too, as one in a dream, so bewildered had her senses grown by all that she had witnessed.

'Speak, Madonna,' the magician calmly urged her. 'I am here to do your will.'

It was encouraging, and would have been still more encouraging had she but held some explanation of the extraordinary manner of his advent. Still overawed, she spoke at last, her voice unsteady.

'I need your help,' said she. 'I need it very sorely.'

'It is yours, Madonna, to the entire extent of my vast science.'

'You – you have great learning?' she half-questioned, half-affirmed.

'The limitless ocean,' he answered modestly, 'is neither so wide nor so deep as my knowledge. What is your need?'

She was mastering herself now; and if she faltered still and hesitated it was because the thing she craved was not such as a maid may boldly speak of. She approached her subject gradually.

'You possess the secret of great medicines,' said she, 'of elixirs that will do their work not only upon the body, but at need upon the very spirit?'

'Madonna,' he answered soberly, 'I can arrest the decay of age, or compel the departed spirit of the dead to return and restore the body's life. And since it is Nature's law that the greater must include the less, let that reply suffice you.'

'But can you –' She paused. Then, impelled by her need, her last fear forgotten now that she was well embarked upon the business, she rose and approached him. 'Can you command love?' she asked, and gulped. 'Can you compel the cold to grow impassioned, the indifferent to be filled with longings? Can you – can you do this?'

He pondered her at some length.

'Is this your need?' quoth he, and there was wonder in his voice. 'Yours or another's?'

'It is my need,' she answered low. 'My own.'

He sat back, and further considered the pale beauty of her, the low brow, the black, lustrous tresses in their golden net, the splendid eyes, the alluring mouth, the noble height and shape.

'Magic I have to do your will at need,' he said slowly; 'but surely no such magic as is Nature's own endowment of you. Can he resist the sorcery of those lips and eyes – this man for whose subjection you desire my aid?'

'Alas! He thinks not of such things. His mind is set on war and armaments. His only mistress is ambition.'

'His name,' quoth the sage imperiously. 'What is his name – his name and his condition?'

She lowered her glance. A faint flush tinged her cheeks. She hesitated, taken by a fluttering panic. Yet she dared not deny him the knowledge he demanded, lest, vexed by her refusal, he should withhold his aid.

'His name,' she faltered at length, 'is Lorenzo Castrocaro – a gentleman of Urbino, a condottiero who serves under the banner of the Duke of Valentinois.'

'A condottiero blind to beauty, blind to such warm loveliness as yours, Madonna?' cried Corvinus. 'So anomalous a being, such a *lusus naturae* will require great medicine.'

'Opportunity has served me none too well,' she explained, almost in self-defence. 'Indeed, circumstance is all against us. My father is the castellan of San Leo, devoted to Duke Guidobaldo, wherefore it is natural that we should see but little of one who serves under the banner of the foe. And so I fear that he may go his ways unless I have that which will bring him to me in despite of all.'

Corvinus considered the matter silently awhile, then sighed. 'I see great difficulties to be overcome,' said that wily mage.

'But you can help me to overcome them?'

His gleaming eyes considered her.

'It will be costly,' he said.

'What's that to me? Do you think I'll count the cost in such a matter?'

The wizard drew back, frowned, and wrapped himself in a great dignity.

'Understand me,' said he with some asperity. 'This is no shop where things are bought and sold. My knowledge and my magic are at the service of all humanity. These I do not sell. I bestow them freely and without fee upon all who need them. But if I give so much, so very much, it cannot be expected that I should give more. The drugs I have assembled from all corners of the earth are often of great price. That price it is yours to bear, since the medicine is for your service.'

'You have such medicine, then!' she cried, her hands clasping in sudden increase of hopefulness.

He nodded his assent.

'Love philtres are common things enough, and easy of preparation in the main. Any rustic hag who deals in witchcraft and preys on fools can brew one.' The contempt of his tone was withering. 'But for your affair, where great obstacles must be surmounted, or ever the affinities can be made to respond, a drug of unusual power is needed. Such a drug I have – though little of it, for in all the world there is none more difficult to obtain. Its chief component is an extract from the brain of a rare bird – *avis rarissima* – of Africa.'

With feverish fingers she plucked a heavy purse from her girdle and splashed it upon the table. It fell against the grinning skull, and thus cheek by jowl with each other, lay Life's two masters – Death and Gold.

'Fifty ducats!' she panted in her excitement. 'Will that suffice?'

'Perhaps,' said he, entirely disdainful. 'Should it fall something short, I will myself add what may be lacking.' And with contemptuous fingers, eloquent of his scorn of mere profit, he pushed the purse aside, a thing of no account in this transaction.

She began to protest that more should be forthcoming. But he nobly overbore her protestations. He rose, revealing the broad, black girdle that clasped his scarlet robe about his waist, all figured with the signs of the zodiac wrought in gold. He stepped to the shelves, and took from one of them a bronze coffer of some size. With this he returned to the table, set it down, opened it, and drew forth a tiny phial – a slender little tube of glass that was plugged and sealed.

It contained no more than a thread of deep amber fluid – a dozen drops at most. He held it up so that it gleamed golden in the light.

'This,' he said, 'is my *elixirium aureum*, my golden elixir, a rare and very subtle potion, sufficient for your need.' Abruptly he proffered it to her.

With a little cry of gratitude and joy she held out avid hands to take the phial. But as her fingers were about to close upon it, he snatched it back, and raised a hand impressively to restrain her.

'Attend to me,' he bade her, his glittering eye regarding her intensely. 'To this golden elixir you shall add two drops of your own blood, neither more nor less; then contrive that Messer Lorenzo drink it in his wine. But all must be done while the moon is waxing; and, in a measure, as the moon continues to grow, so will his passion mount and abide in him. And before that same moon shall have begun to wane again this Lorenzo Castrocaro will come to you, though the whole world lie between you, and he will be your utter and absolute slave. The present is a propitious time. Go, and be you happy.'

She took the phial, which he now relinquished, and broke into thanks.

But imperiously, by a wave of the hand and a forbidding look, he stemmed her gratitude. He smote a little gong that stood by.

There was the sound of an opening door. The curtains parted with a clash, and the white-robed Nubian appeared salaaming on the threshold, waiting to reconduct her.

Madonna Bianca bowed to the great magician, and departed overawed by the majesty of his demeanour. She had passed out, and still the Nubian waited on the threshold – waited for the man he had admitted with her. But Corvinus, knowing naught of his slave's motive for lingering, bade him harshly begone; whereupon the curtains were drawn together again, and the door was closed.

Left alone, the magician flung off the great mantle of overawing dignity, descended from the lofty indifference to gain, natural enough in one who is master of the ages, and became humanly interested in the purse which Madonna Bianca had left him. Drawing wide the mouth of it, he emptied the golden contents on to the vast page of his book of magic. He spread the glittering mass, and fingered it affectionately, chuckling in his red beard. And then, quite suddenly, his chuckle was echoed by a laugh, short, abrupt, contemptuous, and sinister.

With a startled gasp Corvinus looked up, his hands spreading to cover and protect the gold, his eyes dilating with a sudden fear, a fear that swelled at what he saw. Before him, in mid-chamber, surged a tall figure all in black – black cloak, black cap, and black face, out of which two gleaming eyes considered him.

Trembling in every fibre, white of cheek, his mouth and eyes agape, a prey to a terror greater far than any it had ever been his lot to inspire in others, the wizard stared at the dread phantom, and assumed – not unnaturally it must be confessed – that here was Satan come to claim his own at last.

There fell a pause. Corvinus attempted to speak, to challenge the apparition. But courage failed him; terror struck him dumb.

Presently the figure advanced, silent-footed, menacing; and the wizard's knees were loosened under him. He sank gibbering into his high-backed chair, and waited for death with Hell to follow. At least, you see, he knew what he deserved.

The apparition halted at last, before the table, within arm's length of Corvinus, and a voice came to break the awful spell, a voice infinitely mocking yet unquestionably, reassuringly human.

'Greetings, Thrice-Mage!' it said.

It took Corvinus some moments to realize that his visitor was mortal, after all, and some further moments to recover some semblance of self-possession. An incipient chagrin mingling with the remains of his fears, he spoke at last.

'Who art thou?' he cried, the voice, which he would fain have rendered bold, high-pitched and quavering.

The cloak opened, displaying a graceful well-knit figure in sable velvet that was wrought with golden arabesques. From a girdle studded with great fiery rubies hung a long and heavy dagger, whose hilt and scabbard were of richly chiselled gold. On the backs of the black velvet gloves diamonds hung and sparkled like drops of water, to complete the sombre splendour of the man's apparel. One of the hands was raised to pluck away the visor and disclose the youthful, aquiline, and very noble countenance of Cesare Borgia, Duke of Valentinois and Romagna.

Corvinus recognized him on the instant, and recognizing him was far from sure that things would have been worse had his visitor been the devil, as he had at first supposed. 'My lord!' he cried, profoundly amazed, profoundly uneasy. And, thinking aloud in his consternation, he added the question, foolish in a master of all secrets: 'How came you in?'

'I too, know something of magic,' said the tawny-headed young duke, and there was mockery in his voice and in the smile he bent upon the wizard.

He did not think it necessary to explain that all the magic he had employed had been to enter as if in attendance upon Madonna Bianca de' Fioravanti, and then to slip silently behind the black arras with which, to serve his purposes of deception, Messer Corvinus hung his walls.

But the magician was not duped. Who makes the image does not worship it. The truth – the precise truth – of magic was known undoubtedly to Corvinus, and it therefore follows that he could not for a moment suppose that the means by which the Duke had gained admittance had been other than perfectly natural ones. Anon the Nubian should be keenly questioned, and if necessary as keenly whipped. Meanwhile, the Duke himself must claim attention, and Corvinus – knowing himself a rogue – was far from easy.

But if he was not easy at least he was master of an inexhaustible store of impudence, and upon this he made now a heavy draught. To cover his momentary discomfiture, he smiled now as inscrutably as the Duke. Quickly he thrust the gold back into the purse, never heeding a coin that fell and rolled away along the floor. He tossed that purse aside, and, retaining his seat what time his highness remained standing, he combed his long, bifurcate beard.

'Betwixt your magic and mine, Magnificent, there is some difference,' he said, with sly suggestion.

'I should not be here else,' replied the Duke; and abruptly he proceeded to the matter that had brought him. 'It is said you have found an elixir that restores the dead to life.'

'It is rightly said, my lord,' replied the wizard with assurance. He was becoming master of himself again.

'You have tested it?' quoth Cesare.

'In Cyprus, three years ago, I restored life to a man who had been dead two days. He is still living, and will testify.'

13

'Your word suffices me,' said the Duke; and the irony was so sly that Corvinus was left wondering whether irony there had been. 'At need, no doubt, you would make proof of it upon yourself?'

Corvinus turned cold from head to foot, yet answered boldly of very necessity:

'At need, I would.'

Valentinois sighed as one who is content, and Corvinus took heart again.

'You have this elixir at hand?'

'Enough to restore life to one man – just that and no more. It is a rare and very precious liquor, and very costly, as you may perceive, Magnificent.'

'Derived, no doubt, from the brain of some rare bird of Africa?' the Duke mocked him.

By not so much as a flicker of the eyelid did Corvinus acknowledge the hit.

'Not so, Magnificent,' he replied imperturbably. 'It is derived from –'

'No matter!' said the Duke. 'Let me have it!'

The magician rose, turned to his shelves, and sought there awhile. Presently he came back with a phial containing a blood-red liquid.

'It is here,' he said, and he held the slender vessel to the light, so that it glowed like a ruby.

'Force apart the teeth of the dead man, and pour this draught down his throat. Within an hour he will revive, provided the body has first been warmed before a fire.'

Valentinois took the phial slowly in his gloved fingers. He considered it, his countenance very thoughtful.

'It cannot fail to act?' he questioned.

'It cannot fail, Magnificent,' replied the mage.

'No matter how the man may have died?'

'No matter how, provided that no vital organ shall have been destroyed.'

'It can conquer death by poison?'

'It will dissolve and dissipate the poison, no matter what its nature, as vinegar will melt a pearl.'

'Excellent!' said the Duke, and he smiled his cold, inscrutable smile. 'And now another matter, Thrice-Mage.' He thoughtfully fingered his tawny beard. 'There is a rumour afoot in Italy, spread, no doubt, by yourself to further the thieving charlatan's trade you drive, that the Sultan Djem was poisoned by the Holy Father, and that the poison – a poison so subtle and miraculous that it lay inert in the Turk for a month before it slew him – was supplied to his Holiness by you.'

The Duke paused as if for a reply, and Corvinus shivered again in fear, so coldly sinister had been the tone.

'That is not true, Magnificent. I have had no dealings with the Holy Father, and I have supplied him with no poisons. I know not how Messer Djem may have died, nor have I ever said I did.'

'How, then, comes this story current, and your name in it?'

Corvinus hastened to explain. Explanations were a merchandise with which he was well stocked.

'It may be thus. Of such a poison I possess the secret, and some there have been who have sought it from me. Hence, no doubt, knowing that I have it and conceiving that it was used, the vulgar have drawn conclusions, as the vulgar will, unwarrantably.'

Cesare smiled.

' 'Tis very subtle, Trismegistus.' And he nodded gravely. 'And you say that you have such a poison? What, pray, may be its nature?'

'That, Magnificent, is secret,' was the answer.

'I care not. I desire to know, and I have asked you.'

There was no heat in the rejoinder. It was quite cold – deadly cold. But it had more power to compel than any anger. Corvinus fenced no more; he made haste to answer.

'It consists chiefly of the juice of catapuce and the powdered yolk of an egg, but its preparation is not easy.'

'You have it at hand?'

'Here, Magnificent,' replied the mage.

And from the same bronze coffer whence he had taken the love-philtre – the golden elixir – he drew now a tiny cedar box, opened it, and placed it before the Duke. It contained a fine yellow powder.

'One drachm of that will kill thirty days after it has been administered, two drachms in half the time.'

Cesare sniffed it and eyed the mage sardonically.

'I desire to make experiment,' said he. 'How much is here?'

'Two drachms, highness.'

The Duke held out the box to Corvinus.

'Swallow it,' he bade him calmly.

The mage drew back in an alarm that almost argued faith in his own statement. 'My lord!' he cried, aghast.

'Swallow it,' Cesare repeated, without raising his voice. Corvinus blinked and gulped.

'Would you have me die, my lord?'

'Die? Do you, then, confess yourself mortal, Thrice-Mage – you, the great Corvinus Trismegistus, whose knowledge is wide and deep as the limitless ocean, you who are so little sensible to the ills and decay of the flesh that already you have lived two thousand years? Is the potency of this powder such that it can slay even the immortals?'

And now, at last, Corvinus began to apprehend the real scope of Cesare's visit. It was true that he had set it about that the Sultan Djem had been poisoned, and that he had boasted that he himself had supplied the Borgias with the fabulous secret drug that at such a distance of time had killed the Grand Turk's brother; and, as a consequence, he had made great profit by the sale of what he alleged was the same poison – a subtle *veneno a termine*, as he called it – so convenient for wives who were anxious for a change of husbands, so serviceable to husbands grown weary of their wives.

He understood at last that Cesare, informed of the defamatory lie that had procured the mage such profit, had sought him out to punish him. And it is a fact that Corvinus himself, despite his considerable knowledge, actually believed in the drug's fabulous power to slay at such a distance of time. He had found the recipe in an old MS volume, with many another kindred prescription, and he believed in it with all the blind credulity of the Cinquecento in such matters, with, in fact, all the credulity of those who came to seek his magician's aid.

The Duke's sinister mockery, the extraordinary sense which he ever conveyed of his power to compel, of the futility of attempting to resist his commands, filled Corvinus with an abject dread.

'Highness…alas!… I fear it may be as you say!' he cried.

'But even so, of what are you afraid? Come, man, you are trifling! Have you not said of this elixir that it will restore the dead to life? I pledge you my word that I shall see that it is administered to you when you are dead. Come, then; swallow me this powder, and see that you die of it precisely a fortnight hence, or, by my soul's salvation, I'll have you hanged for an impostor without giving you the benefit afterwards of your own dose of resurrection.'

'My lord – my lord!' groaned the unfortunate man.

'Now, understand me,' said the Duke. 'If this powder acts as you say it will, and kills you at the appointed time, your own elixir shall be given to you to bring you back again to life. But if it kills you sooner, you may remain dead; and if it kills you not at all – why, then I'll hang you, and publish the truth of the whole matter, that men may know the falsehood of the manner of Djem's death upon which you have been trading! Refuse me, and – '

The Duke's gesture was significant.

Corvinus looked into the young man's beautiful, relentless eyes, and saw that to hope to turn him from his purpose were worse than idle. As soon, then, risk the powder as accept the certainty of the rope, with perhaps a foretaste of hell upon the rack. Besides, some chemical skill he had, and a timely emetic might save him – that and flight. Which shows the precise extent of his faith in his elixir of life.

With trembling hands he took the powder.

'See that you spill none of it,' Cesare admonished him, 'or the strangler shall valet you, Thrice-Mage!'

'My lord, my lord!' quavered the wretched warlock, his eyes bulging. 'Mercy! I …'

'The poison, or the strangler,' said the Duke.

In despair, and yet heartening himself by the thought of the emetic, Corvinus bore the edge of the box to his ashen lips, and emptied into his mouth the faintly musty contents, Cesare watching him closely the while. When it was done, the appalled magician sank limply to his chair.

The Duke laughed softly, replaced his visor, and, flinging his ample cloak about him, strode towards the curtains that masked the door.

'Sleep easily, Thrice-Mage,' he said, with infinite mockery. 'I shall not fail you.'

Watching him depart, so confidently, so utterly fearless and unconcerned, Corvinus was assailed by rage and a fierce temptation to extinguish the light and try conclusions with Cesare in the dark, summoning the Nubian to his aid. It was with that thought in his mind that he smote the gong. But, whilst the note of it still rang upon the air, he abandoned a notion so desperate. It would not save him if he were poisoned, whilst if he allowed Cesare to depart unmolested he would be the sooner gone, and the sooner Cesare were gone the sooner would Corvinus be free to administer himself the emetic that was now his only hope.

The curtains flashed back, and the Nubian appeared. On the threshold Cesare paused, and over his shoulder, ever mocking, he flung the warlock his valediction:

'Fare you well, Thrice-Mage!' he said; and, with a laugh, passed out.

Corvinus dashed wildly to his shelves in quest of that emetic, fiercely cursing the Duke of Valentinois and all the Borgia brood.

ii

As the Nubian opened the door of the mage's house to give egress to the Duke, he felt himself suddenly caught about the neck in the crook of a steely, strangling arm, whilst the shrill note of a whistle sounded almost in his very ear.

Instantly the hitherto silent and deserted street awoke to life. From out of doorways darted swift-footed men in answer to the Duke's summons. Into the hands of two of these he delivered the writhing Nubian; to the others he issued a brief command, 'In!' he said, waving a hand down the passage. 'In, and take him.' And upon that he stepped out into the street and so departed.

Later that evening word was brought him at the palace of how Messer Corvinus had been taken in the very act of mixing a drug.

'The antidote, no doubt,' said Cesare to the officer who bore him the information. 'You would be just in time to save my experiment from being frustrated. A wicked, faithless, inconsiderate fellow, this Corvinus. Let him be kept in close confinement, guarded by men whom you can trust, until you hear from me again.'

Thereafter Cesare summoned a council of his officers – Corella the Venetian, Naldo the Forlivese, Ramiro de Lorqua, his lieutenant-general of Romagna, Della Volpe the one-eyed, and Lorenzo Castrocaro.

A tall, clean-limbed young man was this last, very proud in his bearing, very splendid in his apparel, with golden hair and handsome, dreamy eyes of a blue as dark as sapphires. Cesare held him in great regard, knowing him valiant, resourceful, and ambitious. Tonight he regarded him with a fresh interest, in view of what at the magician's he had overheard.

The Duke waved his officers to their seats about his council board, and craved of Della Volpe, who was in charge of the siege operations, news of the fortress of San Leo.

The veteran's swarthy face was gloomy. His single eye – he had lost the other in the Duke's service – avoided his master's penetrating glance. He sighed wearily.

'We make no progress,' he confessed, 'nor can make any. San Leo is not a place to be carried by assault, as your magnificence well knows. It stands there upon its mountaintop like a monument upon a plinth, approached by a bridlepath offering no cover. And, for all that it is reported to be held by scarcely more than a score of men, a thousand cannot take it. There is no foothold at the summit for more than a dozen men at a time, and as for using guns against it, it were easier to mount a park of artillery upon a fiddle-string.'

'Yet until San Leo is ours we are not fully masters of Urbino,' said the Duke. 'We cannot leave the place in the hands of Fioravanti.'

'We shall have to starve him out, then,' said Della Volpe.

'And that would take a year at least,' put in Corella, who had been gathering information. 'They have great store of wheat and other victuals and they are watered by a well in the inner bailie of the fortress. With few mouths to feed, as they have, they can hold us in check for ever.'

'There is a rumour today,' said Della Volpe, 'that the Lord Fioravanti is sick, and that it is feared he may not live.'

'Not a doubt but Venice will say I poisoned him,' said Cesare, sneering. 'Still, even if he dies, it will be no gain to us. There is his castellan, Tolentino, to take his place; and Tolentino is the more obstinate of the two. We must consider some way to reduce them. Meanwhile, Taddeo, be vigilant, and hold the path against all.'

Della Volpe inclined his head.

'I have taken all my measures for that,' he said.

And now young Castrocaro stirred in his chair, leaning forward across the table.

'By your leave,' said he, 'those measures may not suffice.'

Della Volpe frowned, rolled his single eye, which was preternaturally fierce, and scowled contemptuously upon this young cockerel whose pretence it seemed to be to teach that war-battered old captain the art of beleaguering.

'There is another way to reach San Leo,' Castrocaro explained; and drew himself upon the attention of all, particularly the Duke, in whose fine eyes there gleamed now an eager interest very unusual in him.

Castrocaro met with a confident smile this sudden and general alertness he had provoked.

'It is not,' he explained, 'such a way by which a company can go, but sufficient to enable a bold man who is acquainted with it to bear messages, and, at need, even victuals into the fortress. Therefore, it will be necessary that Messer della Volpe surround the entire base of the rock if he would be sure that none shall slip through his lines.'

'You are certain of what you tell us?' quoth the Duke sharply.

'Certain!' echoed Castrocaro; and he smiled. 'The way of which I speak lies mainly to the south of the rock. It is perilous even for a goat, yet it is practicable with care to one who knows it. Myself, as a boy, have made the ascent more often than I should have cared to tell my mother. In quest of an eagle's nest I have more than once reached the little plateau that thrusts out under the very wall of the fortress on the southern side. Thence, to enter the castle, all that would be needed would be a rope and a grappling hook; for the wall is extremely low just there – not more than twelve feet high.'

The Duke pondered the young soldier with very thoughtful eyes, in silence, for some moments.

'I shall further consider this,' he said at length. 'Meanwhile, I thank you for the information. You have heard, Della Volpe. You will profit by what Castrocaro tells us, encircling the base entirely with your troops.'

Della Volpe bowed, and upon that the council rose.

Next morning Cesare Borgia summoned Castrocaro to his presence. He received the young condottiero in the noble library of the palace, a spacious chamber, its lofty ceiling gloriously frescoed by Mantegna, its walls hung with costly tapestries and cloth of gold, its shelves stocked with a priceless and imposing array of volumes, all in manuscript; for, although the new German invention of the printing press was already at work, by not a single vulgar production of that machine would Duke Guidobaldo have contaminated his cherished and marvellous collection.

At work at a table spread with papers sat the black-gowned figure of Agabito Gherardi, the Duke's secretary.

'You have the acquaintance, have you not,' quoth Cesare, 'of Madonna Bianca, the daughter of Fioravanti of San Leo?'

The young man, taken by surprise, flushed slightly despite his habitual self-possession, and his blue eyes, avoiding the Duke's, considered the summer sky and the palace gardens through one of the windows that stood open to the broad marble balcony.

'I have that honour in some slight degree,' he answered; and Cesare considered from his air and tone that the magician's golden elixir was scarcely needed here as urgently as Madonna Bianca opined, and that what still was wanting to enchant him the sorcery of her beauty might accomplish unaided, as the magician had supposed.

He smiled gently.

'You may improve that acquaintance, if you so desire.'

The young man threw back his head very haughtily.

'I do not understand your potency,' said he.

'You have my leave,' the Duke explained, 'to convey in person to Madonna Bianca the news we have received that her father lies sick in San Leo.'

Still the young man held himself loftily upon the defensive, as a young lover will.

'To what end this, highness?' he inquired, his tone still haughty.

'Why, to what end but a Christian one, and' – the Duke slightly lowered his voice to a confidential tone, and smiled inscrutably – 'a kindly purpose towards yourself. Still, if you disdain the latter, for the former any other messenger will serve.'

Ill at ease in his self-consciousness, a little mystified, yet well-content at heart, the condottiero bowed.

'I thank your highness,' he said. 'Have I your leave to go?'

The Duke nodded.

'You will wait upon me on your return. I may have other commands for you,' he said, and so dismissed him.

An hour later came Castrocaro back to the palace library in great haste and some excitement to seek the duke again.

'My lord,' he cried, all in a trembling eagerness, 'I have conveyed the message, and I am returned to crave a boon. Madonna Bianca besought of me in her affliction a written order to pass the lines of Della Volpe, that she might repair to her father.'

'And you?' cried the Duke sharply, his level brows drawn together by a sudden frown.

The young captain's glance fell away. Obviously he was discouraged and abashed.

'I answered that I had no power to grant such an order, but – but that I would seek it of your highness; that I knew you would not desire to hold a daughter from her father's side at such time.'

'You know a deal,' said Cesare sourly, 'and you promise rashly. Precipitancy in making promises has never yet helped a man to greatness. Bear that in mind.'

'But she was in such sore affliction!' cried Messer Lorenzo, protesting.

'Aye!' said the Duke dryly. 'And she used you so kindly, eyed you so fondly, gave you such sweet wine to drink, that you had no strength to resist her soft appeal.'

Cesare, watching his condottiero closely, observed the flicker of the young man's eyelids at the mention of the wine, and was satisfied. But even more fully was he to have the assurance that he sought.

'Have I been spied upon?' quoth Messer Lorenzo hotly.

Cesare shrugged contemptuously, not deigning to reply.

'You have leave to go,' he said in curt dismissal.

But Messer Lorenzo was in a daring mood, and slow to obey.

'And the authority for Madonna Bianca to join her father?' he asked.

'There are good reasons why none should enter San Leo at present,' was the cold reply. 'Since you lay such store by it, I regret the necessity to deny you. But in time of war necessity is inexorable.'

Chagrined and downcast, the condottiero bowed and withdrew. Having promised, and finding himself now unable to fulfil the promise made to her over that cup of wine which she had brought him with her own fair hands, he dared not present himself to her again. Instead he dispatched a page to her with the unwelcome news of the Duke's refusal.

Yet in this matter Cesare Borgia was oddly inconsistent. For scarcely had Castrocaro left his presence than he turned to his white-faced secretary.

'Write me three lines to Della Volpe,' said he, 'ordering that if Madonna Bianca de' Fioravanti should attempt to steal through his lines and gain San Leo, he is to offer her no hindrance.'

Agabito's round, pale countenance reflected his amazement at this order. But Cesare, surveying him, smiled inscrutably for all reply, and, from his knowledge of his master and that smile, Agabito perceived that Cesare was embarked upon one of those tortuous, subtle courses whose goal none could perceive until it had been reached. He bent to his task, and his pen scratched and spluttered briskly. Very soon a messenger bearing the order was on his way to Della Volpe's camp.

That very night Madonna Bianca considerately did what the Duke expected of her. She slipped past the Borgia sentinels in the dark, and she was in San Leo by morning, though in Urbino none knew of this but Cesare, who had word of it privately from Della Volpe. Her palace by the Zoccolanti remained opened as if inhabited by her, but to all who came to seek her it was said that she was in ill-health and kept her chamber. And amongst these was Lorenzo Castrocaro, who, upon being denied admittance on this plea, concluded that she was angry with him for having failed to do as he had promised, and thereafter grew oddly silent and morose.

Two days after her flight came news of Fioravanti's death in the grim fortress he defended, and Castrocaro was dispatched by the Duke to Cesena on a mission which might well have been entrusted to a less-important officer. It was ten days later when his immediate return was ordered, and, in view of the terms of that order, he went, upon reaching Urbino, all dust-laden as he was, into the Duke's presence with the dispatches that he bore.

Valentinois sat in council at the time, and Della Volpe from the lines under San Leo was in attendance.

'You are very opportunely returned,' was his greeting of Messer Lorenzo, and he thrust aside, as of no consequence, the dispatches which the latter brought. 'We are met here to consider this resistance of San Leo, which is being conducted now by Tolentino with all the firmness that was Fioravanti's. We must make an end; and you, Messer Lorenzo, are the man to accomplish it.'

'I?' cried the young soldier.

'Sit,' Cesare bade him, and obediently Castrocaro took a chair at the table. 'Listen. You are to understand that I am not commanding you to do this thing, for I command no valued officer of mine so greatly to imperil his life. I but show you what is our need – what might be done by one who has your knowledge and whose heart is stout enough to bid him take the risk which the thing entails.'

The condottiero nodded his understanding, his blue eyes set upon the Duke's calm face.

'You told us here,' Cesare continued, 'of a perilous way into San Leo which is known to few, and to yourself amongst those few. You said that if a man were to gain the plateau on the southern side of the rock's summit he might, with a rope and a grappling hook, effect an entrance. Now, if a man were to do this at dead of night, choosing his time wisely so as to take the sentry unawares, stab that sentry, and thereafter reach the gates and loose the bars, the rest would be an easy task. Della Volpe's troops would, meanwhile, have crept up by the bridlepath to await the signal, upon which they would pour forth against the unbarred gate, and so San Leo might be reduced at last with little loss of life.'

Messer Lorenzo considered for some moments, the Duke watching him.

'It is shrewd,' he said, approvingly. 'It is shrewd and easy, and likely to succeed, provided the man who goes is one who knows the rock and the fortress itself.'

'Provided that, of course,' said Cesare; and he looked steadily at the young man.

Messer Lorenzo bore that look a moment with the self-possession that was natural to him. Then, translating its quiet significance:

'I will go,' he said quietly, 'and, Heaven helping me, I will succeed.'

'You have counted the cost of failure?' said Cesare.

'It needs no counting. It is plain enough. A rope and a beam from the castle wall, or a leap from the rock itself.'

'Then, since who gambles should know not only what he may chance to lose, but also the stake he stands to win,' said the Duke, 'let me say that if you succeed I'll give you the governorship of the fortress with a stipend of ten thousand ducats.'

Messer Lorenzo flushed in his agreeable surprise. His eyes sparkled and his tone rang with youth's ready confidence in its own powers.

'I will not fail,' he promised. 'When do I make the attempt?'

'Tomorrow night, since you have resolved. See that you rest betwixt this and then to fit you for the fatigue of such an enterprise. And so, sirs, let us hope that we have found at last a solution to this riddle of San Leo.'

iii

You see, I hope, what Messer Castrocaro did not yet see, nor for that matter ever saw – knowing nothing of what had happened on the night when the duke visited Messer Corvinus Trismegistus. You see in the Duke's choice of him for this enterprise an instance of that fine discrimination with which Cesare picked his instruments.

Macchiavelli, who studied the Duke at close quarters, and who worshipped him as the very embodiment of all the virtues of princeship, was no doubt inspired by the duke's unerring wisdom in the choice of ministers to devote to the subject a chapter of his 'The Prince'.

'The first conjecture made of a prince and of his intellectual capacity,' he writes, 'should be based upon a consideration of the men by whom he surrounds himself, and when these are faithful to him, and sufficient for his occasions, he is to be accounted a wise prince, for having chosen them sufficient and kept them faithful.'

Macchiavelli writes thus no more than Cesare might, himself, have written had he theorized upon princeship instead of practising it. It is, indeed upon Cesare Borgia's practices – as Macchiavelli half admits in one place – that the Florentine founded his theories. So that it is hardly an over-statement to say that whilst Macchiavelli wrote 'The Prince', Cesare Borgia was its real author, since his were the conceptions and actions that Macchiavelli converted into precepts.

You see him here selecting for this task one who although the youngest among all his captains, was yet undoubtedly the most sufficient for his particular need. And observe the quality of his sufficiency. In a measure it was adventitious, depending upon Castrocaro's chance acquaintance with that back way up the rock of San Leo. But in a still greater measure it was the result of Cesare's clever manipulation of circumstances.

If that is not yet quite clear to you, it shall become abundantly so ere all is told. But do not fall into the error of supposing that anything that befell was the result of chance. From now onward all happens precisely as Cesare had designed. He had discovered certain forces, and he had harnessed them to his needs, setting them upon a course by him predetermined and marked out.

He realized that chance might disturb their career, and fling them out of that course, but he did not depend upon chance to bear them to the goal at which he aimed them.

On the afternoon of the following day, thoroughly rested and refreshed, Messer Lorenzo Castrocaro rode out of Urbino with a bodyguard of a half-dozen of his men-at-arms and took the road to Della Volpe's camp under San Leo. He arrived there without mishap towards nightfall, and having supped with the commander of the beleaguerers in the latter's tent, he thereafter completed his preparations. Towards the third hour of night he set out alone upon his perilous undertaking.

To lessen the risk of being perceived by any watcher in the castle, he had dressed himself entirely in black, taking the precaution to put on under his doublet a shirt of mail, which whilst being dagger-proof, was yet so finely wrought that your two cupped hands might contain it. He was armed with sword and dagger, and bandolier-wise about his body, was coiled a rope, to which he had attached a strong, double-pronged grappling hook very broad in the bend, all swathed in straw. This had been carefully and firmly adjusted upon his back, so that it should not hamper his movements.

With Della Volpe he had concerted that the latter, at the head of fifty men, should quietly approach the fortress by the bridlepath, and, having gained the summit, lie concealed until the gate should be opened by Castrocaro himself. Then they were instantly to spring forward, and so effect an entrance.

It was a fine clear night of summer, and a full moon rode in the heavens, rendering the landscape visible for miles. This was well for the earlier part of Messer Lorenzo's climb; and before midnight, by when he hoped to reach the summit, that moon would have set, and darkness would lend him cover.

Alone, then, he set out, and made his way round to the southern side of the great precipitous hill on the crest of which, like the capital of a column, the bulk and towers of the fortress showed grey in the white moonlight.

At first the ascent was easy, and he was able to go forward swiftly; soon, however, the precipice grew more abrupt, the foothold became scantier, and in places failed almost entirely, so that his progress was retarded and for his life's sake he was compelled to move with infinite caution, husbanding his strength against the still more strenuous labour that lay before him.

Hesitation or doubt he had none. It was a good ten years since last, in boyhood, he had scaled those heights; but boyhood's memories are tenacious, and he was as confident of his way as if he had trodden it but yesterday. Every little projection of that cliff, every fissure that afforded foothold, every gap to be overcome, he knew before he reached it.

At the end of an hour he had not accomplished more than a third of the ascent, and the most difficult part of it was yet to come. He sat down upon a grassy ledge, unusually spacious, and there he rested him awhile and recovered breath.

Thence he viewed the Emilian plain, revealed for miles in the moon's white light, the glittering, silvery spread of sea away in the distance to the east, the glimmering snow-capped peaks of the Apennines to westward. Above him towered the grey cliff, abrupt and sheer as the very walls of the fortress that crowned its summit, a climb that well might have appalled the hardiest mountaineer, that might, indeed, have baffled even a goat. Surveying it with his calm blue eyes, Messer Lorenzo realized that the worst danger he had to face that night was the danger of this climb. By comparison, the rest – the scaling of the castle wall, the poniarding of a sentry or two, and the opening of the gate – were safe and simple matters. Here, however, a false step, a misgiving even, or a moment of giddiness, such as might well beset him, must plunge him down to instant death.

He rose, inhaled the fragrance of the summer night, breathed a short prayer to his patron saint, the Holy Lawrence, and pushed on. Clinging with hands and feet and knees to the face of the cliff, he edged along a narrow strip of rock, for some few yards, to another ledge; there he paused to breathe again, thankful that so much was accomplished.

Thereafter for a while the going was easier. A natural path, some three feet wide, wound upwards along the precipice's face. At the end of this he was confronted by another gap, to be surmounted only by a leap.

Fearing lest his sword should trip him, he unbuckled his belt, and cast the weapon from him. He did so with regret, but constrained to it by the reflection that if he kept it he might never live to need it. Then he took a deep breath, seized his courage in both hands, and jumped across the black unfathomable void at a stunted tree that thrust out from that sheer wall. With arms and legs he clutched like an ape at the frail plant, and had its hold given way under his weight, there would have been an end of him forthwith. It held, however, and clinging to it, he groped for foothold, found it, and went on.

29

This brought him to a narrow fissure in the cliff. Up this fissure he swarmed, supported by just the pressure of knees and forearms against the rock, and only at times finding a projection affording a safer grip for one or the other.

Up, straight up, he went for nearly twenty feet, until at last he reached the fissure's summit; one of its walls permitted him to get astride it, and there he rested, bathed in sweat and winded by the stupendous exertions he had put forth. Seated thus, his breast close against the cliff, he looked sideways and down into the awful depths below him. He shuddered, and clung with his bruised hands to the rock, and it was some time before he could proceed upon the second half of his ascent, for by now he knew that he was a good midway.

At last he resumed his climb, and by similar means, and surmounting similar and constant perils, he pushed on and ever upwards.

One narrow escape he had. As he clung with both hands to that awful wall at a place where the foothold was but a few inches wide, a great brown body, with a shrieking whirr, dashed out of a crevice just above his head, and went cawing and circling in the void beyond. So startled was he that he almost loosed his hold, and a cold sweat broke out upon his roughened skin as he recovered and knew the thing for what it was. And later, when, an hour or so before midnight, the moon went down and left him in utter darkness, fear at last assailed his stout spirit, and for a time he did not dare to move. Presently, however, as he grew accustomed to the gloom, his eyes were able to pierce it to an extent that restored his courage. The night, after all, was clear and starlit, and at close quarters objects were just visible; yet immense care was necessary lest he should now commit the irreparable error of mistaking substance for shadow, or should misjudge his distances, as was so easy.

At long length, towards midnight, utterly spent, with bleeding hands and rent garments, he found himself on the roomy platform at the very foot of the castle's southern wall; and not for all the wealth of the world would he have consented to return by the way he had so miraculously ascended – for miraculous did he now account it that he should have reached his goal in safety. He flung himself down, full length, there at the foot of the wall, to rest awhile before attempting the escalade. And what time he rested, he whispered a prayer of thankfulness for his preservation so far, for a devout soul was this Messer Lorenzo.

He looked up at the twinkling stars, out at the distant sheen of the Adriatic, down at the clustering hamlets in the plain, so far below him, from which so painfully he had climbed. Immediately above his head he could hear the steady measured tread of the sentry, approaching, passing, and receding again, as the man patrolled the embattled parapet. Thrice did the fellow pass that way before Castrocaro stirred; and when at length he rose, as the steps were fading in the distance for the third time, he felt a certain pity for the soldier whose spirit he must inevitably liberate from its earthly prison-house that night.

He uncoiled the rope from his body, stood back, and swung the grappling hook a moment, taking aim, then hurled it upwards. It soared above the wall, and fell beyond, between two merlons, then thudded softly against the masonry, the straw in which he had the foresight to swathe it muffling the sound of the metal.

He pulled gently at the rope, hoping that the hooks would fasten upon some projection in the stone or lodge within some crevice. But neither happened. The hooks came to the summit of the wall, and toppled back, falling at his feet. Again he repeated the operation, with a like result; but at the third attempt the hooks took hold. He swung his entire weight upon the rope to test the grip, and found that it held firmly.

But now the sentry's return warned him that the moment was unpropitious. So he waited, intently listening, crouching at the wall's foot, until the man had passed, and his footsteps were once more receding in the distance.

Then he began the ascent in sailor fashion, hauling himself up hand over hand, his feet against the masonry to lighten the labour of his arms. Thus he came swiftly to the top of the wall, and knelt there, between two merlons, peering down into the black courtyard. All

31

was silent. Save for the tramp of the sentry, who was now turning the north-western angle of the ramparts, as Messer Lorenzo rightly judged, no sound disturbed the stillness of the place.

He loosed the hooks from the crevice in which they had fastened. He flung them wide, the rope with them, and sent them hurtling over the precipice, that there might be no evidence of the manner of his coming. Then he dropped softly down upon the parapet, exulting to realize that his journey was accomplished, and that he was within the fortress.

His mission was all but ended. The rest was easy. Within a few moments the Borgia troops would be pouring into San Leo, and the soldiers of the garrison, surprised in their beds, would make a very ready surrender. It no longer appeared even necessary to Messer Lorenzo to butcher that single sentry. If he but wisely chose his moment for the unbarring of the gates, the whole thing might be done without the man's suspicions being aroused until it was too late. Indeed, it was the safer course; for, after all, if he came to grapple with the soldier, there was always the chance that the fellow might cry out and give the alarm before Castrocaro could dispatch him.

Resolved thus upon that score, he moved forward swiftly yet very cautiously, and gained a flight of stone steps that wound down into the inner bailie. This he descended, and so reached the quadrangle. Round this vast square he moved, keeping well within the shadows, until he came to the gateway opening upon a passage that ran past the guard-room on one side and the chapel on the other, into the outer bailie of the fortress.

In this gateway he crouched, and waited until the sentry, who was coming round again, should have passed once more to the castle's northern side. No window overlooking the courtyard showed a single light; the place was wrapped in slumber.

Messer Lorenzo waited calmly, his pulse quite regular. Should the door be locked, then he must return, deal with the sentry, and make his way to the main gates by the battlements. But it was unlikely that such would be the case.

High up, immediately before him upon the ramparts, he saw the sentry, passing slowly, pike on shoulder, a black shadow dimly outlined against the blue-black, star-flecked dome of sky. He watched him as he passed on and round, all unsuspicious, and so vanished once more. Then, very softly, Messer Lorenzo tried the latch of that big door. It yielded silently to his pressure and a black tunnel gaped before him. He entered it, and very softly closed the door again on the inside. Then he paused, reflecting that were he to go straight forward and pass out into the northern court he must risk detection by the sentry, who was now on the northern battlements. Therefore he must wait until the fellow should come round again.

Interminable seemed his wait this time, and once he fancied that he heard a man's voice coming from the guard-room on his right. The sound momentarily quickened his pulses that had been steady hitherto. But hearing no more, he concluded that his senses, strained by so much dodging, waiting, and listening, had deceived him.

At last he caught the sound of the sentry's step approaching again along the parapet. Satisfied that he had waited long enough he made shift to grope his way through the black darkness of that passage. And then, even as he turned, his heart almost stood still. Upon the chapel door, at the height of some three feet, there was a tiny oval splash of light, along the ground at the same spot a yellow gleam long and narrow as a sword-blade. Instantly he understood. The guard-room, whose windows looked upon the northern court, was still tenanted, and what he beheld was the light that shone through the keyhole and under the door.

A moment he paused, considering. Then he perceived that, having come so far, he must go on. To retreat and reopen the door would be fraught with the greater risk, whilst to linger in the passage would be but to increase the already imminent danger of discovery. His only chance of winning through lay in going forward at once, taking care to make no sound that should reach those within. Thus, no doubt, all would be well. With extremest caution, then, he stepped forward on tip-toe, his hands upon the wall on the chapel side to guide and steady him.

Not more than three of four steps had he taken when, quite suddenly, an oath rang out in a deep male voice, followed by the laughter of several men. With that there was a scraping of chairs, and heavy steps came tramping towards the door.

With this door Messer Lorenzo was now level, and, being startled, he made his one mistake. Had he taken the risk of speeding forward swiftly, he might even now have won safely the outer bailie. But he hung there hesitating, again considering retreat even, his every sinew taut. And that pause was his ruin. In a moment he realized it, saw that he was trapped, that retreat was now utterly hopeless, and that to go forward was no better. Therefore with set teeth, and angry misery in his soul to reflect that he had won so far and at such peril only to fail upon the very threshold of success, he stood at bay, to meet what he no longer could avoid.

The door was pulled open from within, and a flood of light poured out into that black place, revealing Messer Lorenzo, white of face, with staring eyes, one hand instinctively upon his poniard-hilt, poised there as if for a spring.

Thus did the foremost of the five men who issued behold him, and at sight of him all checked abruptly, staring. This foremost one, a big, heavily-built fellow all clad in leather, black-browed and bearded, seemed in some slight measure the superior of those other four. All five were very obviously soldiers.

He fell back a step in sheer amazement, startled even by the sight of Messer Lorenzo. Then, recovering, he set his arms akimbo, planted wide his feet, and looked our gentleman over with an eye of deepest interest. 'Now who the devil may you be?' he demanded.

Messer Lorenzo's wits were ever very ready, and in that moment he had a flash of inspiration. He stepped forward easily in answer to that challenge, and so came more fully into the light.

'I am glad to see there is someone alive and awake in San Leo,' he said; and he seemed to sneer, as one who had the right to utter a reproof.

On the faces of those five men amazement grew and spread. Looking beyond them into the room, which was lighted by torches set in iron sconces in the walls, Messer Lorenzo beheld the explanation of the silence they had kept. There was a table on which remained spread a pack of greasy cards. They had been at play.

'Body of God,' he went on, 'you keep a fine watch here! The Borgia soldiery may be at your very gates. I myself can effect an entrance, and no man to hinder or challenge me, or so much as give the alarm! By the Host! were you men of mine, I should find work for you in the kitchen, and hope that you'd give a better account of yourselves as scullions than you do as soldiers.'

'Now, who the devil may you be, I say?' again demanded the black-browed warrior, scowling more truculently than before.

'And how the devil come you here?' cried another, a slender, loose-lipped fellow, with a wart on his nose, who pushed forward to survey the intruder at closer quarters.

Castrocaro on the instant became very haughty.

'Take me to your captain – to Messer Tolentino,' he demanded. 'He shall learn what manner of watch you keep. You dogs, the place might be burnt about your ears while you sit there cheating one another at cards, and set a fellow who appears to be both deaf and blind to pace your walls.'

The note of cool authority in his voice produced its effect. They were entirely duped by it. That a man should so address them whose right to do so was not entirely beyond question seemed to them – as it might indeed to any – altogether incredible.

'Messer Tolentino is abed,' said the big fellow in a surly voice.

They did not like the laugh with which Messer Castrocaro received that information. It had an unpleasant ring.

'I nothing doubt it from the manner of your watch,' he sneered. 'Well, then, up and rouse him for me!'

'But who is he, after all, Bernardo?' insisted the loose-lipped stripling of their leader; and the others grunted their approval of a question that at least possessed the virtue of being timely.

'Aye,' quoth black-browed Bernardo. 'You have not told us who you are?' His tone lay between truculence and sulky deference.

'I am an envoy from the Lord Guidobaldo, your duke,' was the ready and unfaltering answer; and the young condottiero wondered in his heart whither all this would lead him, and what chance of saving himself might offer yet.

Their deference was obviously increased, as was their interest in him.

'But how came you in?' insisted the one who already had posed that question.

Messer Lorenzo waved the question and questioner impatiently aside.

'What matters that?' quoth he. 'Enough that I am here. Are we to trifle away the night in silly questions? Have I not told you that the Borgia troops may at this moment be at your very gates?'

'By Bacchus, they may stay there,' laughed another. 'The gates of San Leo are strong enough, my master; and should the Borgia rabble venture to knock, we shall know how to answer them.'

But even as the fellow was speaking, Bernardo fetched a lanthorn from the room, and shouted to them to follow him. They went down the passage towards the door leading to the outer bailie. They crossed the courtyard together, pestering the supposed envoy with questions, which he answered curtly and ungraciously, showing them by his every word and gesture that it was not his habit to herd with such as they.

Thus they came to the door of the maschio tower, where Messer Tolentino had his dwelling; and, what time they paused there, Castrocaro sent a fond glance in the direction of the great gates, beyond which Della Volpe and his men were waiting. He was so near them that to reach and unbar those gates would be an instant's work; but the way to rid himself of those five dogs of war was altogether beyond his devising. And now the sentry on the walls above peered down and hailed them to know whom they had with them, and the young condottiero prayed that thus Della Volpe, who must be intently on the watch without, might have warning that he was taken. Yet at the same time he knew full well that, even so, Della Volpe would be powerless to assist him. He had but his own wits upon which he could depend and he realized how desperate was his situation.

Up a winding staircase, the walls and ceilings very rudely frescoed, they led Messer Lorenzo to the apartments of Tolentino, the castellan who had been ruler of San Leo since the death, ten days ago, of the Lord Fioravanti.

As he went the young condottiero took heart once more. So far all had gone well. He had played his part shrewdly, and his demeanour had so successfully imposed upon the men that no shadow of suspicion did they entertain. Could he but succeed in similarly befooling their captain, it might well be that he should be assigned some chamber from which he anon might slip forth still to do the thing he was come to do.

As he went he prepared the tale he was to tell, and he based it upon his knowledge that Fioravanti's resistance of Cesare Borgia had been almost in opposition to the wishes of Duke Guidobaldo – that mild and gentle scholar who had desired all fortresses to make surrender, since no ultimate gain could lie in resistance and naught ensue but a useless sacrifice of life.

The difficulty for Messer Lorenzo lay in the fact that Tolentino would desire to see credentials; and he had none to offer.

He was kept waiting in an ante-chamber what time the big Bernardo went to rouse the castellan and to inform that grumbling captain that an envoy from Duke Guidobaldo had stolen into the castle and was seeking him. No more than just that did Bernardo tell Tolentino. But it was enough.

The castellan roused himself at once, with a wealth of oaths, first incoherent, then horribly coherent; he shook his great night-capped head, thrust out a pair of long hairy legs from the coverlet, and sat up on the bed's edge to receive this envoy, whom he made Bernardo to admit.

Messer Lorenzo, very uneasy in his heart, but very haughty and confident in his bearing, entered and gave the captain a lofty salutation.

'You are from Duke Guidobaldo?' growled Messer Tolentino.

'I am,' said Castrocaro. 'And had I been from Cesare Borgia, with a score of men at my heels, I could by now have been master of San Leo, so zealous are your watchers.'

It was shrewdly conceived, because it seemed to state an obvious truth that was well calculated to disarm suspicion. But the tone he took though well enough with men-at-arms, was a mighty dangerous one to take with a castellan of such importance and such a fierce, ungovernable temper as was notoriously Messer Tolentino's. It flung that gentleman very naturally into a rage, and might well have earned the speaker a broken head upon the instant. This Messer Lorenzo knew and risked; for he also knew that it must earn him confidence, both for the reason already given and also because it must be inferred that only a person very sure of himself would dare to voice such a reproof.

Tolentino stared at him out of fierce, blood-injected eyes, too much taken aback to find an answer for a moment. He was a tall, handsome, big-nosed man, with black hair, an olive, shaven face, and a long, square chin. He stared on awhile, and then exploded.

'Blood of God!' he roared. 'Here is a cockerel with a very noisy cackle! We'll mend that for you ere you leave us,' he promised viciously. 'Who are you?'

'An envoy from Duke Guidobaldo, as you have been informed. As for the rest – the cockerel and the cackle – we will discuss it at some other time.'

The castellan heaved himself up and sought to strike a pose of dignity, no easy matter for a man in his shirt and crowned by a night-cap.

'You pert lap-dog!' said he, between anger and amazement. He breathed gustily, words failing him, and then grew calmer. 'What is your name?'

'Lorenzo Snello,' answered Castrocaro, who had been prepared for the question, and he added sternly: 'I like it better than the one you have just bestowed upon me.'

'Are you come hither to tell me what you like?' bellowed the castellan. 'Look you, young sir, I am the master here, and here my will is law. I can flog you, flay you, or hang you, and give account of it to none. Bear you that in mind, and – '

'Oh, peace!' cried Messer Lorenzo, in his turn, waving a contemptuous hand, and dominating the other by his very tone and manner. 'Whatever I may have come for, I have not come to listen to your vapourings. Have I climbed from the plain, risked my life to get through the Borgia lines, and my neck a score of times in the ascent, to stand here and have you bellow at me of what you imagine you can do? What you cannot do, I have seen for myself.'

'And what may that be?' quoth Tolentino, now wickedly gentle.

'You cannot guard a castle, and you cannot discriminate between a lackey and one who is your peer and perhaps something more.'

The castellan sat down again and rubbed his chin. Here was a very hot fellow, and, like all bullies, Messer Tolentino found that hot fellows put him out of countenance.

In the background, behind Messer Lorenzo, stood Tolentino's men in line, silent but avid witnesses of his discomfiture. The castellan perceived that at all costs he must save his face.

'You'll need a weighty message to justify this insolence and to save you from a whipping,' said he gravely.

'I'll need no weightier a message than the one I bear,' was the sharp answer. 'The duke shall hear of these indignities to which you are subjecting one he loves, and who has run great peril in his service.'

His dignity, his air of injury was now overwhelming. 'And mark you, sir, it is not the way to treat an envoy, this. Were my duty to the duke less than it is, or my message of less moment, I should depart as I have come. But he shall hear of the reception I have had, rest assured of that.'

Tolentino shuffled, ill at ease now.

'Sir,' he cried, protesting, 'I swear the fault is yours. Who pray are you, to visit me with your reproofs? If I have failed in courtesy it was you provoked me. Am I to bear the gibes of every popinjay who thinks he can discharge my duties better than can I? Enough, sir!' He waved a great hand, growing dignified in his turn. 'Deliver the message that you bear.' And he held out that massive hand of his in expectation of a letter.

But Messer Lorenzo's pretence was, of necessity, that he bore his message by word of mouth.

'I am bidden by my lord to enjoin you to make surrender with the honours of war, which shall be conceded you by the Duke of Valentinois,' said he; and seeing the surprise, doubt, and suspicion that instantly began to spread upon Tolentino's face for all to read, he launched himself into explanations. 'Cesare Borgia has made terms with Duke Guidobaldo, and has promised him certain compensations if all the fortresses of his dominions make surrender without more ado. These terms my lord has been advised to accept, since by refusing them nothing can he hope to gain, whilst he may lose all. Perceiving this, and satisfied that by prolonging its resistance San Leo can only be postponing its ultimately inevitable surrender and entailing by that postponement the loss of much valuable life, Duke Guidobaldo has sent me to bid you in his name capitulate forthwith.'

It had a specious ring. It was precisely such a message as the humanitarian duke might well have sent, and the profit to accrue to himself from the surrender he enjoined seemed also a likely enough contingency. Yet the shrewd Tolentino had his doubts, doubts which might never have assailed another.

Wrinkles increased about his fierce black eyes as he bent them now upon the messenger.

'You will have letters of this tenour from my lord?' he said.

'I have none,' replied Messer Lorenzo, dissembling his uneasiness.

'Now, by Bacchus, that is odd!'

'Nay, sir, consider,' said the young man too hastily, 'the danger of my carrying such letters. Should they be found upon me by the Borgia troops, I – '

He checked, somewhat awkwardly, perceiving his mistake. Tolentino smacked his thigh with his open palm, and the room rang with the sound of it. His face grew red. He sprang up.

'Sir, sir,' said he, with a certain grimness, 'we must understand each other better. You say that you bring me certain orders to act upon a certain matter that has been concerted between Valentinois and my lord, and you talk of danger to yourself in bearing such orders in a letter. Be patient with me if I do not understand.' Tolentino's accents were unmistakably sardonic. 'So desirable is it from the point of view of Valentinois that such commands should reach me, that he could not have failed to pass you unmolested through his troops. Can you explain where I am wrong in these conclusions?'

There but remained for Messer Lorenzo to put upon the matter the best face possible. A gap was yawning at his feet. He saw it all too plainly. He was lost, it seemed.

'That explanation, my lord, no doubt, will furnish you, should you seek it from him. I hold it not. It was not given me, nor had I the presumption to request it.' He spoke calmly and proudly, for all that his heart-beats had quickened, and in his last words there was a certain veiled reproof of the other's attitude. 'When,' he continued, 'I said that it would have been dangerous to have given me letters, I but put forward, to answer you, the explanation which occurred to me at the moment. I had not earlier considered the matter. I now see that I was wrong in my assumption.'

Messer Tolentino considered him very searchingly. Throughout his speech, indeed, the castellan's eyes had never left his face. Messer Lorenzo's words all but convinced Tolentino that the man was lying. Yet his calm and easy assurance, his proud demeanour, left the captain still a lingering doubt.

'At least you'll bear some sign by which I am to know that you are indeed my lord's envoy?' said he.

'I bear none. I was dispatched in haste. The duke, it seems, did not reckon upon such a message as this being doubted.'

'Did he not?' quoth Tolentino, and his note was sardonic. Suddenly he asked another question. 'How came you to enter the fortress?'

'I climbed up from the plain on the southern side, where the rock is accounted inaccessible.' And, seeing the look of surprise that overspread the captain's face, 'I am of these parts,' he explained. 'In boyhood I have frequently essayed the climb. It was for this reason that Duke Guidobaldo chose me.'

'And when you had gained the wall, did you bid the sentry lower you a rope?'

'I did not. I had a rope of my own, and grappling hooks.'

'Why this, when you are a messenger from Guidobaldo?' The castellan turned sharply to his men. 'Where did you find him?' he inquired.

It was Bernardo who made haste to answer that they had found him lurking in the passage outside the guard-room as they were coming out.

Tolentino laughed with fierce relish, and swore copiously and humorously.

'So-ho!' he crowed. 'You had passed the sentry unperceived, and you were well within the fortress ere suddenly you were discovered, when, behold! you become a messenger of Guidobaldo's bearing orders to me to surrender the fortress, and you take this high tone about our indifferent watch to cover the sly manner of your entrance. Oh-o! 'Twas shrewdly thought of, but it shall not avail you – though it be a pity to wring the neck of so spirited a cockerel.' And he laughed again.

'You are a fool,' said Castrocaro with finality, 'and you reason like a fool.'

'Do I so? Now, mark me. You said that it was because you knew a secret way into this castle that Guidobaldo chose you for his messenger. Consider now the folly of that statement. You might yourself have construed that Guidobaldo's wish was that you should come hither secretly, though yourself you have admitted the obvious error of such an assumption. But to tell me that an envoy from the duke bidding us surrender to Cesare Borgia, and so do the will of the latter, should need come here by secret ways at the risk of his neck –' Tolentino shrugged and laughed in the white face of Messer Lorenzo.

'Which of us is the fool in this, sir?' he questioned, leering. Then, with an abrupt change of manner, he waved to his men. 'Seize and search him,' he commanded.

In a moment they had him down upon the floor, and they were stripping him of his garments. They made a very thorough search, but it yielded nothing.

'No matter,' said Tolentino as he got into bed again. 'We have more than enough against him already. Make him safe for the night. He shall go down the cliff's face again in the morning, and I swear he shall go down faster than ever he came up.'

And Messer Tolentino rolled over, and settled down comfortably to go to sleep again.

iv

Locked in the guard-house – since a man who was to die so soon was not worth the trouble of consigning to a dungeon, Messer Lorenzo Castrocaro spent, as you may conceive, a somewhat troubled night. He was too young and too full of life and the zest and warmth of it to be indifferent about quitting it, to look with apathy upon death. He had seen death and a deal of it – in the past two years of his martial career. But it had been the death of others, and never until now had it seemed to him that death was a thing that very much concerned himself. Even when he had imagined that he realized the dangers before him in this enterprise of San Leo, he had felt a certain confidence that it was not for him to die. He was, in fact, in that phase of youth and vigour when a man seems to himself immortal. And even now that he lay on the wooden bench in the guard-room, in the dark, he could hardly conceive that the end of him was really at hand. The catastrophe had overtaken him so suddenly, so very casually; and surely death was too great a business to be heralded so quietly.

He sighed wearily, and sought to find a more comfortable position on his pitilessly hard couch. He thought of many things – of his past

43

life, of early boyhood, of his mother, of his companions in arms, and of martial feats accomplished. He saw himself hacking a way through the living barrier that blocked the breach in the wall of Forli, or riding with Valentinois in the mighty charge that routed the Colonna under Capua; and he had a singularly vivid vision of the dead men he had beheld on those occasions and how they had looked in death. So would he look tomorrow, his reason told him. But still his imagination refused to picture it.

Then his thoughts shifted to Madonna Bianca de' Fioravanti, whom he would never see again. For months he had experienced an odd tenderness for that lady, of a sweetly melancholy order, and in secret he had committed some atrocious verses in her honour.

It had been no great affair when all was said; there had been other and more ardent loves in his short life; yet Madonna Bianca had evoked in him a tenderer regard, a holier feeling than any other woman that he had known. Indeed, the contrast was as sharp as that which lies between sacred and profane love. Perhaps it was because she was so unattainable, so distant, so immeasurably above him, the daughter of a great lord, the representative today of a great house, whilst he was but a condottiero, an adventurer who had for patrimony no more than his wits and his sword. He sighed. It would have been sweet to have seen her again before dying – to have poured out the story of his love as a swan pours out its deathsong. Yet, after all, it did not greatly matter.

You see that his examination of conscience in that supreme hour had little to do with the making of his soul.

He wondered would she hear of the end he had made; and whether, hearing, she would pity him a little; whether, indeed, she would do so much as remember him. It was odd he reflected that he should come to meet his end in the very castle that had been her father's; yet he was glad that it was not her father's hand that measured out to him this death that he must die tomorrow.

Physically exhausted as he was by the exertions of his climb, he fell at last into a fitful slumber; and when next he awakened it was to find the morning sunlight pouring through the tall windows of his prison.

He had been aroused by the grating of a key in the lock, and as he sat up, stiff and sore, on his hard couch, the door opened, and to him entered Bernardo, followed by six soldiers, all in their harness.

'A good day to you,' said Bernardo civilly, but a trifle thoughtlessly, considering what the day had in store for Messer Lorenzo.

The young man smiled as he swung his feet to the ground. 'A better day to you,' said he; and thus earned by his pleasantry and his debonair manner, the esteem of the gruff soldier.

It had come to Messer Lorenzo that, since die he must, the thing would be best done jocosely. Lamentations would not avail him. Let him then be blithe. Perhaps, after all, death were not so fearful a business as priests represented it; and as for that flaming hell that lies agape for young men who have drunk of the lusty cup of their youth there would be shrift for him before he went.

He rose, and ran his fingers through his long, fair hair, which had become tousled. Then he looked at his hands, grimy and bruised from yesternight's adventure, and begged Bernardo to fetch him water.

Bernardo's brows went up in surprise. The labour of washing did not seem a reasonable thing to him under the circumstances. Outside in the courtyard a drum began to beat a call. Bernardo thrust out a dubious lip.

'Messer Tolentino is awaiting you,' he said.

'I know,' replied Castrocaro. 'You would not have me present myself thus before him. It were to show a lack of proper respect for the hangman.'

Bernardo shrugged, and gave an order to one of his men. The fellow set his pike in a corner and went out, to return presently with an iron basin full of water. This he placed upon the table. Messer Lorenzo thanked him pleasantly, removed his doublet and shirt, and stripped to the waist he proceeded to make the best toilet that he could as briefly as possible.

Washed and refreshed, his garments dusted and their disarray repaired, he acknowledged himself ready. The men surrounded him at a word from Bernardo, marched him out into the open where the impatient castellan awaited him.

With a firm step, his head high, and his cheeks but little paler than their habit, Messer Lorenzo came into the spacious inner bailie of the castle. He glanced wistfully at the cobalt sky, and then considered the line of soldiers drawn up in the courtyard, all in their harness of steel and leather, with the grey walls of the fortress for their background. Not more than thirty men in all did they number, and they composed the castle's entire garrison.

A little in front of them the tall castellan was pacing slowly. He was all in black, in mourning for his late master, the Lord Fioravanti, and his hand rested easily upon the hilt of his sheathed sword, thrusting the weapon up behind. He halted at the approach of the doomed prisoner, and the men surrounding the latter fell away, leaving him face to face with Messer Tolentino.

The castellan considered him sternly for a little while, and Messer Lorenzo bore the inspection well, his deep blue eyes returning the other's solemn glance intrepidly.

At last the captain spoke:

'I do not know what was your intent in penetrating here last night, save that it was traitorous; that much the lies you told me have made plain, and for that you are to suffer death, as must any man taken as you had been.'

'For death I am prepared,' said Messer Lorenzo coolly; 'but I implore you to spare me the torture of a funeral oration before I go. My fortitude may not be equal to so much, particularly when you consider that I have had no breakfast.'

Tolentino smiled sourly, considering him.

'Very well,' said he. And then: 'You will not tell me who you are and what you sought here?'

'I have told you already, but you choose to discredit what I say. What need, then, for further words? It were but to weary you and me. Let us get to the hanging, which, from the general look of you, is no doubt a matter that you understand better.'

'Ha!' said Tolentino.

But now quite suddenly, from the line of men there was one who, having heard question and answer, made bold to call out:

'Sir captain, I can tell you who he is.'

The captain wheeled sharply upon the man-at-arms who had made the announcement.

'He is Messer Lorenzo Castrocaro.'

'One of Valentinois' condottieri?' exclaimed Tolentino.

'The same, sir captain,' the man assured him; and Messer Lorenzo, looking, recognized one who had served under his own banner some months since.

He shrugged indifferently at the captain's very evident satisfaction.

'What odds?' he said. 'One name will serve as well as another to die under.'

'And how,' quoth the captain, 'would you prefer to die? You shall have your choice.'

'Of old age, I think,' said Messer Lorenzo airily, and heard the titter that responded to his sally. But Tolentino scowled, displeased.

'I mean, sir, will you be hanged, or will you leap from the ledge to which you climbed last night?'

'Why, that now is a very different matter. You circumscribe the choice. Appoint for me, I pray, the death that will afford you the greater diversion.'

Tolentino considered him, stroking his long chin, his brows wrinkled. He liked the fellow for his intrepid daring in the face of death. But – he was Castellan of San Leo, and knew his duty.

'Why,' said he slowly at length, 'we know that you can climb like an ape; let us see if you can fly like a bird. Take him up to the ramparts yonder.'

'Ah, but stay!' cried Messer Castrocaro, with suddenly startled thoughts of those sins of his youth and with a certain corollary hope. 'Are you all pagans in San Leo? Is a Christian to be thrust across the black edge of death unshriven? Am I to have no priest, then?'

Tolentino frowned, as if impatient of this fresh motive for delay; then he signed shortly to Bernardo.

'Go fetch the priest,' said he; and thus dashed that faint, sly hope Messer Lorenzo had been harbouring that the place might contain no priest, and that these men, being faithful children of Mother Church, would never dare to slay unshriven a man who asked for shrift.

Bernardo went. He gained the chapel door on the very pronouncement of the 'Ita Missa est,' just as the morning Mass was ended, and on the threshold, in his haste, he all but stumbled against a lady in black who was coming forth attended by two women. He drew aside and flattened himself against the wall, muttering words of apology.

But the lady did not at once pass on.

'Why all this haste to chapel?' quoth she, accounting it strangely unusual in one of Tolentino's men.

'Messer Father Girolamo is required,' said he. 'There is a man about to die who must be shriven.'

'A man?' said she, with a show of tender solicitude, conceiving that one of the all too slender garrison had been wounded to the death.

'Ay, a captain of Valentino's – one Lorenzo Castrocaro – who came hither in the night. And,' he added vaingloriously, 'it was I, Madonna, who took him.'

But the Lady Bianca de' Fioravanti never heard his last words. She fell back a step, and rested, as if for support, against one of the diminutive pillars of the porch. Her face had become deathly white, her eyes stared dully at the soldier.

'What... What is his name, did you say?' she faltered.

'Lorenzo Castrocaro – a captain of Valentino's,' he repeated.

'Lorenzo Castrocaro?' she said in her turn, but on her lips the name seemed another, so differently did she utter it.

'Ay, Madonna,' he replied.

Suddenly she gripped his arm, so that she hurt him.

'And he is wounded – to the death?' she cried with a sudden fierceness, as it seemed to him.

48

'Nay; not wounded. He is to die, having been captured. That is all. Messer Tolentino will have him jump from the rock. You will have a good view from the battlements, Madonna. It is – '

She released his arm, and fell back from him in horror, cutting short his praise of the entertainment provided.

'Take me to your captain,' she commanded.

He stared at her, bewildered. 'And the priest?' he inquired.

'Let that wait. Take me to your captain.'

The command was so imperious that he dared not disobey her. He bowed, muttering in his beard, and, turning, went up the passage again, and so out into the courtyard, the lady and her women following.

Across the intervening space Madonna Bianca's eyes met the proud glance of Messer Lorenzo's, and saw the sudden abatement of that pride, saw the faint flush that stirred at sight of her in those pale cheeks. For to the young man this was a startling apparition, seeing that – as Cesare Borgia had been careful to provide – he had no knowledge or even suspicion of her presence in San Leo.

A moment she paused, looked at him, her soul in her eyes; then she swept forward, past Bernardo, her women ever following her. Thus came she, very pale but very resolute of mien, to the captain of her fortress.

Messer Tolentino bowed profoundly, uncovering, and at once explained the situation.

'Here is a young adventurer, Madonna, whom we captured last night within these walls,' said he. 'He is a captain in the service of Cesare Borgia.'

She looked at the prisoner again standing rigid before her, and from the prisoner to her officer.

'How came he here?' she asked, her voice curiously strained.

'He climbed the rock on the southern side at the risk of his neck,' said Tolentino.

'And what sought he?'

' 'Tis what we cannot precisely ascertain,' Tolentino admitted. 'Nor will he tell us. When captured last night he pretended to be an envoy from Duke Guidobaldo, which plainly he was not. That was but a subterfuge to escape the consequences of his rashness.'

And the captain explained, with a pardonable parade of his own shrewdness, how he had at once perceived that had Messer Lorenzo been what he pretended, there would have been no need for him to have come to San Leo thus, in secret.

'Nor need to risk his neck, as you have said, by climbing the southern side, had he been employed by Cesare Borgia,' said the lady.

'That is too hasty a conclusion, Madonna,' Tolentino answered. 'It is only on the southern side that it is possible to climb the wall; and along the summit itself there is no way round.'

'To what end, then, do you conceive that he came?'

'To what end? Why, to what end but to betray the castle into the hands of the Borgia troops,' cried Tolentino, a little out of patience at such a superfluity of questions.

'You have proof of that?' she asked him, a rising inflection in her voice.

'To common sense no proof is needed of the obvious,' said he sententiously, snorting a little as he spoke, out of his resentment of this feminine interference in men's affairs. 'We are about to fling him back the way he came,' he ended with a certain grim finality.

But Madonna Bianca paid little heed to his manner.

'Not until I am satisfied that his intentions were as you say,' she replied; and her tone was every whit as firm as his, and was invested with a subtle reminder that she was the mistress paramount of San Leo, and he no more than the castellan.

Tolentino glowered and shrugged.

'Oh, as you please, Madonna. Yet I would make bold to remind you that my ripe experience teaches me best how to deal with such a matter.'

The girl looked that war-worn veteran boldly in the eye.

'Knowledge, sir captain, is surely of more account than mere experience.'

His jaw fell.

'You mean that you – that you have knowledge of why he came?'

'It is possible,' said she, and turned from the astonished captain to the still more astonished prisoner.

Daintily she stepped up to Messer Lorenzo, whose deep sapphire eyes glowed now as they regarded her, reflecting some of the amazement in which he had listened to her words. He had weighed them, seeking to resolve the riddle they contained, and – be it confessed at once – wondering how he might turn the matter to his profit in this present desperate pass.

I fear you may discover here something of the villain in Messer Lorenzo. And I admit that he showed himself but little a hero of romance in that his first thought now was how he might turn to account the lady's interest in him. But if it was not exactly heroic, it was undeniably human, and if I have conveyed to you any notion that Messer Castrocaro was anything more than quite ordinarily human, then my task has been ill-performed indeed.

It was not so much his love of her as his love of himself, youth's natural love of life, that now showed him how he might induce her to open a door for his escape from the peril that encompassed him. And yet, lest you should come to think more ill of him than he deserves, you are to remember that he had raised his eyes to her long since, although accounting her far beyond his adventurer's reach.

She looked at him in silence for a moment. Then, with a calm too complete to be other than assumed she spoke.

'Will you give me your arm to the battlements, Messer Lorenzo?'

A scarlet flush leapt to his cheeks; he stepped forward briskly to her side. Tolentino would still have interposed.

'Consider, Madonna,' he began.

But she waved him peremptorily aside; and, after all, she was the mistress in San Leo.

Side by side the prisoner and the lady paramount moved away towards the staircase that led up to the embattled parapet. Tolentino growled his impatience, cursed himself for being a woman's lackey, dismissed his men in a rage, and sat down by the well in the centre of the courtyard to await the end of that precious interview.

Leaning on the embattled wall, looking out over the vast, sunlit Emilian Plain, Madonna Bianca broke at last the long spell of silence that had endured between herself and Castrocaro.

'I have brought you here, Ser Lorenzo,' she said, 'that you may tell me the true object of your visit to San Leo.' Her eyes were averted from his face, her bosom heaved gently, her voice quivered never so slightly.

He cleared his throat, to answer her. His resolve was now clear and definite.

'I can tell you what I did not come to do, Madonna,' he answered, and his accents were almost harsh. 'I did not come to betray you into the hands of your enemies. Of that I here make oath as I hope for the salvation of my soul.'

It may seem perjury at the first glance; yet it was strictly true, if not the whole truth. As we have seen, he had not dreamt that she was in San Leo, or that in delivering up the castle to Della Volpe's men he would be delivering up Madonna Bianca. Had he known of her presence, he would not, it is certain, have accepted the task. Therefore was he able to swear as he had done, and to swear truly, though he suppressed some truth.

'That much I think I knew,' she answered gently.

The words and the tone if they surprised him emboldened him in his deceit, urged him along the path to which already he had set his foot. At no other time – considering what he was, and what she – would he have dared so much. But his was now the courage of the desperate. He stood to die, and nothing in life daunts him who is face to face with death. He threw boldly that he might at the eleventh hour win back the right to live.

'Ah, ask me not why I came,' he implored her hoarsely. 'I have dared much, thinking that I dared all. But now – here before you, under the glance of your angel eyes – my courage fails me. I am become a coward who was not afraid when they brought me out to die.'

She shivered at his words. This he perceived, and inwardly the villain smiled.

'Look, Madonna.' He held out his hands, bruised, swollen, and gashed. 'I am something in this state from head to foot.' He turned. 'Look yonder.' And he pointed down the sheer face of the cliff. 'That way I came last night – in the dark, risking death at every step. You see that ledge, where there is scarce room to stand. Along that ledge I crept, to yonder wider space, and thence I leapt across that little gulf.' She shuddered as she followed his tale. 'By that crevice I came upwards, tearing knees and elbows, and so until I had gained the platform on the southern side, there.'

'How brave!' she cried.

'How mad!' said he. 'I show you this that you may know what courage then was mine, what indomitable impulse drove me hither. You would not think, Madonna, that having braved so much, I should falter now, and yet – ' He stopped, and covered his face with his hands.

She drew nearer, sidling towards him. 'And yet?' said she softly and encouragingly.

'Oh! I dare not!' he cried out. 'I was mad – mad!' And then by chance his tongue stumbled upon the very words to suit his case. 'Indeed, I do not know what was the spirit of madness that possessed me.'

He did not know! She trembled from head to foot at that admission. He did not know! But she knew. She knew, and hence the confidence with which she had interposed to brush Tolentino aside. For had he died, had the executioner driven him over that ledge in that horrible death-leap, it would have been her hands that had destroyed him.

For was it not she who had bewitched him? Was it not she who had drugged him with a love philtre – the elixirium aureum procured from Messer Corvinus Trismegistus? Did she not know that it was that elixir, burning fiercely and unappeasably in his veins, that had possessed him like a madness and brought him thither, reckless of all danger, so that he might come to her?

The mage had said that he would become her utter slave ere the moon had waned again. What had been the wizard's precise words?

53

She strove to recall them, and succeeded: 'He will come to you though the whole world lie between you and him.'

Again the confident promise rang in her ears, and here, surely, was its fulfilment. Behold how truly had the mage spoken – how well his golden elixir had done its work.

Thus reasoned Madonna Bianca, clearly and confidently. There were tears in her dark eyes as she turned them now upon the bowed head of the young captain at her side; the corners of her gentle mouth drooped wistfully. She put forth a hot hand, and laid it gently upon his fair head, which seemed all turned to gold in the fierce sunlight.

'Poor – poor Lorenzo!' she murmured fondly.

He started round and stared at her, very white.

'Oh, Madonna!' he cried, and sank upon one knee before her. 'You have surprised my secret – my unutterable secret! Ah, let me go! Let them hurl me from the rock, and so end my wretchedness!'

It was supremely well done, the villain knew; and she were no woman but a very harpy did she now permit his death. He was prepared for a pitying gentleness towards an affliction which she must now suppose her own beauty had inspired, and so he had looked for a kindly dismissal. But he was not prepared for any such answer as she made him.

'Dear love, what are you saying? Is there no other happiness for you save that of death? Have I shown anger? Do I show aught but gladness that for me you should have dared so much?'

To Messer Lorenzo it seemed in that moment that something was amiss with the world, or else with his poor brain. Was it conceivable that this noble lady should herself have turned the eyes of favour upon him? Was it possible that she should return this love of his, which he had deemed of such small account that in his urgent need he had not scrupled to parade it for purposes of deceit, where he would not have dared parade it otherwise?

He gave utterance to his overmastering amazement.

'Oh, it is impossible!' he cried; and this time there was no acting in his cry.

'What is impossible?' quoth she; and, setting her hands under his elbows, she raised him gently from his kneeling posture. 'What is impossible?' she repeated when they stood face to face once more.

And now the fire in his eyes was not simulated.

'It is impossible that you should not scorn my love,' said he.

'Scorn it? I? I who have awakened it – I who have desired it?'

'Desired it?' he echoed, almost in a whisper. 'Desired it?' For a spell they stood so, staring each into the other's eyes; then they fell into each other's arms, she sobbing in her extreme joy, and he upon the verge of doing no less, for, as you will perceive, it had been a very trying morning for him.

And it was thus – the Lady of San Leo and the Borgia captain clasped heart to heart under the summer sky – that Messer Tolentino found them.

Marvelling at the long delay, the castellan had thought it well to go after them. And what he now beheld struck him to stone, left him gaping like a foolish image.

They fell apart for very decency, and then the lady, rosily confused, presented Messer Lorenzo to the castellan as her future lord, and explained to him in confidence – and as she understood it – the true reason of that gentleman's visit to San Leo.

That Tolentino profoundly and scornfully discountenanced the whole affair – that he accounted it unpardonable in his mistress, a loyal subject of Duke Guidobaldo's, the holder, indeed, of one of the fortresses of Urbino, to take to husband one whose fortunes followed those of the Borgia usurper – there is no doubt, for Messer Tolentino has left it upon record. And if he did not there and then tell her so, with all that warmth of expression for which he was justly renowned, it was because he was dumbfounded by sheer amazement.

Thereafter, Messer Lorenzo was cared for as became a man in his position. A bath was prepared for him; fresh garments were found to fit him, the richest and most becoming being selected; the garrison was disappointed of its execution, and the Borgia captain went to dine at Madonna's table. For this banquet the choicest viands that the besieged commanded were forthcoming, and the rarest wines from Fioravanti's cellar were procured.

Messer Lorenzo was gay and sprightly, and in the afternoon, basking in the sunshine of Madonna Bianca's smiles, he took up a lute that he discovered in her bower, and sang for her one of the atrocious songs that in her honour he had made. It was a dangerous experiment. And the marvel of it is that, despite a pretty taste of her own in lyric composition, Madonna Bianca seemed well pleased.

In all Italy there was no happier man in that hour than Lorenzo Castrocaro, who, from the very edge of death, saw himself suddenly thrust up to the highest and best that he could have dared to ask of life. His happiness entirely engrossed his mind awhile. All else was forgotten. But suddenly, quite suddenly, remembrance flooded back upon him and left him cold with horror. He had been midway through his second song, Madonna languishing beside him, when the thought struck him, and he checked abruptly. The lute fell clattering from his grasp, which had suddenly grown nerveless.

With a startled cry his mistress leaned over him.

'Enzo! Are you ill?'

He rose precipitately.

'No, no; not ill. But – Oh!' He clenched his hands and groaned.

She too had risen, all sweet solicitude, demanding to know what ailed him. He turned to her a face that was blank with despair.

'What have I done? What have I done?' he cried, thereby increasing her alarm.

It crossed her mind that perhaps the effect of the magician's philtre was beginning to wane. Fearfully, urgently she insisted upon knowing what might be alarming him; and he, seeing himself forced to explain, paused but an instant to choose a middle course in words, to find expressions that would not betray him.

'Why, it is this,' he cried, and there was real chagrin in his voice as there was in his heart. 'In my hot madness to come hither, I never paused to count the cost. I am a Borgia captain, and at this moment no better than a traitor, a deserter who has abandoned his trust and his condotta to go over to the enemy – to sit here and take my ease in the very castle that my Duke is now besieging.'

At once she perceived and apprehended the awful position that was his.

'Gesù!' she cried. 'I had not thought of that.'

'When they take me, they will surely hang me for a traitor!' he exclaimed; and indeed he feared it very genuinely, for what else was he become? All night he had left Della Volpe and his men to await in vain the unbarring of the gate. For having failed there could be no excuse other than death or captivity. That he should not only remain living, but that he should later be discovered to have made alliance with Madonna Bianca de' Fioravanti was a matter that could have no issue but one.

'By heaven, it had been a thousand times better had Tolentino made an end of me this morning as he intended!' Then he checked abruptly, and turned to her penitently. 'Ah, no, no! I meant not that, Madonna! I spoke without reflecting. I were an ingrate to desire that – an ingrate and a fool. For had they killed me I had never known this day of happiness.'

'Yet what is to be done?' she cried, crushing her hands together in her agony of mind. 'What is to be done, my Enzo? To let you now depart would no longer save you. Oh let me think, let me think!' And then, almost at once: 'There is a way!' she cried; and on that cry, which had been one of gladness, she fell suddenly very gloomy and thoughtful.

'What way?' quoth he.

'I fear it is the only way,' she said never so wistfully.

And then he guessed what was in her mind and repudiated the suggestion.

'Ah! Not that,' he protested. 'That way we must not think of. I could not let you – not even to save my life.'

But on the word she looked up at him and her dark eye kindled anew with loving enthusiasm.

57

'To save your life – yes. That is cause enough to justify me. For nothing less would I do it, Enzo; but to save you – you whom I have brought into this pass – '

'What are you saying, sweet?' he cried.

'Why, that the fault is mine, and that I must pay the penalty.'

'The fault?'

'Did I not bring you hither?'

He flushed, something ill at ease to see – as he supposed – his lie recoiling now upon him.

'Listen!' she pursued. 'You shall do as I bid you. You shall go as my envoy to Cesare Borgia, and you shall offer him the surrender of San Leo in my name, stipulating only for the honours of war and the safe-conduct of my garrison.'

'No, no!' he protested still, and honestly, his villainy grown repugnant. 'Besides, how shall that serve me?'

'You shall say that you knew a way to win into San Leo and accomplish this – which,' she added, smiling wistfully, 'is, after all, the truth. The Duke will be too well content with the result to quarrel with the means employed.'

He averted his face.

'Oh! But it is shameful!' he cried out, and meant not what she supposed him to mean.

'In a few days – in a few weeks, at most – it will become inevitable,' she reminded him. 'After all, what do I sacrifice? A little pride, no more than that. And shall that weigh against your life with me? Better surrender now, when I have something to gain from surrender, than later, when I shall have all to lose.'

He considered. Indeed, it was the only way. And, after all, he was robbing her of nothing that she must not yield in time – of nothing, after all, that it might not be his to restore her very soon, in part at least. Considering this, and what the Duke had promised him, he gave her the fruit of his considerations, yet hating himself for the fresh deceit he practised.

'Be it so, my Bianca,' he said; 'but upon terms more generous than you have named. You shall not quit your dwelling here. Let your garrison depart, but you remain!'

'How is that possible?' she asked.

'It shall be,' he assured her confidently, the promised governorship in his mind.

V

That evening, with letters appointing him her plenipotentiary, he rode out of San Leo alone, and made his way down into the valley by the bridlepath. At the foot of this he came upon Della Volpe's pickets, who bore him off to their captain, refusing to believe his statement that he was Lorenzo Castrocaro.

When Della Volpe beheld him, the warrior's single eye expressed at once suspicion and satisfaction.

'Where have you been?' he demanded harshly.

'In San Leo, yonder,' answered Castrocaro simply.

Della Volpe swore picturesquely.

'We had accounted you dead. My men have been searching for your body all day at the foot of the rock.'

'I deplore your disappointment and their wasted labour,' said Lorenzo, smiling; and Della Volpe swore again.

'How came you to fail, and, having failed, how come you out alive?'

'I have not failed,' was the answer. 'I am riding to the Duke with the garrison's terms of capitulation.'

Della Volpe very rudely refused to believe him, whereupon Messer Lorenzo thrust under the condottiero's single eye Madonna Bianca's letters. At that the veteran sneered unpleasantly.

'Ha! By the horns of Satan! I see! You ever had a way with the women, Lorenzo. I see!'

'For a one-eyed man you see too much,' said Messer Lorenzo, and turned away. 'We will speak of this again – when I am wed. Good night!'

It was very late when he reached Urbino. But late as it was – long after midnight – the Duke was not abed. Indeed, Cesare Borgia never seemed to sleep. At any hour of the day or night he was to be found by those whose business was of import.

His highness was working in the library with Agabito preparing dispatches for Rome, when Messer Lorenzo was ushered into his presence.

He looked up as the young captain entered.

'Well,' quoth he sharply. 'Do you bring me news of the capture of San Leo?'

'Not exactly, highness,' replied the condottiero. 'But I bring you a proposal of surrender, and the articles of capitulation. If your highness will sign them, I shall take possession of San Leo in your name tomorrow.'

The Duke's fine eyes scanned the confident young face very searchingly. He smiled quietly.

'*You* will take possession?' he said.

'As the governor appointed by your highness,' Messer Lorenzo blandly explained.

He laid his letters before the Duke, who scanned them with a swift eye, then tossed them to Agabito that the latter might con them more minutely.

'There is a provision that the Lady Bianca de' Fioravanti is to remain in San Leo,' said the secretary, marvelling.

'Why that?' quoth Cesare of Messer Lorenzo. 'Why, indeed, any conditions?'

'Matters have put on a curious complexion,' the condottiero expounded. 'Things went not so smoothly with me as I had hoped. I will spare your highness the details; but, in short, I was caught within the castle walls, and – and I had to make the best terms I could under such circumstances.'

'You do not, I trust, account them disadvantageous to yourself?' said Cesare. 'It would distress me that it should be so. But I cannot think it; for Madonna Bianca is accounted very beautiful.'

Castrocaro crimsoned in his sudden and extreme confusion. For once he was entirely out of countenance.

'You are informed of the circumstances, highness?' was all that he could say.

Cesare's laugh was short and almost contemptuous.

'I am something of a seer,' he replied. 'I could have foretold this end ere ever you set out. You have done well,' he added, 'and the governorship is yours. See to it at once, Agabito. Ser Lorenzo will be in haste to return to Madonna Bianca.'

A half-hour later, after the bewildered yet happy Castrocaro had departed to ride north again, Cesare rose from his writing-table, yawned, and smiled at the secretary, who had his confidence and affection.

'And so, San Leo, that might have held out for a year, is won,' he said, and softly rubbed his hands in satisfaction. 'This Castrocaro thinks it is all his own achievement. The lady imagines that it is all her own – by the aid of that charlatan Trismegistus. Neither dreams that all has fallen out as I had intended, and by my contriving.' He made philosophy for the benefit of Messer Agabito: 'Who would achieve greatness must learn not only to use men, but to use them in such a manner that they never suspect they are being used. Had I not chanced to overhear what I overheard that night at the house of Corvinus Trismegistus, and, knowing what I knew, set the human pieces in this game in motion to yield me this result, matters might have been different indeed, and lives would have been lost ere San Leo threw up its gates. And I have seen to it that the wizard's elixir of love should do precisely as he promised for it. Madonna Bianca, at least, believes in that impostor.'

'You had foreseen this, highness, when you sent Castrocaro on that dangerous errand?' Agabito ventured to inquire.

'What else? Where should I have found me a man for whom the matter was less dangerous? He did not know that Madonna Bianca was there. I had the foresight to keep that matter secret. I sent him, confident that, should he fail to open the gates to Della Volpe and be taken, he was crafty enough not to betray himself, and Madonna must, of course, assume that it was her love philtre had brought him to her irresistibly. Could she have hanged him, knowing that? Could she have done other than she has done?'

'Indeed, Corvinus has served you well.'

'So well that he shall have his life. The precious poison has failed to kill him, and this is the sixteenth day.' The Duke laughed shortly, and thrust his thumbs into the girdle of his robe, which was of cloth of gold, reversed with ermine. 'Give the order for his release to-morrow, Agabito. But bid them keep me his tongue and his right hand as remembrances. Thus he will never write or speak another lie.

San Leo capitulated on the morrow. Tolentino and his men rode out with the honours of war, lance on thigh, the captain very surly at the affair, which he contemptuously admitted passed his understanding.

Into the fortress came then Messer Lorenzo Castrocaro at the head of a troop of his own men, to lay his governorship at the feet of Madonna Bianca.

They were married that very day in the chapel of the fortress, and although it was some years before each made to the other the confession of the deceit which each had practised, the surviving evidence all shows – and to the moralists this may seem deplorable – that they were none the less happy in the meantime.

THE PERUGIAN

i

The Secretary of State of the Signory of Florence urged his mule across the bridge that spans the Misa, and drawing rein upon the threshold of the town of Sinigaglia, stood there at gaze. On his right to westward the sun was sinking to the distant hazy line of the Apennines, casting across the heaven an incendiary glow to blend with that of the flames that rose above the city.

The secretary hesitated. His nature was gentle and almost timid, as becomes a student and a man of thought, being in his own case in violent contrast to the ruthless directness of his theories. Scanning the scene before him with the wide-set, observant eyes that moved so deliberately in his astute, olive-tinted face, he wondered uneasily how things might have fared with Cesare Borgia. Uproar reached him, completing the tale of violence which was borne to his senses already by the sight of the flames. The uneasy guards at the gate who had watched him closely, mistrusting his hesitation, hailed him at last, demanding to know his business. He disclosed himself, whereupon they respectfully bade him to pass on and enjoy an ambassador's immunity.

Thus bidden he conquered his hesitation, touched his mule with the spur and pushed on through the slush and snow that had accumulated about the gateway into the borgo, where he found a comparative calm, past the market-place which was deserted, and on towards the palace.

The clamour, he observed, came all from the eastern quarter of the town, which he knew – for he was a surprisingly well-informed gentleman, this Florentine – to be inhabited by the Venetian traders and the prosperous Jews. Hence he argued logically – for he was ever logical – that the main issue was decided and that the uproar was that of looting soldiery; and knowing as he did the rigour with which looting was forbidden to the followers of the Duke of Valentinois, the only sane conclusion seemed to him to be that notwithstanding all the guile and craft at his command, the Duke had been worsted in the encounter with his mutinous condottieri. And yet in his wisdom and in his knowledge of men Messer Macchiavelli hesitated to accept such a conclusion, however much the facts might seem to thrust it upon him. He guessed something of Cesare Borgia's design in coming to Sinigaglia to make peace with the rebels and settle terms for the future. He knew that the Duke had been prepared for treachery – that he had done no more than pretend to walk into a trap, having taken care first to make himself master of its springs. That in spite of this those springs should have snapped upon him, the secretary could not believe. And yet undoubtedly pillage was toward, and pillage was forbidden by the Duke.

Marvelling, then, Messer Macchiavelli rode on up the steep street towards the palace. Soon his progress was arrested. The narrow way was thronged and solid with humanity; a great mob surged before the palace. Upon one of its balconies in the distance he could faintly discern the figure of a man, and since this man was gesticulating, the secretary concluded that he was haranguing the multitude.

Messer Macchiavelli leaned from the saddle to question a rustic on the outskirts of the mob.

'What is happening?' quoth he.

'The devil knows,' answered the man addressed. 'His Potency the Duke with Messer Vitellozzo and some others went into the palace two hours since. Then comes one of his captains – they say it was Messer da Corella – with soldiery, and they went down into the borgo where they say they have fallen upon the troops of the Lord of Fermo, and the Lord of Fermo is in the palace too, and it is New Year's Day tomorrow. By the Madonna, an ugly beginning to the new year this, whatever may be happening! They are burning and looting and fighting down there, until they have made the borgo into the likeness of hell, and in the palace the devil knows what may be happening. Gesù Maria! These be dread times, sir. They do say...'

Abruptly he checked his loquaciousness under the discomposingly fixed gaze of those sombre, observant eyes. He examined his questioner more closely, noted his sable, clerkly garments heavily trimmed with fur, mistrusted instinctively that crafty, shaven face with its prominent cheekbones, and bethought him that he were perhaps wiser not to make himself further the mouthpiece of popular rumour.

'But then,' he ended abruptly, therefore, 'they say so much that I know not what they say.'

The thin lines of Macchiavelli's lips lengthened slightly in a smile, as he penetrated the reasons of the man's sudden reticence. He pressed for no further information, for indeed he needed no more than already he had received. If the duke's men under Corella had fallen upon Oliverotto da Fermo's troops, then his expectations had been realized, and Cesare Borgia, meeting treachery with treachery, had stricken down the mutinous condottieri.

A sudden surge of the crowd drove the Florentine orator and the rustic apart. A roar rose from the throat of the multitude.

'Duca! Duca!'

Standing in his stirrups, Macchiavelli beheld in the distance before the palace a glitter of arms and the fluttering of bannerols bearing the bull device of the House of Borgia. The lances formed into a double file, and this clove a way through that human press, coming rapidly down the street towards the spot where the secretary's progress had been arrested.

The crowd was flung violently back like water before the prow of a swift-sailing ship. Men stumbled against one another, each in turn cursing the one who thrust against him, and in a moment all was fierce clamour and seething anger; yet above it all rang the acclaiming shout:

'Duca! Duca!'

On came the glittering riders, jingling and clanking, and at their head on a powerful black charger rode a splendid figure, all steel from head to foot. His visor was open, and the pale young face within was set and stern. The beautiful hazel eyes looked neither to right nor left, taking no heed of the acclamations thundering all about him. Yet those eyes saw everything whilst seeming to see nothing. They saw the Florentine orator, and seeing him, they kindled suddenly.

Macchiavelli swept off his bonnet, and bowed to the very withers of his mule to salute the conqueror. The pale young face smiled almost with a certain conscious pride, for the Duke was well pleased to have as it were the very eyes of Florence upon him in such a moment. He drew rein on a level with the envoy.

'Olà, Ser Niccoló!' he called.

The lances cleared a path speedily, flinging the crowd still farther back, and Messer Macchiavelli walked his mule forward in answer to that summons.

'It is done,' the Duke announced. 'I have fulfilled no less than I promised. What it was I promised you will now understand. I made my opportunity, and having made it I employed it – so well that I hold them fast, Vitelli, Oliverotto, Gravina and Giangiordano's bastard. The other Orsini, Gianpaolo Baglioni and Petrucci will follow. My net is wide flung, and to the last man they shall pay the price of treachery.'

He paused, waiting for words that should tell him not what opinion might be Messer Macchiavelli's own, but what reception such news was likely to receive in Florence. The secretary, however, had all the caution of the astute. He was not addicted to any unnecessary expressions of opinion. His face remained inscrutable. He bowed in silence, as one who accepts a statement without consciousness of the right to comment.

A frown flickered between the splendid eyes that were considering him.

'I have done a very great service to your masters, the Signory of Florence,' he said, almost in a tone of challenge.

'The Signory shall be informed, Magnificent,' was the orator's evasive answer, 'and I shall await the honour of conveying to your potency the Signory's felicitations.'

'Much has been done,' the Duke resumed. 'But much is yet to do, and who shall tell me what?' He looked at Macchiavelli, and his eyes invited counsel.

'Does your potency ask me?'

'Indeed,' said the Duke.

'For theory?'

The Duke stared; then laughed. 'For theory,' he said. 'The practice you can leave to me.'

Macchiavelli's eyes narrowed. 'When I speak of theory,' he explained, 'I mean an opinion personal to myself – not a pronouncement of the Florentine Secretary.' He leaned a little nearer. 'When a prince has enemies,' he said quietly, 'he must deal with them in one of two ways; he must either convert them into friends or put it beyond their power to continue his enemies.'

The Duke smiled slowly. 'Where learnt you that?' he asked.

'I have watched with admiration your potency's rise to greatness,' said the Florentine.

'And you have melted down my actions into maxims to govern my future?'

'More, Magnificent, to govern all future princes.'

The Duke looked squarely into that sallow, astute face with its sombre eyes and prominent cheekbones.

'I sometimes wonder which you are – courtier or philosopher,' he said. 'But your advice is timely – either make them my friends or put it beyond their power to continue my enemies. I could not again trust them as my friends. You will see that. Therefore...' He broke off. 'But we will talk of this again, when I return. Corella's troops have got out of hand; they are burning and looting in the borgo, and

I go to set a term to it, or else peddling Venice will be in arms to recover the ducats plundered from her shopkeepers. You will find entertainment in the palace. Await me there.'

He made a sign to his lances, wheeled, and rode on briskly about his task, while Macchiavelli in his turn went off in the opposite direction, through the lane opened out for him very readily in the crowd, since all had seen that he was one who enjoyed the exalted honour of the Duke's acquaintance. The Florentine made his way to the palace as he had been bidden, and thence he indited his famous letter to the Signory of Florence, in which he announced these happenings to his masters. He informed them of the manner adopted by Cesare Borgia to turn the tables upon those who had not kept faith with him, he told them how his master-stroke had resulted in the seizure of the three Orsini, of Vitellozzo Vitelli, and Oliverotto, Lord of Fermo, and he concluded with the opinion: 'I greatly doubt if any of them will be alive by morning.'

Anon he was to realize that for all his penetration he had failed to plumb to its full depth the craft and guile of Cesare Borgia. So astute an observer should have perceived that to have wrung the necks of the Orsini out of hand would have been to spread consternation and alarm in the lair of the bear in Rome, and that being alarmed the powerful Cardinal Orsini, his brother Giulio and his nephew Matteo (with whom we are more particularly concerned) might seek safety in flight, and in that safety concert reprisals.

Macchiavelli's failure to foresee the course which such considerations must dictate to Cesare is another proof of how much the Duke was the Florentine's master in statecraft.

The Lords of Fermo and Castello were dealt with as Macchiavelli expected. They were formally judged, found guilty of treason against their overlord, and strangled that same night – back to back, with the same rope, it is said – in the Palace of the Prefecture of Sinigaglia, whereafter their bodies were ceremoniously borne to the Misericordia Hospital. But the Orsini did not share just yet the fate of their fellow-traitors. They were accorded another ten days of life, until, that is, Cesare had received advices from Rome that the

Cardinal Orsini and the rest of the Orsini brood were safely captured. Thereupon at Assisi – whither the Duke had removed himself by then, Gravina and Paolo Orsini were delivered over to the strangler.

The Duke's net had been wide flung, as he told Macchiavelli on that evening in Sinigaglia. Yet four there were who had escaped its meshes: Gianpaolo Baglioni, prevented from waiting upon the Duke in Sinigaglia by an illness which had proved less fatal to him than had their health to his associates; Pandolfo Petrucci, Tyrant of Siena – the only one of them all who seems to have had the wit to mistrust the Duke's intentions – who armed at all points had taken refuge behind the ramparts of his city, there to wait upon events; Fabio Orsini, who had gone after Petrucci; and Matteo Orsini, the latter's cousin and the cardinal's nephew, who had vanished no man knew whither.

The Duke set himself the task of hunting down the first three, whose whereabouts were known to him. Matteo mattered less, and could be left until later.

'But I swear to God,' Cesare informed Fra Serafino, the minorite friar who discharged the functions of secretary in the absence of the moonfaced Agabito. 'I swear to God, that there is no hole in Italy into which I shall not pursue him.'

This was at Assisi on the very day that he ordered the strangling of Gravina and Giangiordano's bastard. On that same evening came one of his spies with information that Matteo Orsini was in hiding at Pievano, the castle of his distant kinsman Almerico – an Orsini this last, too aged and too inactive to be worthy the Duke's attention, a studious man, living almost in seclusion with his books and his daughter, untouched by ambition, asking but to be left in peace, undisturbed by all the strife and bloodshed that were afflicting Italy.

The Duke was housed in the Rocca Maggiore, that grey embattled fortress crowning the steep hill above the city, and from the height of its scarred and rugged slopes dominating the Umbrian plain. He received the messenger in a vast stone-flagged chamber that was very bare and chill. A great fire roared in the cavernous fireplace, shedding an orange glow upon the empty spaces and driving the shadows before it to seek refuge in the groins of the ceiling overhead. Yet the Duke, pacing thoughtfully back and forth whilst the messenger related what he had discovered, was tightly wrapped for greater warmth in a scarlet mantle lined with lynx fur. Fra Serafino occupied an oaken writing pulpit near one of the windows, and sat cutting a quill, apparently lost in his task, yet missing no word of what was being said.

The messenger was intelligent, and he had been diligent. Not content with learning that Matteo Orsini was believed to be at Pievano, he had scoured the borgo for scraps of gossip, anticipating out of his own knowledge the very question which the Duke now asked him – though not directly – and seeing to it that he came equipped with a ready answer.

'This, then, is mere gossip,' Cesare sneered. ' "It is said" that Matteo Orsini is at Pievano. I am sick to death of "It is said", and all his family. I have known him long, and never found him other than a liar.'

'But the tale, may it please your potency, has its probabilities,' said the messenger.

The Duke halted in his pacing. He stood before the flaming logs, and put out a hand to its genial warmth – a hand so delicate and slender that you would never have supposed its tapering fingers to possess a strength that could snap a horseshoe. Standing thus, the leaping firelight playing over his scarlet cloak, he seemed himself a thing of fire. He threw back his tawny young head, and his lovely eyes lost their dreamy thoughtfulness as they fastened now upon the messenger.

'Probabilities?' said he. 'Discover them.'

The messenger was prepared to do so.

'The Count Almerico has a daughter,' he said promptly. 'It is the common talk of Pievano that this lady – Madonna Fulvia she is called – and Ser Matteo are to be married. The kinship between them is none so close as to forbid it. The old count approves, loving Ser Matteo as a son. And so, where else in Italy should Ser Matteo be safer than with those who love him? Then, too, Pievano is remote, its lord is a man of books, taking no part in worldly turbulence; therefore Pievano, being of all places the last in which one would think of looking for Ser Matteo is the likeliest to which he would run for shelter. Thus circumstances confirm the rumour of his presence there.'

The Duke considered the fellow in silence for a moment, weighing what he said.

'You reason well,' he admitted at length, and the messenger bowed himself double, overwhelmed by so much commendation. 'You have leave to go. Bid them tell Messer da Corella to attend me.'

The man bowed again, stepped softly to the door and vanished. As the heavy curtain quivered to rest, Cesare sauntered across to one of the windows and stared out upon the bleak landscape stretching for miles before him in the cold light of that January afternoon. Above the distant blue-grey mass of the Apennines the brooding sky was slashed with gold. The River Chiagi winding its way to the Tiber lay like a silver ribbon upon the dull green plain. Cesare stared before him a while seeing nothing of all this. Then abruptly he turned to Fra Serafino, who was now testing the quill he had cut.

'What is to be done to take this fellow?' he asked.

It was his way to seek advice of all men, yet never following any but such as jumped with his own wishes. And where no man's advice consorted with his own notions, he acted upon his own notions none the less.

The gaunt-faced monk looked up, almost startled by the suddenness of the question. Knowing the Duke's way, and knowing that Corella had been sent for, Fra Serafino put two and two together, and presented the Duke with what he conceived to be the total sum.

'Send ten lances to fetch him from Pievano,' he replied.

'Ten lances – fifty men... Hum! And if Pievano were to throw up its bridges, and resist?'

'Send another twenty lances and a gun,' said Fra Serafino.

The Duke considered him, smiling faintly.

'You prove to me that you know nothing of Pievano, and still less of men, Fra Serafino. I wonder do you know anything of women?'

'God forbid!' ejaculated the monk, utterly scandalized.

'Then are you worthless as a counsellor in this,' was the Duke's conclusion. 'I had hoped you could have imagined yourself a woman for a moment.'

'Imagine myself a woman?' quoth Fra Serafino, his deep-set eyes staring.

'That you might tell me what manner of man would be likeliest to delude you. You see, Pievano is a rabbit warren. You might conceal an army there, how much more easily a single man. And I do not intend to alarm the Count Almerico into sending to earth a guest whom we are not absolutely sure that he is harbouring. You see the difficulty, I trust? To resolve it I shall need a man of little heart and less conscience; a scoundrel who is swayed by nothing but his own ambition, who cares for nothing but his own advancement; and it is an inevitable condition that he should be of an exterior that is pleasing to a woman and likely to command her confidence. Now where shall I find me such a paragon?'

But Fra Serafino had no answer. He was lost in an amazed consideration of the crooked underground ways by which Cesare burrowed to his ends. And then Corella clanked in, booted, bearded, stalwart and stiff, the very type of the condottiero.

The Duke turned, and considered him in silence at long length. In the end he shook his head.

'No,' he said, 'you are not the man. You are too much the soldier, too little the courtier, too much the swordsman, too little the lute-player, and I think that you are almost ugly. If you were a woman, Fra Serafino, should you not consider him an ugly fellow?'

'I am not a woman, Magnificent…'

'That is all too evident,' the Duke deplored.

'And I do not know what I should think if I were a woman. Probably I should not think at all, for I do not believe that women think.'

'Misogynist,' said the Duke.

'God be thanked,' said Fra Serafino devoutly.

The Duke returned to the consideration of his captain.

'No,' he said again. 'The essence of success is to choose the right tools for the work in hand; and you are not the tool for this, Michele. I want a handsome, greedy, unscrupulous scoundrel, who can both ply a sword and lisp a sonnet. Where shall I find one answering that description. Ferrante da Isola would have been the very man, but poor Ferrante died of one of his own jests.'

'What is the task, Magnificent?' ventured Corella.

'I'll tell that to the man I send to do it, when I have found him. Is Ramirez here?' he asked suddenly.

'He is at Urbino, my lord,' Corella answered. 'But there is Pantaleone degli Uberti, who seems in some way such a man as you describe.'

The Duke considered. 'Send him hither,' he said shortly and Corella bowed stiffly, and departed on that errand.

Cesare paced slowly back to the fire, and stood warming himself until Pantaleone came – a tall, handsome fellow this, with sleek black hair and bold black eyes, martial at once in bearing and apparel yet with a certain foppishness not unbecoming to his youth.

The interview was short. 'From information that I have received,' said Cesare, 'I will wager a thousand ducats to a horseshoe that Matteo Orsini is with his uncle at Pievano. I offer that thousand ducats for his head. Go and earn it.'

Pantaleone was taken aback. He blinked his bold black eyes.

'What men shall I take?' he stammered.

'What men you please. But understand the thing is not to be done by force. At the first show of it, Matteo, if he is there, will go to earth like a mole, and not all your questing shall discover him. This is an affair for wits, not lances. There is a woman at Pievano who loves Matteo, or whom Matteo loves... But you will see for yourself what opportunities there are, and you will use them. Corella thinks you have the wit to accomplish such a task. Afford me proof of it, and I will make your fortune.' He waved his hand in dismissal, and

73

Pantaleone stifled a hundred questions that were bubbling in his mind, and departed.

Fra Serafino stroked his lean nose thoughtfully with his quill. 'I would not trust that fellow with a woman, nor a woman with that fellow,' he delivered himself. 'He is too full in the lips.'

'That,' said Cesare, 'is why I chose him.'

'In a woman's hands he will be so much wax,' the monk continued.

'I am stiffening him with a thousand ducats,' said the Duke.

But the friar's pessimism was nothing lessened. 'A woman's arts can melt gold until it runs,' said he.

The Duke looked at him a moment. 'You know too much about women, Fra Serafino,' he said, and under that rebuke the monkish secretary shuddered and fell silent.

ii

Pantaleone degli Uberti arrived at Pievano on the wings of a snowstorm that swept across the Perugian foothills, and he arrived alone. Within a couple of leagues of the little town he had parted company with the ten knaves he had brought with him from Assisi. He gave them orders to break up into groups of twos and threes and thus follow him to Pievano, each group seeking different quarters and pretending no acquaintance with the others. He concerted signals by which at need he could rally them to himself, and arranged that of the group of three who were to take up their quarters at the Osteria del Toro one at least should remain constantly at the inn where at any moment Pantaleone could find him.

Messer Pantaleone, you see, was a man of method.

He bade them, further, dissemble their true estate, and, himself adopting this course which he imposed upon his followers, he staggered some hours later over the drawbridge into the courtyard of the citadel on foot, a bedraggled, footsore man who seemed to be upon the point of utter exhaustion. Admitted by a groom, he reeled into the presence of the Lord Almerico Orsini and gasped out as if with his last breath an urgent prayer for sanctuary.

'I am a hunted man, my lord,' he lied. 'That bloody despot Valentino clamours for this poor life of mine to swell his hecatomb.'

The old Lord of Pievano's white hands clawed the carved ebony arms of his great chair. From under shaggy brows his piercing dark eyes were bent upon this visitor. He knew well what was the hecatomb to which Messer Pantaleone referred; no need for him to ask; absorbed though he might be in his studies and removed in mind, as in body, from all worldly turbulence, yet, being an Orsini, it was not in human nature that he should remain ignorant of and indifferent to the shedding of Orsini blood. And since here was a man who, as it seemed, was come straight from the scene of strife, he was to be welcomed as one bringing news on matters closely touching the Lord of Pievano.

Yet it was as characteristic of old Almerico Orsini as it was anomalous in his day – when life was cheap and the misfortunes of others troubled men but little – that his first thought should be for this stranger's condition. Seeing him so piteously bedraggled, so white and haggard, swaying like a drunkard where he stood and breathing with obvious difficulty – in short, a man who had reached the uttermost limits of endurance – the Lord Almerico made a swift sign to the groom who had admitted him. The lackey thrust forward a rush-seated chair, and into this Messer Pantaleone sank limply yet gratefully, dropping his sodden cap upon the marbled floor and loosening his great red cloak so that his soldier's leather harness was revealed.

He looked at the Lord Almerico with a faint smile that seemed to express his thanks, and then his bold eyes, seeming very weary now under their heavy drooping lids, passed on to the lady who stood beside her father's chair. She was a girl, no more, of a willowy, virginal slenderness, very simply clad in a wine-coloured gown cut square across her white young breast, and caught about her slender waist by a silver girdle with a beryl clasp. Her blue-black hair was held in a clump behind by a net of golden cord; her eyes, of a blue so deep that they seemed almost black, considered him piteously from out of her pale face.

Thus Messer Pantaleone first beheld her, and since his taste in women was of the rude sort that craves for swelling amplitudes of form, his questing glance passed on without reluctance to rake the shadows of that noble chamber, looking for another who was not present.

'Why are you come to me?' Almerico asked him with inscrutable simplicity.

'Why?' Messer Pantaleone blinked as though the oddness of the question afforded him surprise. 'Because you are an Orsini, and because my cause is the cause of the Orsini.' He proceeded to explain himself. 'Paolo Orsini was my friend.'

'*Was?*' The question came sharply from Madonna Fulvia.

Pantaleone fetched a deep sigh, and sank together like a man in the uttermost depths of dejection. 'I see you have not heard. Yet I should have thought that by now such evil news had travelled o'er the face of all Italy. Paolo was strangled yesterday at Assisi, and with him was strangled too the Duke of Gravina.'

The old man uttered a sharp cry. He half-rose from his seat, supporting himself upon trembling arms; then, bereft of strength, he sank back again.

'God's curse upon me who am the bearer of ill-tidings,' growled the crafty Pantaleone savagely.

But the old man, recovering from his momentary collapse under the shock of that news, reproved him for his words, whilst Madonna Fulvia stood immobile and rigid in a grief that was after all impersonal, for, although they were her kinsmen, she had known neither of those whose death this fugitive announced.

'That is not yet all,' Pantaleone pursued, as if defending himself against the Lord Almerico's reproof. 'From Rome comes news that the Cardinal is in a dungeon of Sant' Angelo, that Giangiordano is taken, together with Santacroce and I know not whom besides. We know what mercy the Borgia will display. The Pope and his bastard will

never rest as long as in the House of Orsini one stone remains upon
another.'

'Then will he never rest indeed,' said Madonna Fulvia proudly.

'I pray so, Madonna, devoutly do I pray it – I who was Paolo
Orsini's friend and who to my undying shame have served the Borgia
tyrant with him. For that – because Valentino knows that if I served
him it was but because I served Orsini and that I am to be reckoned
as of the Orsini's family – I am now proscribed and hunted, and if I
am taken I shall perish as Paolo and Gravina perished and as men say
that Matteo Orsini perished too.'

In nothing perhaps does the craft of the man appear so starkly as
in this probing statement. As he spoke these words he watched father
and daughter closely, seeming but to consider them with eyes of
concern and pity. He saw the sudden movement of astonishment that
neither could repress. Then came the girl's question, laden with a
sudden and betraying eagerness.

'Do men say that?' she cried, her eyes kindling and her bosom
quickening in her faint excitement.

'It is the common talk,' said that swindler sorrowfully. 'I pray God
and the saints it be untrue.'

'Indeed…' Almerico began gravely, as if to reassure him, and then
caution supervening, he abruptly checked. Unworldly and guileless
though he might be, yet some knowledge of his fellow-man had
come to him with his years, and this fugitive inspired him with little
trust, awakening in him an unusual caution. Obeying it, he altered
the tone and current of his phrase. 'I thank you, sir, for that prayer.'

But Pantaleone accounted himself answered concluded that
Cesare Borgia's suspicions were correct, and that Matteo Orsini was
in hiding here at Pievano or hereabouts. He reasoned syllogistically.
The woman who loved Matteo Orsini would not have received the
news of his death with such equanimity had she not been positively
assured that he was living. Such assurance in such times nothing
short of the man's presence at Peivano could afford. The very
eagerness with which she had received the rumour Pantaleone had

77

invented of Matteo Orsini's death showed how welcome would be a tale that might diminish the hunt for that proscribed fugitive.

Wearing outwardly his mask of dejection, Messer Pantaleone's treacherous heart rejoiced in this assurance that he was hot upon the trail, and that soon Matteo Orsini and a thousand ducats would be his.

But now he had to submit to questionings from his host. Almerico's mistrust demanded to know more of him.

'You are from Assisi?' he inquired.

'From the Lord Duke of Valentinois' camp there,' answered the emissary.

'And you fled incontinently when they strangled Paolo and Gravina?'

'Not so.' Messer Pantaleone saw the trap. In a game of wits he was a match for any ten such recluse students as the Lord of Pievano. 'That, as I have said, was yesterday – before Cesare Borgia had proof of my devotion to the Orsini. But for that same devotion and the need to act upon it, I might have remained a captain in the tyrant's service. But it happened that I knew of Valentino's designs upon Petrucci at Siena. I attempted to send a letter of warning to Petrucci. That letter was intercepted, and I had but time to get to horse before the hangman's grooms should come to fetch me. I rode that beast to death a league from here. My notion was to get to Siena and Petrucci; but, being unhorsed and in hourly danger of capture, I bethought me that I would turn aside and seek sanctuary here. Yet, my lord,' he ended, rising with elaborate show of physical pain and difficulty, 'if so be you think that by my presence I shall draw down upon you Valentino's vengeful justice, then...' He gathered his cloak about him, like a man about to take his leave.

'A moment, sir – a moment,' said Almerico, hesitating; and he put forth a hand to stay the soldier.

'What matters Valentino?' cried the girl, and quick anger blazed in her eyes, transmuting them into fiery sapphires. 'Who fears him? We were base indeed did we let you suffer for your generous impulse, sir, to turn you hence who have been our kinsman's friend. While there is a roof on Pievano you may sleep tranquilly under it.'

Don Almerico shifted in his chair and grunted as she brought that impulsive speech to its conclusion. His daughter went too fast, he thought. Whilst himself he should have been reluctant to have driven out this man who came in quest of sanctuary, yet Madonna Fulvia outstripped him altogether in the matter of hospitality.

He spread a white transparent hand to the blazing logs, and with the other stroked his shaven chin cogitating. Then, looking squarely at the stranger:

'What is your name, sir?' he asked him bluntly.

'I am called Pantaleone degli Uberti,' said the adventurer, who had enough worldly wisdom never to make use of lies where truth could be employed with safety.

'An honourable name,' the old man murmured, nodding as to himself. 'Well, well! I will leave it, sir, to your discretion not to tarry at Pievano longer than need be. I think not of myself.' He shrugged and smiled deprecatingly, a smile of singular charm that illumined as with a light of lingering youth within the venerable old face. 'I am too old to weigh the paltry sum of life remaining me against a service due to an honourable man. But there is this child to consider, and the risk of your discovery here...'

But at that she interrupted him, breaking in with the impulsiveness of her generous youth and womanly compassion.

'Who runs great risks may disregard such lesser ones,' she cried, whereat Ser Pantaleone became all ears.

'By the Host! not so,' her father answered. 'We dare add nothing at present to draw attention upon ourselves. You see...'

He checked under the suddenly tightened curb of reawakening caution, and his eyes flashed keenly upon his visitor.

But Pantaleone's face was dull and wooden, a mask betraying nothing of his inward satisfaction. For his quick wits had without difficulty completed the Lord of Pievano's broken sentence, and found it confirming the assurance he had already formed of Matteo Orsini's presence there.

Seeing himself scanned with mistrust, he chose that moment to stagger where he stood. He reeled sideways, one hand to his brow, the other groping feebly for support. Thus he crashed against a bronze table that stood near him, sent it slithering a yard or so along the marble tiles, and, missing its resistance, he fell heavily beside it and lay at full stretch upon the floor.

'I am spent,' he groaned.

They sprang to him at once – all three: Almerico, his daughter and the groom, who had remained in the background awaiting his dismissal. And whilst her father went down on his old joints to lend immediate aid, Madonna Fulvia issued orders briskly to the gaping lackey.

'Fetch Mario, quickly,' she commanded. 'Bid them bring wine and vinegar and napkins. Run!'

Pantaleone raised his lolling head and supported it against Almerico's knee. He opened dull eyes, and babbled incoherent excuses for thus discomposing them. This manifestation of concern for them at such a moment touched them profoundly when coupled with his condition: it melted the old Orsini's lingering mistrust as snow upon the hills is melted by the April suns. The man's extremity was dire and obvious – and what could have produced it but the tribulations of which he told?

Came Mario – a short, sturdy fellow with a face that was the colour of clay, and so ridged and pitted by smallpox that it seemed no more than a hideous mask, a grotesque simulacrum of a human countenance. He was nominally the castellan of Pievano; in effect he was many things, a factotum including in his manifold accomplishments the arts of chirurgeon, horse-leech, and barber. He was rigidly honest, faithful, self-sufficient, and ignorant.

In his wake now as acolytes came a groom, Madonna Fulvia's own woman, and Raffaele the page. Among them they bore flasks and flagons, napkins and a silver basin. With the others they made a group about Ser Pantaleone, whilst Mario went down on one knee beside him and fumbled his pulse, his countenance grave and oracular.

This pulse-feeling was a piece of impressive mummery, no more. For whatever irregularity Mario had discovered there, his prescription would have varied nothing. Finding no irregularity whatever, it still varied nothing.

'Exhaustion. Ha!' he diagnosed. 'A little blood-letting will revive him. I'll ease him of some six ounces, and all will be well.' He rose. 'Vincenzo, lend a hand, and we'll carry him to bed. You, Raffaele, light the way for us.'

So Mario and the groom lifted up our gentleman between them. The page took up one of the gilt candlesticks that stood taller than himself upon the floor, and went ahead. The rear was brought up by Virginia, the waiting-maid, and thus in some sort of state was Messer Pantaleone degli Uberti carried to bed and established at Pievano.

iii

Pantaleone awoke refreshed upon the morrow, none the worse for the loss of the six ounces of blood upon which Mario's chirurgy had insisted and to which he himself had been forced to submit that he might play out his part.

He found his room suffused with the pale sunshine of a January morning and fragrant with the subtle refreshing perfume of lemon verbena steeped in potent vinegar; he found it occupied by the page Raffaele, a graceful stripling with a lovely impudent face and smooth hair that was the colour of buttercups.

'For lack of a man to serve you they have sent me,' the page explained himself.

Pantaleone considered the supple figure in its suit of green that fitted it like a skin.

'And what are you?' he wondered. 'A lizard?'

'I am glad to see you are mending,' said the boy. 'Impudence, they tell me, is a sign of health.'

'And they tell it you often, I've no doubt, and find you healthy in excess,' said Pantaleone, smiling grimly.

'Gesù!' said the boy, with uplifted eyes. 'I'll bear news of your complete recovery to my lord.'

'Stay,' Pantaleone bade him, desiring to have a certain matter explained. 'Since you were sent to serve, give me first to eat. I may be an indifferent Christian, seeing that I have in a sense been in the service of the Pope; but I find it difficult to fast in Lent and impossible in any other season. There is a bowl yonder, steaming. Let it be employed in the service for which it was designed.'

Raffaele fetched the bowl which contained a measure of broth, and with it a platter bearing a small wheaten loaf. He also fetched a silver basin with water and a napkin. But these Pantaleone waved impatiently away. He had been reared in camps, not courts, and was out of sympathy with the affectations of mincing fellows who carry washing to excess.

He drank a portion of the soup noisily, broke bread and munched it, considered the page gravely, and set out upon his quest of the information which he conceived was to be gathered.

'For lack of men they sent you to me,' he said, pondering. 'How come they to lack men at Pievano? The Lord Almerico is a great and potent lord, such as should not want for lackeys. Whence, then, this lack of men?'

The boy perched himself upon the bed. 'Whence are you, Messer Pantaleone?' he inquired.

'I? I am from Perugia,' said the condottiero.

'And is it not known in Perugia that the Lord Almerico is above all things a man of peace – of peace and books. He is more concerned with Seneca than with any tyrant in Italy.'

'With whom?' asked Pantaleone.

'With Seneca,' the boy repeated.

'Who is he?' quoth Pantaleone, staring.

'A philosopher,' said Raffaele. 'My lord loves all philosophers.'

'Then he will love me,' said Pantaleone, and drank the remainder of his broth. 'But you haven't answered my question.'

'I have, indeed. I conveyed to you that my lord keeps here no such family as might be expected in one of his estate. There are but four grooms in his service.'

'Even so,' said Pantaleone. 'Out of four one might have been spared me.'

'Ah, but then, Vincenzo who helped to carry you to bed is my lord's own body servant; Giannone has his duties in the stables, and Andrea has gone down to the borgo on an errand for Madonna.'

'That makes but three, and you said there were four.'

'The fourth is Giuberti; but then Giuberti has vanished; he disappeared a week ago.'

Pantaleone looked at the ceiling dreamily, reflecting how the vanishing of this Giuberti chanced to coincide with the vanishing of Matteo Orsini and wondering whether a link existed that would connect the two.

'He was dismissed, you mean?' he grumbled.

'I do not think so. It is a mystery. There was a great ado that morning here, and I have not seen Giuberti since. But he has not been dismissed for I have been to his room and his garments are all there. Nor did he leave Pievano, unless he went on foot, for there is no horse missing from the stables. On the contrary – and that is another mystery which none can solve for me – on the morning after Giuberti's disappearance I found seven horses in the stables instead of the usual six. I went there to count them that I might discover whether Giuberti had gone away. As I set little faith in wizardry I am not prepared to accept the simple explanation that Giuberti has been changed into a horse. Had it been an ass, now, I could have believed it – for no great metamorphosis would have been needed. But there it is: we have lost a biped and acquired a quadruped. An engaging mystery.'

Pantaleone's face showed nothing of the keenness with which he listened to this fresh piece of indirect information of the fugitive's presence at Pievano. He smiled lazily at the boy and encouraged him with flattery to let the stream of his chatter flow more freely.

'By the Host,' he approved him, 'although you may be no more than a lad you have a man's wit; indeed, more wit than many a man that I have known. You should go far.'

The boy curled his green legs under him upon the bed, and smiled well gratified.

'You miss nothing,' Pantaleone spurred him on.

'Indeed, not much,' the boy agreed. 'And I could tell you more. For instance, it happens that Mario's wife has also disappeared. Mario is our castellan – he with the pock-marked face, who bore you to bed last night and bled you. Mario's wife had charge of the kitchen, and she vanished together with Giuberti. Now that is a circumstance that intrigues me greatly.'

'It might intrigue you less if you were older,' said Pantaleone, implying something which he did not himself believe, and implying it solely as a goad.

Raffaele threw back his head, and considered the soldier with some scorn.

'You said well when you said that I had more wit than many a man,' he informed Pantaleone with pointed significance. 'A man, of course, would blunder here to a prompt and lewd conclusion. Bah, sir! I am a boy, not a cherub in a fresco. You have but to see Colomba – Mario's wife – to be assured of the chastity of her relations with Giuberti or with any man. You have seen Mario's lovely countenance, looking as if the devil had stamped on it with his hoofs and a red-hot horseshoe on each hoof. His wife's is even more uncomely, for she took the smallpox from him when he had it, which leaves them still the fit mates for each other that they were originally.'

'Precocious ape,' said Pantaleone. 'Your discourse is a scandal to a poor soldier's ears. I'd have the rods to you if you were boy of mine.' He flung back the bedclothes so that the lad was momentarily smothered in them, and rose to dress himself. He had learnt all that Raffaele could tell him.

'It is the mystery of it all that intrigues me,' babbled the page unabashed. 'Can you solve the riddle, Ser Pantaleone?'

'I'll try,' said Pantaleone struggling with his hose, but Raffaele for all his precocity missed the grimness of that answer.

Thus, then, you see our adventurer in possession of certain facts that seemed to him tolerably clear: the disappearance of the groom, Giuberti, and of the woman, Colomba, synchronizing with the appearance of an additional horse in the stables and hence, presumably, with the arrival at Pievano of Matteo Orsini, indicated that the care of him had been entrusted to those two servants. Now since had Matteo Orsini remained in the castle itself, so much would have been unnecessary, it was further to be inferred that – no doubt for greater secrecy – he had been lodged elsewhere, though doubtlessly (and the presence of the horse confirmed this) somewhere within the precincts of the citadel.

So far Ser Pantaleone was clear, and already he accounted the half of his task accomplished. His next step must be to ascertain what quarters outside the actual rocca the place contained.

He dressed himself with care in the garments which the page had brought him from the kitchen, where they had been sedulously dried. Having no shoes he must perforce resume his boots, and since the weather was chill and he would presently be taking a turn out of doors he buckled on his leather hacketon over his apricot-coloured doublet. Finally, with his long sword hanging from his steel girdle and a heavy dagger over his right hip, he made his way below, a handsome cavalier, swaggering and arrogant of port, in whom it was scarcely possible to recognize the fainting bedraggled fugitive that but yesternight had implored sanctuary of the Lord of Pievano.

The pert Raffaele ushered him into the presence of Messer Almerico and Madonna Fulvia. They received him cordially, expressing genuine pleasure at his evident recovery. All hesitation and mistrust appeared to have vanished from the old man's demeanour, whence Ser Pantaleone inferred that meanwhile the Lord of Pievano had consulted with Matteo, and that Matteo had told him – since in fact no man could have denied it – that his story was very possibly true, and that he had been friendly with Paolo Orsini as he said. Hence, superfluously now, the circumstance of Matteo's presence was confirmed to him yet again.

Intent upon his task, he would have gone forth at once claiming the need to take the air. But here the clay-faced Mario interposed with all the pompous authority of a medical adviser.

'What, sir? Go forth – in your condition? It were a madness. Last night you had the fever, and you were bled. You must rest and recover, or I will not answer for your life.'

Pantaleone laughed – he had a deeply tuneful laugh that was readily provoked, for when he was not laughing with you he would laugh at you. He scorned the notion that he was weak or that the frosty air would injure him. Was not the sun shining? Was he not quite himself again?

But Mario's opposition was nothing shaken, rather did it gather strength in argument.

'Since it is to my skill that you owe it that you feel recovered, let my skill guide you when I say that the feeling is an illusion, a lightness ensuing upon the relief of an excess of blood which I have procured you. Forth you do not go save at your peril, at the peril of undoing all the good I have done.'

And then to Mario's persuasions were added those of Orsini and his daughter, until in the end, seeing that to insist further might be to awaken suspicions dormant now, Ser Pantaleone, chafing inwardly but still laughing outwardly, submitted. He spent the day indoors, and found the time hang heavily, despite the kindly efforts exerted by his host and his host's daughter to lighten it for him.

The kindness which they lavished upon him, the fact that he sat at table and broke bread with them, made no slightest impression upon Ser Pantaleone. The hideous treachery of the thing he did, the vileness of the manner in which he had insinuated himself into their confidence, left him untouched. It was naught to him that he should sit there in Pievano receiving the hospitality that is bestowed upon a friend.

This Pantaleone was a man without sensibilities, an egotist with a brutally practical mind which harboured no considerations but those of worldly advancement. Honour to him was no more than one of the infirmities of vain men. Shame was a sentiment unknown to him. Macchiavelli might have honoured him for the fine singleness of purpose by which he was ever guided towards the given end in view.

On the morrow at last he had his way, despite Mario's lingering doubts that it was unwise for him to go abroad. He would have taken the page with him for company, thinking that the chatterbox might be of service to him, but the excessive hospitality of Pievano ordained otherwise. Since he would not be denied his desire to take the air, Madonna Fulvia should be his guide. He protested that it was to do him too much – as indeed it was. Nevertheless she insisted, and together they went forth.

The gardens of Pievano ran in a flight of terraces up the steep sides of the hill behind the castle, the whole of it enclosed by massive, grey, machicolated walls that had stood two hundred years and more, and resisted more than one siege in the past – though that was before the days of such artillery as Cesare Borgia now commanded. In summer these terraces were cool lemon groves and cooler galleries of vine; but now all was bare, a mere network of ramage to fret the January sunshine. Yet there were spaces of green turf, whilst the mountain above them showed brightly emerald where the snows had melted. Below them a little to the north was spread the shining face of Lake Trasimene.

They came slowly to the topmost terrace – there were six of them in all, whence a fine view was to be commanded of all that broad valley. Here they found a sheltered spot under the western wall, where a seat hewn out of granite was set before a deep tank sunk to its rim into the ground – one of a series that were used in summer for irrigation purposes. Above the seat in a little semicircular niche there was a figure of the Virgin Mother in baked earth, painted red and blue, that had become mottled by alternate rain and sunshine.

Ser Pantaleone slipped his great red cloak from his shoulders, and spread it on the seat for his companion. She demurred awhile. Was he wise to sit, was not the air too chill and was he not perhaps heated from his walk? Thus, shaping her tender solicitude in questions she warned him. But he reassured her with a buoyant laugh that made a mock of any assumption of weakness in his own condition.

So side by side they sat on that hewn granite seat, beneath the image of the Virgin Mother above the granite tank where the water slept, a crystal mirror. So might a pair of lovers have sat; but if she had no thoughts of love for her companion – her devotion being all given to another, as we know – he had still less for her. It was not that he was usually sluggish to dalliance. Those full red lips of his told a different story, as Fra Serafino had observed. But, in the first place, his taste was all for generously-hipped deep-bosomed Hebes, and in the second his thoughts were all concerned with the enucleation of this problem of Matteo Orsini's hiding-place.

They commanded from that height a noble view of hills and valley, of lake and river, as we have seen. But with this again Ser Pantaleone was no whit concerned. His bold, black eyes were questing nearer home, raking the disposition of the outbuildings to the left of the rocca, and an odd pavilion on the other side occupying the middle of a quadrangular terrain that was all walled about so as to form, as it were, a *hortus inclusus*.

He stretched his long, lithe legs, and took a deep breath of the clean mountain air, noisily like a draught that is relished. Then he sighed.

'Heigh-o! If it were mine to choose my estate in life, I would be lord of some such lordship as this of Pievano.'

'The ambition is a modest one,' said she.

'To have more is to have the power to work mischief, and who works mischief raises up enemies, and who raises up enemies goes in anxiety and may not know the pure joys of a contented life.'

'My father would agree with you. Such is his own philosophy. That is why he has lived ever here, nor ever troubled himself to strive for more.'

'He chose the better part, indeed,' Ser Pantaleone agreed. 'He has enough, and who has enough is happy.'

'Ah, but whoever thinks that he has enough?'

'Your father thought so, and so should I think were I lord of Pievano. To one in your station bearing your name it may seem no more than mediocrity. Compared with what might be yours mediocrity it is. Therein lies the secret of your happiness.'

'You make sure that I am happy,' said she.

He looked at her, and for a moment was in peril of straying into by-ways concerned with her own affairs. But he conquered this.

'I were blind not to see it,' he said in a tone of finality. 'Though when I said "you" I meant not only yourself but your father also. And here lies cause enough. A noble lordship, commodious yet compact, the villeins in the borgo yonder paying tribute and fealty, the rocca itself with all accessory buildings close-packed under its mothering wing – saving perhaps that pavilion yonder in the enclosed garden,' he excepted, waving his hand and speaking idly, giving no sign that thus at last, having reached it by slow and careful degrees, he came upon the goal which had been his since first he took his seat beside her. 'That now,' he continued, musing, 'is an odd construction. I cannot think for what purpose it can have been built.'

There was a question plainly in the statement, and at once she answered it.

'It is a lazar-house,' she said.

Startled, Ser Pantaleone shifted uneasily, and there was no boldness now in the black eyes that stared at her. There was a sinister ring in the word that brought horrors leaping before the eyes of a man's imagination.

'A lazar-house?' he said, aghast.

She explained: 'It happened in the days when my father was no more than a boy. There was the plague in Florence, and it was carried thither to the borgo. Men were dying like flies at close of autumn. To succour them my grandfather ordered that pavilion to be built with others that have since been demolished, and he had the place enclosed by walls. There was a saintly minorite, one Fra Cristofero, who came to tend the plague-ridden, and who himself was miraculously preserved from the contagion.'

Ser Pantaleone twisted his features in a grimace of disgust. 'And do you keep that as a monument in honour of so ugly an event?' he asked.

'Why, no. There were other buildings there; but, as I have told you, they were demolished. That was the only one retained.'

'But why?' he asked.

'It has its uses.'

He looked at her with raised eyebrows, expressing a faint incredulity.

'You will not tell me that it is tenanted?' he asked in a note that was faintly jesting.

'No, no.'

She spoke too quickly, he noted; and her voice had trembled, whilst those deep loyal eyes of hers had fallen guiltily away from his regard.

'No, no,' she repeated. 'Of course, it is not tenanted now.' He looked idly away towards the spot. She had lied to him, he was convinced already. Yet he would make assurance doubly sure. Suddenly he drew his legs under him and started half-rising with a sudden exclamation, his face averted from her and turned towards the enclosed garden.

And then he felt her hand upon his sleeve.

'What is it?' she asked, and her voice was breathless.

'Surely… Surely, you are wrong,' he said. 'It is tenanted. It seemed to me that I saw something or someone move there in the shadow.'

'Oh, no, no – impossible! You were mistaken! There is no one there!' Agitation quivered in every syllable of that breathless denial.

He had drawn from her the answer to the question he had not asked. Satisfied, he craftily made haste to reassure her.

'Why, no,' he said, and laughed in self-derision. 'I see now what it is – the shadow of that gnarled olive deceived me.' He looked at her, a smile on his full lips. 'Alas!' he said. 'You have laid what might have become the ghost of Fra…what was his name?'

'Of Fra Cristofero?' said she, and smiled back at him in her relief. But she rose. 'Come, sir, you have sat here too long for one in your condition.'

'Long enough,' said Pantaleone with more truth than she suspected, and he rose obediently to depart.

It was as he said. He had sat there long enough to achieve his ends, and the very suddenness with which now she urged his departure was yet a further confirmation of what he had discovered. She desired to draw him from that spot before he should chance, indeed, to see what she believed him to have imagined he had seen. Very willingly, then, he went.

iv

A fool never doubts his judgement or questions its findings. He reaches a conclusion at a leap, and having reached it acts forthwith upon it. And that is why he is a fool. But your really astute fellow moves more slowly and with caution, testing the ground at every step, mistrusting his inferences until he has exhausted confirmation of them. Even where he is swift to conclude he will still be slow to act unless urged by necessity to immediate action.

Thus Pantaleone. He had added link to link until he held in his hands a fairly solid chain of circumstantial evidence, from which he was entitled to infer, firstly – and this most positively – that Matteo Orsini was sheltered at Pievano; secondly – and not quite so positively – that he was bestowed in the lazar-house in that *hortus inclusus*.

A rash fellow would have summoned his men and forthwith stormed the place. But Pantaleone was not rash. He counted first the cost of error. He considered that in spite of all indications it was yet possible that his quarry might not be in that lazar-house. And in that case did he take any such action he would find himself in the position of a gamester who staking all upon a single throw has seen the dice turn up ambs-ace. He would have discovered himself in his true character, and must submit to being driven forth in ignominy to bear his tale of failure to his master.

Therefore, despite his stout convictions, Pantaleone waited and watched, what time he took his ease at Pievano and savoured the hospitality of the Lord Almerico. He walked in the gardens with Madonna in the mornings, in the afternoon he would either permit Raffaele to teach him chess or repay these lessons by showing the golden-haired lad how to use a sword in conjunction with a dagger, and by what tricks – not tricks of swordsmanship, indeed, but of pure knavery – an adversary might be done to death; in the evenings he would converse with his host, which is to say that he would listen to the Lord Almerico's learned disquisitions upon life culled from the philosophy of Seneca or the teachings of Epictetus as preserved in the writings of Flavius Arrianus.

Pantaleone it must be confessed was a little bewildered and wearied by these discourses. A man with his full lips, and all the qualities those full lips implied, could find scant sense in the austere philosophy of the stoic, though he was faintly interested to observe the hold which that teaching had gained upon his host, and how his host appeared to have modelled the conduct of his life upon it, purchasing tranquillity as the stoic teaches. Although it was not thus that Pantaleone understood existence, yet he forbore argument and feigned agreement, knowing in his crafty way that agreement with a man is the short road to his esteem and confidence.

He earned, however, little discernible reward for all his patient pains. No such confidences as he hoped for were ever reposed in him. Matteo Orsini's name was never mentioned in his presence, and when once he mentioned it himself to speak in glowing praise of the man and in a proper sorrow at his reported death, he was met by a silence that showed him how far indeed he was, their amiability notwithstanding, from having earned their trust. And he had other signs of this. On more occasions than one his sudden coming into their presence was marked by as sudden an interruption of the conversation between them, and the ensuing of a constrained silence.

Thus a week passed in which his mission made no progress, whereat he was beginning to grow restive, feeling that if his inaction endured much longer it might end by thrusting him into a rashness. No single shred of confirmation had his conclusions received, no single grain of independent evidence that the lazar-house was tenanted. And then, at last, one night as he was taking his way to bed lighted by Raffaele, who was now become his body-servant, he chanced upon a small discovery.

His own room was over the rocca's vast courtyard, and commanded no other view but that. But as on his way to it he passed one of the windows of the gallery facing southward towards that *hortus inclusus*, and as idly he looked in that direction, he caught the yellow glint of a point of light that was moving towards it through the darkness.

He was satisfied that what he did any man in his place would have done, and, therefore, that it could awaken no suspicion. He stood still, looking at that light a moment, and then drew the page's attention to it.

'Someone is roving in the gardens very late,' said he.

Raffaele came to stand beside him, and pressed his face against the glass, the better to peer into the darkness.

'It will be Mario,' said the boy. 'I saw him standing by the door when I came up.'

'And what the devil does he do in the garden at such an hour? He can hardly be gathering snails at this season of the year.'

'Indeed, no,' agreed Raffaele, clearly intrigued.

'Ah, well,' said Pantaleone, who perceived that he was wasting time, since Raffaele had no knowledge to betray. 'It is no affair of ours.' He yawned. 'Come on, my lad, or I shall sleep where I stand.'

First he thought of alluding to the matter casually upon the morrow, watching the effect upon Almerico and his daughter. But sleep brought sounder counsels, and when the morrow came he held his peace. He walked as usual with Madonna in the garden, though never now on the upper terraces whence a view was obtained of the enclosure about the lazar-house. She had refused to repeat that visit of theirs to the garden's heights, ever pleading that she found the ascent excessively fatiguing.

Pantaleone habitually wore a tiny gold pomander ball, no larger than a cherry, suspended from his neck by a slender chain of gold. He wore it as usual that morning when they went forth together; but had Madonna observed him closely she would have noted that at a stage of their sauntering it vanished.

Pantaleone remained apparently unconscious of its disappearance until towards the third hour of night – after they had supped and when it was usual for them to retire to bed, the hour, in fact, at which last night he had observed that mysterious light in the garden. Then it was that quite suddenly he leapt to his feet with an exclamation of dismay that provoked their concerned inquiries.

'My pomander!' he cried, with all the air of a man whom some great mischance has overwhelmed. 'I have lost it.'

My Lord Almerico recovered from his concern and smiled. He quoted the stoic.

'In this life, my friend, we never lose anything. Sometimes we return a thing. That is the proper view. Why, then, all this concern about a pomander, a trifle that may be replaced by a ducat.'

'Should I be so concerned if that were all?' cried Pantaleone, with a faint show of impatience at the philosophy with which Orsini bore another's loss. 'It was my talisman – a potent charm against the evil eye given me by my sainted mother. For her sake I hold it sacred. I would sooner lose all I have than that.'

It made a difference, Madonna Fulvia agreed, admiring the filial piety he displayed; and even her father had no more to say.

'Let me think, now; let me think,' said Pantaleone, standing rapt, fingering the cleft in his shaven chin. 'I had it this morning in the garden – at least I had it when I went forth. I… Yes!' He smote fist into palm. 'It was in the garden – it must have been in the garden that I lost it.' And without a by-your-leave to his host he swung to the page.

'A lantern, Raffaele.'

'Were it not wiser to wait until daylight?' wondered Almerico.

'Sir, sir,' cried Pantaleone wildly, 'I could not rest, I could not sleep in my suspense, in my uncertainty as to whether I shall recover it or not. I will hunt for it all night if need be.'

They attempted further to dissuade him, but before his wild insistence and his general air of distraction, they gave way, the old nobleman scarcely troubling to veil a sneer at superstitions that could take such potent hold upon a man. Since nothing less than to go forth at once would satisfy him, they bade Raffaele go with him, and whether this was a measure of kindly concern or whether of precaution, Pantaleone was by no means sure.

Forth into the night sallied he and Raffaele, each armed with a lantern, and straight they went to the first terrace. With their double light they searched every foot of the long walk, all to no purpose.

'Five ducats, Raffaele, if you find it,' said Pantaleone. 'Let us divide our forces, thus are we likely to shorten the search. Do you go up to the next terrace, and search that carefully, foot by foot. Five ducats if you find it.'

'Five ducats!' Raffaele was a little breathless. 'Why the thing isn't worth more than half a ducat!'

'Nevertheless five shall you have if you find it me. I value it far above its price.'

Raffaele sped upwards with his lantern, leaving Pantaleone in the act of resuming his search over ground that had been covered already. The adventurer waited until the sound of the lad's footsteps had grown distant and until from where he stood the other's light was no longer visible. Then he passed behind a stiff box hedge, that would screen his own light from any windows of the house, and there without more ado he extinguished it. That done he crossed the garden with as much speed as was consistent with his care to make no sound. By a clump of larches within a dozen paces of the wall of the enclosure he came to a halt, effaced himself among the trees, and waited, watchful and listening.

Moments passed in utter silence. In the distance he could perceive the faint gleam of Raffaele's lantern moving at a snail's pace along the third terrace on the hillside. Raffaele he knew was safely engaged for the next hour. That promise of five ducats would sustain his patience against failure. Whilst any who might be spying from the house would be able to make out no more than a glimmer of light up yonder, and would suppose that Raffaele and himself were engaged together.

Reassured on that score, then, Pantaleone was patient on his side, and waited. Nor was his patience sorely taxed. Some ten minutes or so after he had gained his point of observation, he heard the creaking of a door, and from the postern in the inner barbican he beheld the gleam of another lantern. It advanced swiftly towards him – for a pathway ran beside the larches – and presently there came the sound of feet. Soon Pantaleone could discern the figure of a man faintly outlined against the all-pervading gloom.

Immovable he stood screened by the larches, unseen yet observing. The figure advanced; it passed so closely by him that by putting forth his arm he might have touched it. He recognized the livid pock-marked face of the castellan, and he noted that the fellow carried a basket slung on the crook of his left arm. He caught the faint gleam of napery atop of it, and thrusting forth from this the neck of a wine-flask.

The man passed on, and reached the wall. A green door was set in it just thereabouts, and Pantaleone was prepared to see him vanish through, preparing indeed to follow. Instead, however, Mario paused at the wall's foot some ten paces away from that door, and Pantaleone caught the sound of hands softly clapped, and a voice softly calling:

'Are you there, Colomba?'

Instantly from beyond the wall floated the answer in a woman's voice:

'I am here.'

What followed was none so distinct, and asked for guesswork on Pantaleone's part. Partly he saw and partly he inferred that Mario had taken a ladder that lay at the wall's foot, set it against the wall, mounted it, and from the summit slung down his basket to his wife within the enclosure.

That was all. The thing being done, Mario descended again, removed the ladder, and returned unencumbered now and moving swiftly.

Pantaleone found his every suspicion confirmed. As he had supposed, Colomba and the groom Giuberti were ministering to the concealed Matteo Orsini, whose food was borne to him thus in the night by Mario – and no doubt in the raw, to be cooked and prepared by Mario's wife – so that none in Pievano should share the secret with those who already and perforce were in possession of it.

All this was clear as daylight. But on the other hand the affair had its dark and mysterious side. Why should Mario employ a ladder to scale a wall when there was a door there ready to his hand. It was very odd, but it was some detail of precaution, he supposed, and dismissed the matter with that explanation.

Moreover something was happening that suddenly drew his attention to himself and his own position. Mario, instead of returning to the house, had paused midway a moment, as if hesitating, and then had struck across the gardens towards the light that marked the spot where Raffaele hunted.

Now this to Messer Pantaleone was a serious matter. It might, unless he were careful, lead to the discovery of his own real pursuits. He came forth from his concealment and very softly set himself to follow Mario. Thus as far as the second terrace. Then as Mario still went on upwards, Pantaleone turned quickly away to the right, thus returning to the very spot where he had extinguished his lantern. Arrived there, he turned and came running back shouting as he ran:

'Raffaele! Raffaele!'

He saw the swinging lantern of Mario arrested in its progress, and a moment later farther along the upper terrace gleamed Raffaele's light, as the boy approached the edge in answer to that summons.

'I have found it!' cried Pantaleone, as indeed he had found it – in his pocket where it had been safely bestowed.

'I have found it…found it!' he repeated on a note of ridiculous triumph, as if he were Columbus announcing that he had found the New World.

He advanced to the foot of the flight of steps that led upward, and there he awaited them.

'You have found it?' quoth Raffaele, crestfallen.

Pantaleone dangled it aloft by the chain.

'Behold!' he said, and added – 'but you shall have a ducat for your pains none the less. So comfort you.'

'Did you find it in the dark?' It was Mario's voice that growled the question, and Pantaleone was quick to catch the note of suspicion running through it.

'Fool,' he answered, preferring to take him literally. 'How could I have found it in the dark? I upset my lantern in my excitement.'

Mario was scanning his face closely.

'It is very odd,' said he, 'that as I came this way I saw no light.'

'I was beyond the hedge yonder. That may have screened it,' Pantaleone explained, and added no word more, for he knew that who explains himself too much accuses himself.

They trooped back to the house together; Raffaele silenced by his disappointment, Mario thoughtful and suspicious of all this ado, Pantaleone babbling naively in his delight at the recovery of his precious amulet, and recounting the circumstances under which his mother had set it round his neck, with what words she had enjoined him to keep it safe, and against what dreadful perils it had been his shield – all lies that came bubbling from his fertile mind like water from a spring.

But despite all this, when at length he came to bid good night to Mario, he saw that clay-coloured face grimly set in lines of mistrust.

He went thoughtfully to bed in consequence. He lay awake some time considering his discovery and considering still more deeply that part of it which left him mystified. At another time he might have delayed his action until he had cleared that up. But here he decided that to delay further might be dangerous. He told himself again that he had discovered all that mattered, and he fell asleep promising himself that upon the morrow he would act upon that discovery and lay Messer Matteo Orsini snugly by the heels.

V

The manner adopted by Messer Pantaleone in which to do the thing he had been sent to do was startling and yet precisely such as was to have been looked for in a man of his temper.

He had been that day – the day following upon the affair of the lost amulet – down into the borgo of Pievano for the first time since his coming to the castle. As a pretext for this he had urged the need to mend the leg of one of his boots which had become torn during his search last night. (Himself he had ripped it with his dagger.)

He had made his way in the first place to a cobbler, with whom perforce he remained until the required repairs had been effected. From the cobbler's he went to the Osteria del Orso, ostensibly to refresh himself, actually to issue his orders to his knaves through the one he had posted there. It resulted from these movements of his that as dusk was falling his tenesbirri wandered singly and unchallenged over the drawbridge into the empty courtyard of the castle. No guards were kept at Pievano, as we know, and so this furtive and piecemeal invasion was neither hindered nor yet so much as observed.

When he had assured himself that these knaves of his were at hand, Messer Pantaleone, armed, booted, spurred, cap in hand, and wrapped in his ample red cloak – obviously ready to take the road forthwith – strode into the hall of the rocca, that noble chamber where a week ago he had been so charitably received. Now, as then, he found the Lord Almerico engrossed in a volume of manuscript, and Madonna Fulvia with him.

They looked up sharply, inexplicably startled by the manner of his advent. There was a subtle change in his air. It was more arrogant and self-assertive than usual; here was no longer the guest with just so much swagger as was inseparable from a soldier of fortune, but one who seemed to come mantled in authority. He did not long intrigue them.

99

'My lord,' he announced bluntly, 'I have a duty to perform and ten stout fellows below to help me against the need of help. Will you summon your nephew Matteo Orsini who is hiding here?'

They stared at him in utter silence, whilst for as long as it would take a man to say a paternoster. They were like people stupefied. Then at last the girl spoke, her brows contracted, her eyes flashing like sombre jewels in her white face.

'What is your purpose with Matteo?'

'The Lord Cesare Borgia's purpose,' he answered brutally. The mask of guile having served its turn was now discarded, and there was no tinge of shame upon the uncovered face of his real self which he now showed them. 'I was sent hither to arrest Ser Matteo by order of the Duke.'

Again there fell a pause, what time those four eyes searched his bold countenance. The Lord Almerico closed his book upon his forefinger, and a faint yet intensely scornful smile broke upon the grey old face.

'Then,' said Madonna Fulvia, 'all this time we…we have been your dupes. You lied to us. Your faintness, the persecution of which you were the victim, was all so much pretence?' There was a note of incredulity in her voice.

'Necessity,' he reminded her, 'knows no law.' And although he was neither shamed nor daunted by their steadfast scornful stare, yet he grew weary of it. 'Come,' he added roughly. 'You have had your fill of looking at me. Let us get to business. Send for this traitor you are harbouring.'

Madonna Fulvia drew herself stiffly up. 'My God!' she exclaimed. 'A base Judas, a dirty spy! And I have sat at table with you. We have housed you here as an equal.' Her voice soared upwards, from the low note of horror and disgust upon which she had spoken. 'O vile, O pitiful dog!' she cried. 'Was this your errand? Was this…'

Her father's hand fell gently upon her arm, and silenced her by its mute command. The stoic in him was equal even to so bitter an occasion. It was not for nothing that he had assimilated the wisdom of the ancients.

'Hush, child, self-respect forbids that you should address so base a creature even to upbraid it.' His voice was calm and level. 'What is it to you that he is vile and treacherous, a shameless thing of shame? Does that hurt you? Does it hurt any but himself?'

It did not seem to her to be a time for stoicisms. She swung upon her father in a blaze of passion.

'Aye, does it hurt me,' she cried. 'It hurts me and it hurts Matteo.'

'Can it really hurt a man to die?' wondered Almerico. 'Matteo being dead, shall yet live. But that poor thing being living is yet dead.'

'Shall we come to business?' quoth Pantaleone, breaking in upon what promised to develop into an eloquent discourse upon life and death, chiefly derived from Seneca. 'Will you send for Matteo Orsini, or shall I bid my men drag him from the lazar-home where he skulks. It is idle to resist, futile to delay. My knaves have hemmed the place about, and none goes in or out save at my pleasure.'

He saw a change of expression sweep across both faces. The girl's eyes dilated – with fear, as he supposed; the old man uttered a short, sharp laugh – of stoicism he opined.

'Why, sir,' said Almerico, 'since you are so well informed, you had best yourself complete your task of infamy.'

Pantaleone looked at him a moment, and then shrugged.

'Be it so,' he said shortly, and swung upon his heel to go about it.

'No, no!' It was Madonna Fulvia who arrested him with that cry, sharp with a new anxiety. 'Wait, sir! Wait!'

He paused obediently, and half-turned. He beheld her standing tense and straight, one hand pressed upon her bosom as if to quell its tumult, the other held out to him in a gesture of supplication.

'Give me leave to speak with my father alone, ere…ere we decide,' she panted.

Pantaleone sniffed, and raised his eyebrows.

'Decide?' quoth he. 'What remains to be decided?'

She wrung her hands in a pathetic intensity of mental stress.

'We…we may have a proposal to make to you, sir.'

'A proposal?' He said, and scowled. Did they seek to bribe him? 'By the Host…' he began hotly, and there checked. The cupidity of his nature leapt up instantly, aroused and alert. After all, he bethought him, there would be no harm in hearing this proposal. The man is a fool who neglects to learn anything from which he may cull personal advantage. He considered further. After all, none save himself was aware of Matteo Orsini's presence at Pievano, and if the price were high enough – who knew? – he might be induced to keep that knowledge to himself. But the price must needs be high to compensate him not only for the loss of the thousand ducats offered by the Duke but for the hurt his vanity would suffer in the admission of failure.

Seeing him silent, and conceiving that he hesitated, Madonna renewed her prayer.

'What harm can it do to grant me this?' she asked. 'Have you not said yourself that the place is hemmed about by your men? Are you not therefore master of the situation?'

He bowed stiffly.

'I will concede it you,' he said. 'I shall await your pleasure in the ante-chamber.' And upon that he went out, his spurs jingling musically.

Left alone father and daughter looked long at each other.

'Why did you hinder him?' asked the Lord of Pievano at length. 'Surely you were not moved by any thought of pity for such a man?'

Her lip curled in a scornful smile. 'You cannot think that – not in your heart,' she said.

'It is because I cannot think it that I ask. I am all bewildered.'

'Had we allowed him to go, consider what in his vengeance he might have done. He might have summoned these men of his, and ransacked the rocca until he discovered Matteo indeed.'

'But surely that must inevitably follow now. How can we prevent it?'

She leaned towards him. 'To what purpose do you study so deeply the lore of human nature if in practice you cannot probe the shallow murky depth of such a nature as this dog's?'

He shrank back, staring at her, feeling that his philosophy had taught him nothing indeed if in an extremity such as the present one, this child could show him how it should be handled.

'Do you not know – does it not say so in any of those pages – that who betrays once, will betray again and yet again? Do you not see that a man so vile as to have played that knave's part will be vile enough to sell his own master, will be true to naught save his own base interests?'

'You mean that we should bribe him?'

She drew herself up and uttered a short laugh. 'I mean that we should seem to bribe him. Oh!' She pressed her hands to her white brow. 'I have a vision of something that lies before us here. It is as if a door had been opened, a weapon thrust into my hand by means of which I can smite and at a blow avenge all the wrongs of the Orsini.'

'Pish, you are fevered, child! Here is no work for a weak maid…'

'Not for a weak maid – no; but for a strong one,' she broke in impetuously; 'work for a woman of the Orsini. Listen.' She leaned towards him again, lowering her voice instinctively because of the secret thing she had to communicate. Speaking quickly now she expounded the whole plan that had flashed into her ready witted mind, a plan complete in its every detail, a chain whose every link was soundly forged.

He listened, hunched in his chair, and the farther she proceeded the more hunched he became, like one who instinctively gathers himself together against a blow that is about to fall.

'My God!' he gasped when she had done, and his old eyes stared at her between amazement and dismay. 'My God! And your pure virgin mind has conceived this horror! In all these years I have not known you, Fulvia. I have deemed you a child, and you…' Words eluded him. Limply he waved his old transparent hands. The stoic in him had succumbed to the parent.

He would have dissuaded her out of his deep concern for her, his only child. But she was not to be dissuaded. She argued on, gathering enthusiasm as she dwelt upon the means by which she would at a single blow strike down this base betrayer and his master

103

the Duke of Valentinois. She urged that there was no safety for her or him or any Orsini in her refraining from this step upon which she was resolved. She reminded him that as long as Cesare Borgia lived no single Orsini would be safe, and she concluded by announcing that she believed her mission inspired by Heaven itself, that she a maid and the weakest of the Orsini should avenge the wrongs of their house and stay its further ruin.

At last his shocked, bruised mind became infected by something of her ardour; enough at least to wring from him a grudging fearful consent to let her have her way.

'Leave me,' she said, 'to deal with Cesare Borgia and his lackey, and do you pray for the souls of both.'

Upon that she kissed him, and swept out to the impatient Pantaleone waiting in the sparsely furnished ante-chamber.

He was seated in a high-backed chair by a carved table that bore a cluster of candles in a silver branch. He rose as she entered, marking her pallor and obvious agitation. To the stately beauty of her, her slim height and the fine poise of her lovely head, he remained indifferent.

She came to lean against the table, facing him across it, considering him with a glance that was steady despite the tremors agitating all the rest of her.

Pantaleone was shrewd and crafty as we know, but his craft was a shallow business when compared with her own; his shrewdness was mere low cunning when contrasted with the agile wits which her frail exterior dissembled.

In the moment in which he had revealed himself for what he was she had judged him, and she had judged him to the weight of a hair of his vile head. Upon that judgement she now went to work.

'Consider me well, Ser Pantaleone,' she invited him, her voice level and calm.

He did so, wondering whither this might lead.

'Tell me now, do you not find me fair to see, and am I not shapely?'

He bowed, his face almost sardonic. 'Fair as an angel, assuredly, Madonna. The Duke's own sister, Madonna Lucrezia, would suffer by comparison. But what has this to do with...?'

'In short, sir, do you account me desirable?'

The question robbed him of breath, so amazing was it. It was a moment ere he found an answer, and by then the sardonic smile had passed entirely from his face. His pulses were quickened under her steady glance and her no less steady invitation to appraise her. He pondered her now, and discovered a thousand graces in her to which he had hitherto been blind. He may even have realized that her chaste frail beauty held a subtler appeal than the grosser femininity to which his senses more usually responded.

'Desirable as Paradise,' said he at last, dropping his voice.

'And to render me so, there is not merely this perishable beauty that is mine. I am well dowered.'

'It is fitting that so noble a jewel should be nobly set.' In his mind stirred now some inkling of whither she was leading him, and his pulses throbbed the faster.

'A matter of ten thousand ducats goes with me to the man I wed,' she informed him, and turned him giddy by the mention of so vast a sum.

'Ten thousand ducats?' he repeated slowly, awe-stricken.

'To the man who weds me,' she insisted, and added quietly – 'Will you be that man?'

'Will I...?' He checked. No, no. The thing was incredible. The shock of that question almost stunned him. He gaped at her, and his handsome face turned pale under its tan.

'Upon the condition, of course,' she pursued, 'that you abandon this quest for Ser Matteo, and bear word to your master that he is not to be found.'

'Of course, of course,' he mumbled foolishly. Then he reassembled his scattered wits and set them to read him this riddle. She was Matteo's betrothed. She loved Matteo. And yet... Or could it be that her love was of that great self-sacrificing kind of which he had heard – but in which he had never believed – that will surrender all for the sake of the beloved? He could not swallow that. It was not in his nature to be so credulous. And then he threw up his head, his nostrils quivering. Suddenly he scented danger. A trap was being baited for him. Bluntly he said so, laughing short and scornfully.

But her reply disarmed his last suspicion.

'Take your own measures,' she invited him serenely. 'I understand your fears. But we are honourable folk, and if I swear to you that Matteo Orsini shall not stir him hence until this matter is done beyond recalling, so shall it be. Yet take your measures. You have the men and the power. Let them remain at their post surrounding that garden. Do that tonight, and tomorrow I will ride with you to Castel della Pieve to become your wife.'

Slowly he licked his lips, and his bold eyes narrowed as they surveyed her greedily. Yet still he was suspicious. Still he could not believe in so much good fortune.

'Why at Castel della Pieve?' he asked. 'Why not here?'

'Because I must be sure that you will keep faith. Castel della Pieve is the nearest place – yet far enough to leave Matteo a clear road of flight.'

'I understand,' he said slowly.

'And you agree?'

His keen black eyes stabbed into her calm white face as though they would pierce to her very soul and probe its secrets. It was incredible. To have fortune thrust upon him thus, fortune and a wife, and such a wife; for in his eyes she was growing more desirable moment by moment as he considered her. Had not Fra Serafino warned the Duke that this man would be as wax in the hands of a woman?

What greater profit – what profit one-tenth as great could he look for in taking Ser Matteo, in keeping faith with Valentinois? He made, you see, no attempt to struggle with the temptation. He did not give so much as a thought to a young woman in the Bolognese – one Leocadia by name – who kept a wine-shop at Laveno, who had borne him a son and whom he had promised to marry. But all that had happened before he had risen to the rank of a condottiero and earned the regard and trust of Cesare Borgia; and of late in his new-found importance it had shrunk into a dim and distant background. It did not trouble him now. If he hesitated, it was only because the thing proposed him was beyond belief. It bewildered him; a fog settled down upon his wits. By the Host! how she must love this fellow Matteo! Or was it – was it perhaps that he himself…

Now here was a possibility hitherto unregarded; here something that might explain her singular attitude towards him. In saving Matteo she performed a duty, and by the very manner of it placed a barrier between herself and a lover of whom she had wearied.

Thus his vanity to complete the rout of his perspicuity, to convince him where cold reason failed.

'Agree?' he cried after that long pause. 'Agree? By the Eyes of God? Am I a wooden image, or a purblind fool to refuse? I'll set a seal forthwith upon that contract.' And with arms flung wide he swooped down upon her like a hawk upon a dove, and caught her to him.

She suffered it, stiff and cold with sudden terror and repressed loathing. He held her close and muttered foolish fondnesses. Then the awakened passion mounting, it became suffused with tenderness, and he told her of a future in which he should be the slave of her slightest whim, her devout and worshipping lover always.

At length she released herself from those lithe arms, and drew away from him, a hectic spot on either cheek, deep shame in her soul and a sense of defilement pervading all her being. He watched her, abashed a little, mistrustful even.

But when she had gained the door she paused, and there for an instant her iciness melted. Her laugh trilled softly across the chamber to him.

'Tomorrow!' she flung at him, and vanished leaving him distracted.

vi

Perplexed, yet true to his adventurer's character, determined to follow his fortunes and accept such chances as there might be, Pantaleone took his measures against possible treachery, posted his men for the night so as to make quite certain that his prey did not escape until Madonna Fulvia and himself should be on their way to the nuptials, and that done went to bed to dream of a roseate future ennobled by ten thousand ducats.

It is the test of your true adventurer in all ages and of all kinds that ducats are with him the sole standard of nobility. A man may pawn his honour, pledge his proper pride and sell his immortal soul, so that he drives a good bargain in the matter of ducats. Thus it was with Pantaleone. Unless you are yourself one of those who measure worth – your own or another's – by ducats, you will pity a little this man who set such store by profit. For the thousand ducats offered him by the Duke he had consented to act the part of a Judas and a traitor. For the ten thousand ducats now dangled before his eyes he was ready to betray the hand that had hired him; and the sad part of it all is that he was convinced he did a shrewd and clever thing. That is why I invite your pity for him. He needs it both in this and in what is to follow out of it. Had he realized his baseness, he would have been just a villain. But far from it, since his baseness brought him profit he accounted himself a clever and deserving man. He was a true product of his age, and yet his kind has existed multitudinously in all ages.

Whilst he dreamt his aureate dreams, Madonna Fulvia below stairs was planning his destruction and another's. She indited a note calculatedly enigmatic and brief that it might provoke curiosity and through this the response which she desired. She couched it in an odd mixture of curial Latin and the common language of the people.

Magnificent (*Magnifice Vir*) – You are betrayed by one whom you hired to a betrayal. Before the Duomo of Castel della Pieve punctually at high noon tomorrow I will afford you proof of it if your Illustrious Magnificence is pleased to be there to receive it.

Your Servant (Servitrix vestra),
FULVIA ORSINI.

From the Rocca of Pievano this 20th day of January, 1503.

And under her signature she added the two words 'Manu propria,' which her self-respect seemed to demand of her.

Then came the superscription:

To the Illustrious Prince, the Duke of Valentinois these
Quickly
Quickly
Quickly.'

As she shook the pounce over the wet ink, she called Raffaele, who lay prone upon an Eastern rug before the fire, kicking his heels in the air. Instantly he leapt to her summons.

She set her hands upon his shoulders, and looked steadily into his lovely face.

'Will you do a man's work for me, Raffaele? I have need of a man, and there is none here whom I can spare. Will you ride tonight to Cesare Borgia's camp at Castel della Pieve with this letter?'

'If that be all that is needed to prove myself a man, account it proven,' said he.

'Good lad! Dear lad! Now listen. There may be spies about the gate, and so it were best you went forth on foot from here. If you can slip out unseen it will be better still. Then go down into the borgo to the house of Villanelli. Bid him lend you a horse for my service, but say no word even to him of whither you ride. Be circumspect and swift.'

'Trust me, Madonna,' said the lad, slipping the letter into the breast of his doublet.

109

'I do, else I should not charge you with this message. God watch over you! Send Mario to me as you go.'

He went forthwith, and soon came Mario in answer to her summons.

'How is it with Giuberti tonight?' she asked the seneschal as he entered.

He shrugged despondently. 'I doubt if the poor fellow will be alive by morning,' he answered.

Her face was drawn and grave, her eyes sad. 'Poor lad!' she said. 'Is the end indeed so near.'

'A miracle might save him. Nothing less. But miracles do not happen now.'

She paced slowly to the hearth, her face thoughtful, her eyes bent upon the ground. Thus she stood for a long moment, Mario waiting.

'Mario,' she said at last, speaking very quietly. 'There is a service I require of you this night – of you and Colomba.'

'We are yours to command, Madonna,' he replied.

Yet when she had told him what the service was she saw him recoil, aghast, horror stamped upon that face which the ravages of disease had made so horrible.

At that she fell to pleading with him, and with a burning eloquence she set forth the wrongs her house had suffered, spoke of the Orsini blood that had been shed to gratify Borgian ambition and to satiate Borgian vengeance, and so in the end won him to her will.

'Be it so, then, Madonna, since you desire it,' he said, but he shuddered even as he spoke. 'Have you the letter written?'

'Not yet. Come to me again soon, and it shall be ready.'

In silence he departed, and she returned to the writing pulpit. For awhile she could not write, such was the tremor of her hand as a consequence of the agitation her interview with Mario had produced in her. Presently, however, she recovered her self-control, and thereafter for a spell there was no sound in the chamber, save the occasional splutter and crackle of the burning logs and the scratch of her busy quill.

Mario returned before she had finished, and stood waiting patiently until rising she flung down her pen, and proffered him the accomplished document.

'You understand?' she said.

'I understand, Madonna. God knows it is simple – terribly simple.' And he looked at her with eyes of sorrow, conveying by his glance that what he found so terrible was that one so young and lovely should have conceived a notion so diabolical as this in which she had besought his aid.

'And you will instruct Colomba carefully so that there is no mistake.'

'There will be none,' he promised. 'I have the cane, and I myself will prepare it. A thorn is easily procured.'

'Let me have it, then, at daybreak. Bring it to my chamber. You will find me risen, and ready for a journey.'

At that he was gripped by a fresh alarm. 'You are not yourself to be the bearer of it?' he cried out.

'Whom else?' she asked him. 'Could I demand such a service of any other?'

'Gesù!' he wailed. 'Does my lord know of this?'

'Something of it. Enough of it. Not a word more now, Mario. Away with you, and see it done.'

'Ah, but consider, Madonna, what you risk! Consider, Madonna, I beseech you.'

'I have considered. I am an Orsini. Orsini have been strangled at Assisi, others are gaoled in Rome. Matteo's life is sought by this insatiable monster of revenge. I go there both to save and to avenge. I shall not fail.'

'Ah, but Madonna mine…' he began, his voice quavering, tears of intercession gathering in his eyes.

'No more, as you love me, Mario. Do my will. You cannot alter it.'

The tone invested with a stern inflexibility that never before had he known in her – and he had known her from her very birth – made an end of his protests. She was the mistress, he the servant, almost the slave, owing unquestioning obedience. And so Mario, heavy hearted, went his ways to do as she commanded, whilst she followed soon thereafter to seek what sleep she could, and in that sleep the strength to perform the task that lay before her.

The morning found her pale but calm when she came to confront her bridegroom in the hall.

The Lord of Pievano kept his chamber. Not all his stoicism was equal to the ordeal of sitting down to meat again with such a thing as Pantaleone, or witnessing the humiliation to which his daughter was to subject herself. However much he might esteem the end in view – since he was an Orsini before being a philosopher – he abhorred the means, and took the course of refusing them his countenance, and remaining passive. Yet – in justice to him be it said – of a certainty he would not have remained so had he known her full intent. A part of it only had she revealed to him.

Pantaleone was tortured between elation at the extraordinary good fortune that had so unexpectedly been flung into his lap and an irrepressible misgiving, an incredulity, a doubt as to its genuineness. Something of this was reflected in his glance as he came now into her presence. It had lost much of its habitual arrogant confidence; it seemed even a little strained.

He crossed to her, swaggering, since to swagger was natural to him; but there was none of the air of proprietorship that naturally was to be looked for in such a man towards the woman whom he had won to wife. Indeed, it was almost with humility that he took her hand, and bore it to his lips, she suffering it in the same icy detachment in which last night she had suffered his terrible embrace.

They sat down to table to break their fast, with none to wait upon them but the silent sphinx-like Mario. Even Raffaele was absent, and Pantaleone had missed the pert lad's ministrations on that morning of mornings.

He commented upon this, as much to ease the increasing strain of their silence as because he desired to know what had become of the page. Madonna excused the boy, saying that he was none so well and kept his bed. The truth was that he had but sought it a half-hour ago, upon his return from his ride to Castel della Pieve and the safe delivery of his letter.

They set out soon after, and took the road by the marsh towards Castel della Pieve. With them went Pantaleone's ten knaves, and Mario as Madonna's equerry by her insistence. Pantaleone disliked and mistrusted the silent clay-faced servant and would gladly have been rid of his presence. Yet he deemed it wise to humour her at least until a priest should have given her fully into his possession.

As they cantered briskly forward in the bright sunshine of that January morning, and the miles were flung behind them, Pantaleone's spirits rose, and conquered his last misgiving. Of treachery he had now no shadow of fear. Had she not delivered herself up to him? Were they not surrounded by men of his own? And must not the ducats and the rest follow as inevitably as the rising of tomorrow's sun? In this assurance he attempted to play the gallant, as befits a bridegroom: but he found her cold and haughty and reserved, and when he remonstrated, pointing out that she did not use him at all like one who was to be her husband by noontide, she retorted with a reminder that between them was naught but a bargain that had been struck.

This chilled him, and for a while he rode amain sulkily, with bent head and furrowed brows. But that soon passed. His abiding humour was too bouyant to suffer any permanent overclouding. Let her be as cold as ice at present. Anon he would know how to kindle her into living woman. He had so kindled a many in his day, and he was confident of his natural gifts in that direction. Not that it would greatly matter if she were to remain proof against his ardour. There were her ducats for ample consolation, and with her ducats he might procure elsewhere an abundance of the tenderness that she denied him.

They toiled up a gentle hill, and then from its summit the gleaming ruddy roofs of Castel della Pieve broke at last upon their view, some two leagues distant. It wanted yet an hour to noon, and if they maintained their present pace they would arrive too soon for Madonna's schemes. Therefore she now delayed by slacking her pace a little, pleading fatigue as a result of a ride that was something arduous for one so little used to the saddle. And she contrived so well that noon was striking from the Duomo as they rode under the deep archway of the Porta Pia and entered the town.

vii

The Duke's army was encamped upon the eastern side of the city, so that Pantaleone had no inkling of his master's presence there until they had entered the main street and saw the abundant evidences of it in the soldiers that thronged everywhere chattering in all the dialects of Middle Italy. The part he had played at Pievano had so isolated Pantaleone from the outside world, that he had remained without precise knowledge of Cesare Borgia's whereabouts. His sudden realization that he had ridden almost into the very presence of the Duke was as a shower of cold water upon his heated body. For you will understand that engaged as he was he had every reason to avoid the Duke as he would avoid the devil.

He reined in sharply, and his eyes glared mistrustfully at Madonna, instinctively feeling that here was some trap into which like a fool he had been lured by this white-faced girl. It flashed across his mind that it had been his lifelong practice to mistrust lean women. Their very leanness was in his eyes an outward sign of their lack of femininity, and a woman that lacks femininity – as all the world knows – is as often as not a very devil.

'By your leave, Madonna,' said he grimly, 'we will seek a priest elsewhere.'

'Why so?' she asked.

'Because it is my will,' he snarled back.

She smiled a crooked little smile. She was calm and mistress of herself.

'It is early yet to impose your will upon me, and if you are over-insistent now, perhaps you never shall – for I marry you at Castel della Pieve or I do not marry you at all.'

He looked at her blenching with anger. 'God's Blood!' he swore, and gave tongue to that thought of his. 'I never yet knew a lean woman that was not sly and a very bag of devil's tricks. What is in that mind of yours?'

And then suddenly a hoarse voice hailed him, and from among the passers-by there rolled forward a grizzled veteran upon sturdy bowed legs, a swarthy one-eyed fellow, who creaked and clanked as he walked, being all mail and leather. It was Valentinois' captain, Taddeo della Volpe.

'Well returned, my Pantaleone!' he cried. 'The Duke named you but yesterday, wondering how you fared.'

'Did he so?' said Pantaleone since he must say something, raging inwardly to find his retreat cut off by this most inopportune encounter.

The veteran rolled his single eye in the direction of Madonna Fulvia. 'Is this the prisoner you were sent to capture?' quoth he, and Pantaleone could not be sure that he was not being mocked. 'But I delay you. You'll be for the Duke. I'll go with you'.

Now here was Pantaleone in desperate straits. Mechanically he moved forward with Taddeo, since to obey his very natural impulse and turn about to retreat by the way he had come was now utterly impossible. Nor could he question Madonna as he desired to do whilst Della Volpe stalked there beside him.

A dozen paces brought them to the open space before the Duomo, and there Pantaleone grew cold with fear to find himself almost face to face with Cesare Borgia himself, who rode amid a group of courtiers followed by a file of men-at-arms from whose lances fluttered the bannerols with the Borgia device of the Red Bull.

He was in the trap. He had been led into it by the nose like a fool by this whey-faced Orsini girl, and he lacked even the strength to brace himself against the snapping of its springs. As he checked his horse, mechanically in his dismay, Madonna Fulvia dealt her own a cut across the hams that launched it forward as from a catapult.

'Justice!' she cried, brandishing above her head what looked like a short truncheon. 'Lord Duke of Valentinois, justice!'

There was a commotion in the magnificent group about his Highness. The wild bound of her horse had brought her almost into the midst of it.

The Duke raised his hand, and the cavalcade came to a sudden halt. His splendid eyes swept over her, and there was something in his glance that seemed to scorch her.

She beheld now for the first time this man, the enemy of her house, one whom she had come to consider a very monster. He was dressed in black, in the Spanish fashion, his doublet scrolled with golden arabesques, his velvet cap laced with a string of smouldering rubies large as sparrow's eggs. From under this the wave of his bronze-coloured hair fell to his shoulders. The delicate yet essentially male beauty of his young face was such that for a moment it checked her cruel purpose.

A smile, gentle, almost wistful, broke upon that noble countenance, and he spoke in a voice that was soft and full of melody.

'What justice do you seek, Madonna?'

To combat the sweet seduction of his face and voice she had need in that hour to bethink her of her cousins strangled at Assisi, of those other kinsmen gaoled in Rome and like to die, and of her own lover, Matteo, in peril of capture and death. What, then, if this man were a very miracle of male beauty? Was he not the enemy of her race? Did he not seek Matteo's life? Had he not set that foul hound of his to track Matteo down.

Upon the unuttered answer to those unuttered questions she braced herself, steeled her resolve and held out the tube she carried.

'It is all set down here, Magnificent, in this petition.'

He moved his horse forward some paces from amid his attendant courtiers, and without haste put forth his gauntleted hand to receive the thing she proffered. He balanced it in his palm a moment, as if weighing it, considering. It was a hollow can, sealed at both ends. A faint smile moved his lips under cover of his auburn beard.

'Here are great precautions,' was his gentle comment, and his eyes stabbed her with questions.

'I would not have it polluted on its way to your august hands,' she explained.

His smile broadened. He inclined his head as if to acknowledge the courtliness of her speech. Then his glance went beyond her and rested on the scared and savage Pantaleone.

'What fellow is that who is skulking there behind you?' said he. 'You there!' he called. 'Olà! Approach!'

Pantaleone gave a nervous hitch to his reins and walked his horse forward. His bronzed face was pallid, his glance furtive and uneasy; indeed, extreme uneasiness was writ large in every line of him.

Cesare's brows were faintly raised. 'Why, Messer Pantaleone!' he cried. 'You are well returned, and most opportunely. Here, break me these seals and read me the parchment this tube contains.'

There was a sudden stir of interest in the gay flock of attendants, a movement of horses and a craning of necks which quickened when Madonna Fulvia intervened.

'No, no, Magnificent!' Her voice was sharp with a sudden anxiety. 'It is for your eyes alone.'

He pondered her white face until she felt as she would faint under his regard, such was the terror with which it was beginning to inspire her. He smiled with a sweetness as ineffable as it was terrible and he addressed her in his silkiest accents.

'Since beholding you, Madonna, my eyes are something dazzled. I must borrow Ser Pantaleone's, there, and be content to employ my ears.' Then to Pantaleone on a sudden note of sharp command: 'Come, sir,' he said, 'we wait.'

Pantaleone a little dazed by his terror took the thing in his shaking hands, and not daring to demur or show hesitation, broke one of the seals with clumsy fumbling fingers. A silken cord protruded from the tube. He seized it to pull forth the parchment, then with a sharp exclamation he drew back his hand as if he had been stung – as indeed he had been. There was a speck of blood on his thumb and another on his fore-finger.

Madonna Fulvia shot a fearful glance at Valentinois. She saw here the miscarriage of her crafty plan, through the one factor which she had left out of consideration – the circumstance that Cesare Borgia living and moving in an environment of treachery, amid foes both secret and avowed, took no chances of falling a victim either to their force or their guile. She had not reckoned that he would appoint Pantaleone in this matter to an office akin to that filled at his table by the venom-taster.

'Come, come,' the Duke was admonishing the hesitating Pantaleone, more sharply now. 'Are we to wait here in the cold all day? The petition, man!'

Desperately Pantaleone now grasped the cord, taking care this time to avoid the thorn that accident or design – and he did not greatly care which, since he counted himself lost in any case – had lodged in the strands of the silk. He drew forth a cylinder of parchment, let fall the cane that had contained it, unrolled the petition with shaking hands, and studied it awhile, his brow wrinkled by the effort, for he was an indifferent scholar.

'Well, sir? Will you read?'

Precipitately he responded to that command, and fell to reading aloud, his voice hoarse.

'Magnificent – By these present I make appeal to you for justice against one who has proved as treacherous to you in the performance of the task to which you set him as was treacherous that task itself...'

He broke off abruptly, looking up with the wild eyes of a hunted thing.

'It...it is not true!' he protested, faltering. 'I...'

'Who bade you judge?' Cesare asked. 'I bade you read; no more. Read on, then. Should it prove to concern you your answer to it can follow.'

Under the suasion of that imperious will, Pantaleone bent his eyes to the parchment again, and pursued his reading.

'...Believing that Matteo Orsini whom he was bidden to arrest is in hiding at Pievano, he has consented to connive at his escape and thus betray your trust in him upon the condition that I become his wife and my dowry his possession.'

Again he broke off. 'By the Eyes of God, it is false! As false as hell!' he cried, a sob of agony breaking his voice.

'Read on!' The Duke's voice and mien were alike terrible. Dominated once more, Pantaleone returned yet again to the parchment.

'...Escape may or may not be for Matteo, but at least there can be no escape for you who read, by the time you have read thus far. We have another guest at Pievano in our lazar-house there – the small-pox. And these present have lain an hour upon the breast of one who is dying of it, and...'

On a sudden outcry of terror Pantaleone brought his reading abruptly to an end. The plague-laden parchment floated from his hands that were suddenly turned limp. It reached the ground, and there was a sudden alarmed movement on all sides to back away beyond the radius of its venom, beyond the danger of the dread scourge that it exuded.

Dully through Pantaleone's benumbed wits the realization thrust itself that the thorn in the silk had been no accident. It had been set there of intent, so that it might open a way by which the terrible infection should travel the more swiftly and surely into the reader's veins. He knew himself for a doomed man, one who might count himself under sentence of death, since the chances of winning alive through an attack of that pestilence were so slight as to be almost negligible. Ashen-faced he stared straight before him, what time indignation and horror found voice on every side, and continued clamant until the Duke raised an imperious hand to demand silence.

He alone remained unmoved, or at least showed no outward sign of such anger as he may have felt. When next he addressed the white-faced lady, who had made this desperate attempt upon his life, his voice was as smooth and silken as it had been before, his returning smile as sweet. And perhaps because of that the doom he pronounced was the more awful.

'Of course,' he said, 'since Ser Pantaleone has fulfilled his part of the bargain, you, Madonna, will now fulfil yours. You will wed him as you undertook.'

119

Wide-eyed, she stared, and it was a long moment ere she understood the poetic justice that he meted out to her. When at last her voice came it came in a hoarse cry of horror.

'Wed him? Wed him! He is infected…'

'With your venom,' Cesare cut in crisply. And he continued calmly as one reasoning with a wayward child: 'It is your duty to yourself and him. You are in honour bound by your compact. The poor fellow could not foresee all this. You had not made him privy to you plans.'

He was mocking her. She perceived it, and rage surged through her at the ruthless cruelty of it. She had ever heard that he was pitiless, but in no imagining of hers could she ever have conceived a pitilessness to compare with this. Her sudden surge of anger heartened her a little, yet it lent her no words in which to answer him, for in truth he was unanswerable – his justice ever was, wherefore men hated him the more.

'You called to me for justice, Madonna,' he reminded her. 'Thus you receive it. It is complete, I think. I hope it satisfies you.'

Her anger shivered itself unuttered against that iron dominance of his. Before it her spirit left her utterly, her high courage ebbed like water, and she became again the prey of fear and horror.

'Oh, not that! not that!' she cried to him. 'Mercy! Mercy! as you would hope for mercy in your need, have mercy on me now.' He looked sardonically at Ser Pantaleone, who sat his horse, benumbed in body and in brain.

'Madonna Fulvia does not flatter you, Pantaleone,' said he. 'She has little fancy for you as a bridegroom, it appears. Yet, fool, you believed her when she promised to take you to husband. You believed her! Ha! What was it Fra Serafino said of you?' He fell thoughtful. 'I remember! He found you too full in the lips to be trusted with a woman. He knows his world, Fra Serafino. A cloister is a good coign of observation. So you succumbed to her promises! But be comforted. She shall fulfil them, where she thought to cheat you. She shall take you to that white breast of hers – you and the plague you carry with you.'

'Oh, God!' she panted. 'Will you wed me to death?'

'Is it possible,' he wondered, 'that you can find death more repulsive than Pantaleone? Yet consider,' he begged her, reasoning dispassionately, 'that I do naught by you that you would not have done by me.' He began with infinite caution to peel off the heavy gauntlet of buffalo hide with which he had handled that death-dealing tube. 'After all,' he resumed, 'if to keep your word is beyond measure odious to you – a family trait with you, Madonna, as I have cause to know – I may show you the way to escape its consequences.'

She looked at him, but there was no hope in her glance.

'You mock me!' she cried.

'Not so. There is a way that some would account to be consistent with honour. Cancel the bargain that you made with him, and thus cancel the obligation to fulfil your part and to submit to his embrace.'

'Cancel it? How cancel it?' she asked.

'Is it not plain? By surrendering Matteo Orsini to me. Deliver him up to me this day, and the night shall be free from nuptials that are distasteful to you.'

She understood at once the satanic subtlety of this man; she saw how far removed he was from any petty vengeance such as she had suspected him to be gratifying: she was but an insignificant pawn in the deep game he played; her feelings were to him no more than the means to the one end of which never for an instant had he lost sight – the capture of Matteo Orsini. That was all that mattered to him, and he was not to be turned aside by any considerations of anger towards herself. He had terrified her with the threat of this unutterable marriage, simply that he might render her pliant to his will, ready to pay any price of treachery to escape that ghastly fate.

'Deliver him up to you?' she said, and it was her turn to smile at last, but with infinitely bitter scorn.

'Could aught be easier?' he asked. 'There is no need to tell me even where he lurks. I do not ask you to betray him, or do aught that would hurt your tender Orsini sensibilities.' His sarcasm was a sword of fire. 'You need but to send him word of the plight into which your essay in poisoning has landed you. That is all. As he is a man, he must come hither to ransom you from the consequences of your deed. Let him come before nightfall, or else – ' he shrugged, flung his gauntlets down into the mud, and nodded his head towards the stricken Pantaleone – 'you keep your bargain; you pay the price agreed upon for his escape, and myself I shall provide the nuptial banquet.'

She looked at him with a deep malignity aroused by his own relentlessness and by the hateful suavity in which he cloaked it. And then her wits roused themselves to do battle with his own. She saw how subtlety might yet defeat subtlety. And as the idea crept into her fevered mind, the blood came slowly back into her livid cheeks, her glance grew bold and resolute as it met his own.

'Be it so,' she said. 'You leave me no choice, Magnificent.' Her voice came harsh and something mocking. 'It shall be as you desire. I will send my servant to him now.'

He gave her a long, searching glance which at first was grave and doubting, and ended by becoming almost contemptuous. He made a sign to his cavaliers.

'Let us on, sirs. Here is no more to do.' But he stooped from his saddle to issue an order in an undertone to Della Volpe who throughout had stood beside him. Then flicking his horse with the slight whip which he carried, he moved on across the square, his fluttering attendants with him. He knew this Orsini brood. They were all the same. Bold to devise, but craven to execute; their brains were stouter than their hearts. Their stiffness crumpled at the touch.

viii

Erect and stiff upon her horse sat Madonna Fulvia, her eyes following the Duke as he rode away across the square, to vanish down the street that opened out of it. She remained thus, bemused, half-dazed, indifferent to the gaping crowd that by now surrounded her, but keeping its distance out of respect for the disease with which Pantaleone was accounted laden.

She was roused at length by a groom dressed in black with a bull wrought in red upon the breast of his doublet, who stepped forward to take her reins, whilst at the same time Della Volpe addressed her, his tone respectful but his single eye contemptuous.

'Madonna,' he said, 'I pray you go with us. I have my lord's commands for your entertainment.'

She looked at him, sneering at first at the euphemism he had employed by which to convey to her that she was a prisoner. But something in that veteran's rugged face struck the sneer from her lips. Two things she read in that countenance: the first, that he was honest; the second, that he contemned her action.

Her glance grew troubled, and it fell away from him. 'Do you lead the way then, sir,' she said. 'My equerry here accompanies me, I think.' And she indicated Mario, who sat his horse rigidly behind her, a dumb anguish in his dark eyes.

'Naturally, Madonna, since he is to be your messenger. Forward, Giasone,' he commanded, and upon that, the groom leading her horse, Della Volpe striding grimly beside her and Mario riding as grimly in her wake, she moved forward towards the Communal Palace whither by Cesare's orders they were taking her.

As for the wretched Pantaleone, she scarce bestowed another thought upon him. He had been no more than a pawn in this game of hers, even as she was become one now in the deeper game of the Duke's. He had served his miserable turn, though not quite as she had intended. In view of the resolve she had taken, it was unlikely that she would be troubled with him again, she thought.

She had observed, though with but faint interest, that a half-dozen arbalisters had charge of him. These men, under the command of an antient, showed no relish for their task of apprehending one who was so armed that without raising a finger he could fling death about him. Accordingly they kept their distance. They made a wide ring about their prisoner, each with a quarrel laid to his arbalest, and thus they urged him away, threatening to shoot him if he were disobedient.

123

When at last he had been removed in this fashion, a man in the Borgia livery came forward with a flaming torch to within a couple of yards of the pestilential parchment that still lay where it had fallen. Thence he flung his torch upon it, nor went to recover it again. Torch and plague-laden parchment were consumed together, in spite of which, so runs the story, the good folk of Città della Pieve went wide of the spot for days thereafter.

Meanwhile Madonna Fulvia had been conducted to the Communal, and found herself housed in a long low-ceilinged chamber of the mezzanine of the old palace, an austere room in the matter of equipment, for Città della Pieve was a modest township that had not kept pace with the luxurious development of the great Italian States.

A guard was placed outside the door, and another was set to pace beneath her windows; but at least she was given the freedom of that spacious chamber, and of course Mario was admitted to her presence, since he was to be her messenger to Matteo Orsini. The Duke had judged it well that it should be so, since to the testimony of such letters as she might write Mario would add the confirmation of his own evidence of a fact which might be disbelieved if related by another.

Alone with his mistress, this frail child whom he had known from her cradle, the old servant now broke down utterly. His grimness deserted him utterly, and the tears rolled down his ghastly furrowed face.

'Madonna mine! Madonna mine!' he sobbed brokenly, and held out his arms as if he would have taken her to them, paternally to comfort her. 'I warned you. I told you here was no work for such gentleness as yours. I implored you to let me do this thing in your stead. What do I matter? I am old; my life has reached its evening; my loss of a few days more would be nobody's gain. But you... O God of Pity!'

'Calm, Mario! Be calm,' she bade him gently.

'Calm?' he cried. 'Can I be calm when before you lies the choice between betrayal and death, and, Gesù! such a death. Had I carried an arbalest I should have put a bolt through his devil's heart when he pronounced your doom; the fiend, the monster!'

'A beautiful devil he is,' she said. Then she dropped her voice. 'Mario!' she called him softly. Her eyes flashed to the door, then she drew still farther from it, over to the window overlooking the square, beckoning him to follow. He went silently, staring, impressed by the mystery of her bearing.

By the window, in lowered murmuring accents she addressed him.

'There may yet be a way out of this,' she said. 'You shall bear no letters, because you will need none. Listen now.' And she gave him her commands.

By the time she had done he was staring at her, his jaw fallen. Then he stirred himself out of his amazement. He broke into protests that she was but making her ruin doubly certain; he sought to dissuade her, reminded her that it was through a disregard of his counsels that she came into her present ghastly pass, and besought her not again to disregard them.

But in her headstrong way she remained unmoved, her resolve a rock upon which the torment of his loving eloquence broke and was dissipated. And so in the end she had her way with him against his better judgement, even as last night. That there might be no mistake she repeated all to him in brief at parting.

'And to my lord? What shall I say to my lord?' he asked.

'As little as you can, and nothing to alarm him.'

'I am to lie, then.'

'Even that if need be, out of charity to him.'

He departed at last, and throughout the long afternoon she sat alone in that room of the mezzanine, save for one interruption when a couple of slender vermilion striplings of the Duke's household brought her food and wine in golden vessels upon salvers of beaten gold.

She drank a little of the wine, but though she had not eaten since leaving Pievano early that morning, the suffocation of suspense was upon her and she refused all food.

She sat on by the window, and towards evening she saw the Duke returning with his gay cavalcade. Later, as the twilight was deepening, the two vermilion pages returned to bid her in the Duke's name to the supper that was spread below. She excused herself. But the pages were gently insistent.

'It is his potency's wish,' one of them informed her, in a tone that quietly implied that what his potency wished none might withstand.

Perceiving not only the uselessness of further denial, but, further, that her very presence below might advance the thing she had set herself to do, she rose and signed to the pages to lead the way. In the corridor another pair awaited her, each bearing a lighted taper, who went on ahead. In this ceremonious fashion was she conducted below to the great hall, where a courtly crowd of cavaliers and ladies were assembled, making her instantly conscious – very woman that she was – of her own plain and dusty raiment, so out of place amid all this glittering splendour.

The Duke himself, tall and graceful in a suit of sulphur-coloured silk with silver bands at throat and waist, advanced to the foot of the stairs to receive her, bowing to her with the deference he might have used to a princess. By the hand, which she did not dream of denying him, he led her through the throng to the double doors that were thrown open upon an inner room. Here long tables were set for supper upon a dais that formed the three sides of a parallelogram.

At the table's head, in the middle of the short upper limb, he took his seat with her beside him, whilst those who had trooped in after them found for themselves the places that had been allotted them. It was as if the company had but awaited the arrival of herself as of an honoured guest, and the vengeful mockery of it stabbed her to the soul. Yet she strove that naught of this should appear, and she succeeded. White-faced she sat between Valentinois and the portly Capello, Orator of Venice, braving the curious glances that were flashed towards her from every side.

That room of the Communal, which in normal times was bare and cheerless as a barn, had been transmogrified under the deft hands of Cesare's familiars until none who knew its ordinary appearance could now have recognized it. You might have supposed yourself in one of the chambers of the Vatican. The walls were hung with costly arras, Byzantine carpets had been spread upon the stone floor, and the tables themselves gleamed and flashed with broidered naperies, vessels of gold and silver, costly crystal and massive candlesticks in which candles of painted and scented wax were burning. Add to this that gorgeous company in silk and velvet, in cloth of gold and silver, in ermines and miniver, the women in gem-encrusted bodices and jewelled hair-nets, the flock of splendidly liveried servants below the dais, the cloud of fluttering pages, and you will understand how Madonna Fulvia reared far from the world of courts in the claustral seclusion of Pievano, was dazzled by the spectacle.

From a fretted gallery above the doorway came a sound of lutes, archlutes and viols, and under cover of the music – his voice so melodious that it almost seemed to sing to it – the Duke addressed her.

'I rejoice for you, Madonna,' he said, 'that here is spread no nuptial feast.'

She looked at him, and shivered slightly as she turned away again.

'It would break my heart,' he pursued on that murmuring, caressing note of his that lent his voice a wooing quality, 'it would break my heart to see so much beauty delivered into the arms of foul infection. Hence do I fervently pray that Matteo Orsini comes tonight.'

'And for no other reason?' she asked him scornfully, stung by what seemed to her such stark hypocrisy.

He smiled, his beautiful sombre eyes enveloping her white face in their regard. 'I confess the other,' he admitted, 'but I swear as I am living man and worship all things lovely, the reason that I gave weighs the heavier.' He sighed. 'It is to save you that I pray Matteo Orsini may come tonight.'

'He will come,' she answered him. 'Have no doubt of that.'

'He owes no less to his manhood,' he said quietly. Then turned his attention to more immediate matter. 'You do not eat,' he reproved her.

'I should choke, I think,' she answered frankly.

'A cup of wine at least,' he urged, and signed to a cellarer who bore a gold vessel of soft Puglia wine. But, seeing her gesture of refusal, he put forth a hand to stay the servant's pouring. 'Wait,' he said, and beckoned a page to him. 'A moss-agate cup for Madonna Fulvia, here,' he bade the stripling, and the page vanished upon his errand.

Madonna's lip curled a little. 'There is no need for the precaution,' she said – for moss-agate cups were said to burst if poison touched them – 'I neither suspect venom nor do I fear it.'

'So much I might have known,' he answered, 'since you have displayed yourself so subtly learned in the uses of it.'

He spoke quietly and gravely, but at the words she felt herself go hot and cold at once. A scarlet wave suffused her face, then ebbed, to leave it deathly pale. His words made her perhaps realize that she had no just cause for grievance; she was a poisoner caught *flagrante*, and the steely treatment he meted out to her in his silken fashion was no more than her desert.

Back came the page with the gleaming moss-agate cup, which he set down before her. The waiting cellarer brimmed it at a sign from him, and his glance now inviting her she drank to steady her sudden weakness.

But the meats they placed before her continued unheeded, nor did she thereafter heed the Duke when he leaned aside to mock her still with that dread gentleness of his. Her staring eyes were set expectantly upon the doors at the room's end. It waxed late, and her impatience mounted. Why did they not come, and thus put an end to the unbearable strain of suspense that racked her very soul?

Came pages now with silver basins, ewers, and napkins. Gallants and ladies dipped their hands and washed their fingers against the serving of the sweetmeats, and then without warning – but obeying, no doubt, the orders that the Duke had left – those portals upon which Madonna's eyes had so long been fastened swung open, and between two men-at arms in steel she beheld her clay-faced equerry, the faithful Mario, haggard and dust-stained, returned at last.

The hum of conversation sank down and was stilled as the sturdy fellow advanced up the long room between the tables and came, still flanked by his guards, to stand immediately before the Duke. Not to the Duke, however, but to Madonna Fulvia did he address himself when at length he spoke.

'Madonna, I have done your bidding. I have brought Ser Matteo.'

A silence followed and a pause, ended at last by Cesare's short laugh.

'Body of God! Did he need bringing?'

'He did, my lord.'

The Duke's glance swept over the noble company. 'You hear,' he called to them, raising his voice. 'You perceive the lofty spirit of these Orsini. An Orsini must needs be brought to ransom his mistress and kinswoman from the fate decreed her.' He turned to the equerry. 'Fetch him hither,' he said shortly, with a wave of his fine hand.

But Mario was slow to obey. Not upon the Duke but upon Madonna were his eyes set, as if awaiting her confirmation of that command. She nodded, whereupon he turned and strode down the room again upon his errand and so out.

The doors closed after him, but the silence continued. No man or woman there but felt the oppression of the impending drama, but awaited in suspense the climax and conclusion that were close at hand. The very minstrels in the gallery had ceased their music, and not a sound disturbed the general brooding hush.

Cesare leaned back in his high gilded chair, his slender fingers toying delicately with the strands of his auburn beard, his narrowed eyes glancing aslant at Madonna Fulvia. He found her manner very odd. It contained some quality that intrigued him, and eluded his miraculous penetration.

She sat there with ashen face and wide, staring eyes; so might a corpse have sat, and a corpse you might have deemed her but for the convulsive heave of her slight bosom.

And then a sound of voices beyond the door – of voices raised in sudden altercation – broke upon the general expectancy.

'You cannot enter!' came a gruff shout. 'You cannot take…'

And then they heard Mario's voice, harsh, vibrant and compelling, interrupting and overbearing the objector.

'Did you not hear the Duke's express commands that I should bear Matteo Orsini to him? I have Matteo Orsini here, and I but obey his potency's commands. Out of my way, then.'

But other voices broke in upon him, all speaking together so that they made no more than a confused and bawling chorus whose purport was not to be discerned.

Suddenly Cesare rose in his place, his eyes flaming. 'What's this?' he cried, 'By the Host! am I kept waiting? Set me wide those doors!'

There was a scurry of lackeys to obey that imperious voice. The Duke sank back into his chair as the doors were violently pulled open. Beyond it a line of a half-dozen men-at-arms made a screen that concealed whatever lay behind them.

'My lord…' began one of these, a grizzled antient, raising his hand in appeal.

But Cesare let him get no further. His clenched hand descended violently upon the table. 'Stand back, I say, and let him enter.'

Instantly that line of steel-clad men melted and vanished, and where it had been stood Mario now. He paused a moment on the threshold, his face set and grim. Then he stalked forward up the long room again between the tables. But no one heeded him. Every eye was fixed in amazed and uncomprehending horror upon that which followed after him.

Came four brothers of the Misericordia in black, funereal habits, their heads cowled, their eyes gleaming faintly from the eyeholes cut in their shapeless vizors. Among them they carried a bier, whose trappings of black velvet edged with silver swept the ground as they solemnly advanced.

They were midway up that room before the company broke from the spell of horror which this grim spectacle had laid upon it. A loud outcry seemed to burst from every throat at once. Then the Duke leapt to his feet, and the whole company with him, and in the sudden stir and confusion none observed that Madonna Fulvia left her place at the Duke's side.

The bearers halted and set down their ghastly burden. Mario stood slightly aside, lest his body should screen the bier from the eyes of the Duke.

'What's this?' his potency demanded, anger ringing in his voice. 'What jest is this you dare to put upon me?' And as he spoke he swung aside to where Madonna Fulvia had been, then, finding her place now vacant, his flaming eyes swept round in quest of her, and discovered her at last standing there beside the bier.

'No jest, Magnificent,' she answered him, her head thrown back, a smile of bitter, tragic triumph on her white face. 'Faithful and utter compliance with your behest – no more. You commanded that Matteo Orsini should be delivered into your hands. Provided I did that you would release me of my compact to wed your jackal Pantaleone degli Uberti. I hold you to your word, my lord. I have done my part. Matteo Orsini is here.' And she flung an arm out and downwards to indicate the bier.

He stared at her, his eyes narrowing, oddly out of countenance for one habitually so calm, so master of every circumstance.

'Here?' he questioned, and added the further question – 'Dead?'

For answer she stooped and swept the velvet pall aside, laying bare the coffin underneath. That done she faced him again, defiance in her every slender line, a ghastly smile on her pale lips.

'Bid your guards hack off the lid that you may assure yourself 'tis he. I promise you he will offer no resistance now.'

Considering him, she took satisfaction in the perception that at last she had wiped that hateful, gently mocking smile from his face. He was scowling upon her, his eyes ablaze with such a passion as no man in all Italy would willingly have confronted. His hands, resting upon the table before him, were clenched so that the knuckles showed like knobs of marble.

The rest of them, the whole of that splendid company, was ranged against the walls as far as possible from that hideous thing below. In their minds, as in Cesare's, there stirred a memory of what had befallen earlier that day – of that letter that had been infected and of the manner of that infection – and a suspicion of what was yet to follow began to form in the thoughts of all.

Thus for a spell of awful silence, then Cesare's voice rasped out a question harshly – a question that voiced in part that general and terrible suspicion:

'How died he?'

Came like a thunderbolt her answer, shrilly delivered on a high note of fierce exaltation – 'He died of the smallpox yesternight. Hack off the lid,' she added. 'Hack off the lid, and take him.'

But that last mocking invitation which she hurled at the Duke was lost in the sudden uproar in the noise of the wild stampede that followed her announcement. Mad with fear, men who had shown themselves fearless upon a field of stricken battle turned this way and that, seeking a way out. Cursing, they hurled themselves against the long windows that opened upon the little claustral garden of the Communal, and screaming, fainting women crowded after them to avail themselves of this shortest way out that was being forced open.

It would have needed more even than the presence of that terrible duke to have restrained them in their wild panic, in their mad frenzy to breathe the clean cold air, to quit this tainted atmosphere, to fly this hideous plague-spot. Nor did Cesare make any effort to delay their flight.

With shivering of glass and crashing of splintered timbers those long window-doors were swept away. Out of the room headlong, as a river that has burst its dam, surged that courtly, terror-stricken mob; into it rushed the pure, keen air of the January night.

Cesare alone, at his place beyond the board, in the flickering light of wind-blown, guttering candles, remained even after the last lackey had fled, conquered by his panic. Indomitable, the Duke stood there to face the woman who dared to bring a plague-ridden corpse to set at naught his authority and make a mock of his power.

'Well?' she asked him, and her laugh made him shudder, man of iron though he was. 'Have you the courage to face Matteo Orsini now? Or do you lack it still, for all that he is dead?'

'Living I never feared him,' he blazed out, unworthily it must be confessed.

'Then you will not fear him dead,' said she, and turned fiercely upon her equerry. 'Here, Mario, you who have had the scourge and therefore need no longer fear it, prize off this lid. Give Matteo room to strike even in death.'

But the Duke waited for no more. Panic took him, too; and he was known to confess to it thereafter, adding that it was the only occasion in all his life upon which he had been face to face with fear, he who so often had looked death in the eyes without quailing.

'Blood of God!' he cried, and on that fierce oath he sprang from the table, and flung through the nearest window in the wake of his vanished court. Outside they heard him shouting for his horse, and they heard too the clamour of answering voices.

Within ten minutes he and his noble company were in the saddle, scudding through the night away from Castel della Pieve and the dread plague it harboured.

As that thunder of hoofs receded, Madonna Fulvia, who had remained by the coffin with no word spoken, bade the men take up their burden once more. Laden with it they passed out of that room, all littered with the now unheeded treasures that had been assembled in the Duke's honour. Madonna and Mario walked ahead, the coffin was borne after them. They crossed the hall and quitted the palace, none hindering, indeed all fleeing before their approach. Horses were found for herself and Mario; the bearers came on foot with their burden. Thus they took the road by the marshes back to Pievano in the dark.

When they had put a league or so between themselves and Città della Pieve, she spoke for the first time.

'How was it with Giuberti today, Mario?' she asked.

'He died at noon, Madonna,' was the answer. 'God be praised, there is no other case of smallpox yet, and by His Grace there will be none. Our precautions were well taken, and they will be to the end. Colomba herself dug his grave and gave him burial deep in the enclosed garden. The lazar-house was in flames when I left Pievano, so that all source of infection may be destroyed, and Colomba herself will set up a tent in the enclosure and abide there until all danger of her carrying the scourge is overpast.'

'The good Colomba shall be rewarded, Mario. We are profoundly in her debt.'

'A faithful soul,' Mario admitted. 'But there was no risk to her, since like myself, she too has paid the price of immunity.'

'That cannot lessen our gratitude,' she said. And then she sighed. 'Poor Giuberti! God rest his loyal soul! A faithful servant ever, he has served us even in death. Heaven has blessed us in the matter of servants, Mario. There is yourself...'

'I? I am but a clod,' he interrupted. 'I had not the wit to trust you today. Had you been dependent upon my service all must have miscarried and Heaven knows what fatality had been the end of this adventure.'

'Which reminds me,' said she, 'that these poor fellows are unnecessarily laden. We have no pursuit to fear, and we shall make the better speed if we ease them of their burden.' She drew rein as she spoke, and Mario with her. 'Enough!' she called to those cowled figures that swung along behind her. 'Empty it out.'

Obediently they set down the coffin, forced up the lid, tilted it over, and rolled out the load of earth and stones that it contained.

She laughed softly in the dark when this was done. But Mario shuddered, bethinking him of the risk she had taken.

'God and His saints be thanked he did not dare to look,' he said with fervour. 'He has a reputation for high courage, and I feared... By the Host! how I feared!'

'Not more than I feared, Mario,' she confessed, 'but I also hoped; and if the chance was a desperate one it was still the only chance.'

At Pievano some hours later she found her father so racked with anxiety by her continued absence and the circumstance that Mario had come and gone again that afternoon that he had summoned the fugitive Matteo Orsini from his hiding place to consult with him as to what measures should be taken.

Her appearance ended their travail of spirit, and the sight of them made an end of the fortitude that had so long upheld her. She flung herself upon her lover's breast, panting and trembling.

'You may sleep quiet now of nights, Matteo mine,' she said. 'He believes you dead, and fears you dead more than he could ever have feared you living.' And on that she fainted in his arms, her strength of body and of spirit alike exhausted.

And that, so far as I can discover, is the only instance in which man or woman defeated the Duke of Valentinois in an encounter of wits; nor does it lessen my high opinion of his penetration, for it must surely be admitted that the dice were heavily cogged against him, and that he fell a victim to a fraud rendered possible by circumstances. There is also responsible for this failure the fact that for once he did not choose his tool with that discrimination which Macchiavelli enjoins upon princes. He overlooked the significance of those excessively full lips of Pantaleone's and left unheeded the warning Fra Serafino uttered on the score of them. Or perhaps, on the other hand... But why speculate? I have laid the facts before you, and you may draw your own inferences.

As for Pantaleone, if he still interests you, he fared on the whole perhaps better than he deserved, though that is purely a matter of the point of view from which he is to be judged. For, as the Lord Almerico's favourite philosopher has said, a man does not choose the part he shall play in life, he simply plays the part that is allotted to him.

He was entirely overlooked when Cesare with all his following left Città della Pieve, and he was left there in the gaol into which he had been flung until it should be ascertained whether he was to be required as a bridegroom. Anon Cesare remembered him, and was about to order him to be strangled when he learnt that the fellow had developed the smallpox and had been, very properly, taken to a lazar-house. It is recorded that upon hearing this the Duke shuddered at the memory of his own escape, and was content to leave the rascal to the fate that had overtaken him – perhaps because he knew of no one who in the circumstances would undertake to strangle him.

Pantaleone's lusty youth stood him in such good stead that he made one of those rare recoveries from that pitiless scourge. But he came forth into the world again broken in health and strength, and no longer to be recognized for the same swaggering, arrogant captain who had sought sanctuary on that January evening at Pievano.

His career as a captain of fortune being ended, realizing that he was a broken and useless man, he dragged himself wearily back to the village of Laveno in the Bolognese, and stumbled one April morning into Leocadia's wine-shop; there he flung himself upon the charity and the ample bosom of the woman whom in prosperity he had forsaken. And such is the ever-forgiving and generous nature of your true woman that Leocadia put her arms about him and wept silently in thanksgiving for his return, blessing the disease that had made him weak and hideous since it had restored him to her.

Since it sorted well with his interest, I do not doubt that he made an honest woman of her.

THE VENETIAN

i

He who is great shall never lack for enemies. He has to reckon first with lesser great ones, whose ambitions he thwarts by his own success, outstripping and overshadowing them; and he has to reckon further with those insignificant parasites of humanity who, themselves utterly unproductive of aught that shall benefit their race, destitute alike of the wit to conceive for themselves or the energy and capacity to execute the conceptions of their betters, writhe in the secret consciousness of their utter worthlessness and spit the venom of their malice at him who has achieved renown. In this they no more than obey the impulses of their paltry natures, the dictates of their foolish narrow vanity. The greatness of another wounds them in their own self-love. They readily become detractors and defamers, conceiving that if in the public mind they can pull down the object of their envy, they have lessened the gulf between themselves and him. Fluent – if undeceiving – liars, they go to work through the medium of that their sole and very questionable gift. They lie of their own prowess, importance and achievement, that thus they may puff themselves up to an apparently greater stature, and they lie maliciously and cruelly concerning the object of their envy, belittling his attainments, slandering the object of their envy, belittling his attainments, slandering him in his private and public life, and smothering his repute in the slime of their foul inventions.

By such signs shall you know them – for a fool is ever to be known by those two qualities: his inordinate vanity and his falsehood, which usually is no more than an expression of that vanity. But his falsehood, being naturally of the measure of his poor intelligence, deceives none but his own kind.

Such a thing was Messer Paolo Capello, Orator of the Most Serene Republic, a servant chosen to forward the Venetian hatred of Cesare Borgia. Venice watched the Duke's growing power in Italy with ever-increasing dismay. She saw herself threatened by a serious rival in the peninsula, by one indeed who might come to eclipse her own resplendent glory, even if he did not encroach upon her mainland territories of which indeed she was by no means sure. That jealousy of hers distorted her judgement of him, for she permitted herself judgement and applied to him the only canons that she knew, as if men of genius are to be judged by the standards that govern the lives of haberdashers and spice-merchants. Thus Venice became Cesare's most crafty, implacable enemy in Italy, and an enemy for whose hand no weapon was too vile.

Gladly would the Venetians have moved in arms against him, to attempt to crush this man who snatched the Romagna from under their covetous traders' eyes; but in view of the league with France they dared not. Yet what they dared they did. They sought to disturb his relations with King Louis, and failing there, they sought alliances with other States to which normally they were hostile, and when there again they failed, thanks to a guile more keen and intelligent than their own, they had recourse to the common weapons of the assassin and the slanderer.

For the latter task they had a ready tool in that ineffable and worthless Messer Capello, sometime their Orator at the Vatican; for the former, another of whom we shall hear more presently.

This Capello was of the slipperiness of all slimy things. And he worked in the dark, burrowing underground and never affording the Duke a plain reason that should have justified extreme measures against the sacred person of an ambassador. How he came to escape assassination in the early days of his infamous career I have never understood. I look upon its omission as one of Cesare Borgia's few really great blunders. A hired bravo with a dagger on some dark night might have stemmed that source of foulness, leaving the name of Cesare Borgia and of every member of his family less odious to posterity.

When Giovanni Borgia, Duke of Gandia, was murdered in the pursuit of one of his frivolous amours, and no murderer could be discovered – though many possible ones were named, from his own brother Gioffredo to Ascanio Sforza, the Cardinal Vice-Chancellor – there came at last from Venice a year after the deed the accusation unsupported by any single shred of evidence that the deed of fratricide was Cesare's. When Pedro Caldes – or Perrotto, as he was called – the Pope's chamberlain, fell into the Tiber and was drowned, came from Venice a lurid tale – supplied as we know from the fertile, unscrupulous pen of Messer Capello – of how Cesare had stabbed the wretch in the Pope's very arms; and although no man admittedly had witnessed the deed, yet Messer Capello gave the most circumstantial details, even to how the blood had spurted up into the face of his Holiness. When the unfortunate Turkish prince, the Sultan Djem, died of a colic at Naples, it is Capello who starts the outrageous story that he was poisoned by Cesare, and again he circulated the like calumny when the Cardinal Giovanni Borgia succumbed to a fever in the course of a journey through Romagna. And if this were all – or if all the calumny that Capello invented had been concerned with no more than steel and poison – we might be patient in our judgement of him. But there was worse, far worse. There was indeed no dunghill of calumny too foul to be exploited by him in the interests of the Most Serene. His filthy pen grew, fevered in the elaboration of the gossip that he picked up in curial ante-chambers, and in marking out Cesare Borgia for its victim, it yet spared no member of his family but included all in the abominations it invented or magnified. Most of them have passed into history where they may be read, but not necessarily believed. I will not sully this fair sheet nor your decent mind with their recapitulation.

Thus was it that Messer Paolo Capello served the Most Serene Republic. But because his services, frenzied though they were, seemed slow to bear the fruit which the Most Serene so ardently desired, other and more direct methods than those of calumny were resolved upon. The Venetians took this resolve in mid-October of the year 1500 of the Incarnation and VIII of the Papacy of Roderigo Borgia, who ruled from the Chair of St Peter as Alexander VI; and what urged them to it was to see Pandolfo Malatesta, whom they had protected, driven out of his tyranny of Rimini, and that tyranny of his, which they had coveted, pass by right of conquest – based upon certain legal papal rights – into the possession of Cesare Borgia, further to swell his dominions and his might.

The Most Serene Republic conceived that the hour had come for sharper measures than such as were afforded her by the scurrilous gleanings and inventions of her Orator. As her agent in this sinister affair she employed a patrician who held the interests of Venice very dear; a man who was bold, resolute and resourceful, and whose hatred of the Duke of Valentinois was notoriously so intense as to seem an almost personal matter. This man – the Prince Marcantonio Sinibaldi – she dispatched to Rimini as her envoy-extraordinary for the express purpose, ostensibly, of conveying her lying felicitations to the Duke upon his conquest.

As if to emphasize the peaceful and friendly character of his mission, Sinibaldi was accompanied by his princess, a very beautiful and accomplished lady of the noble house of Alviano. The pair made their appearance in Rimini surrounded by a pomp and luxury of retinue that was extraordinary even for the pompous and wealthy Republic which they represented.

The princess was borne in a horse-litter carried by two milk-white Barbary jennets, whose embroidered trappings of crimson velvet swept the ground. The litter itself was a gorgeous construction, gilded and painted like a bride's coffer and hung with curtains that were of cloth of gold, upon each of which was woven in red the device of the winged lion of St Mark. About this litter swarmed a host of pages, all of them lads of patrician estate, in the livery of the Republic.

There were mounted Nubian swordsmen in magnificent barbaric garments, very terrifying of aspect; there were some dozen turbaned Moorish slaves on foot, and finally there was a company of a score of arbalisters on horseback as a bodyguard of honour for the splendid prince himself. The prince, a handsome, resplendent figure, towered upon a magnificent charger with a groom trotting afoot at either of his stirrups. After him came a group of his personal familiars – his secretary, his venom-taster, his chaplain and his almoner, which last flung handfuls of silver coins at the mob to impress it with his master's munificence and to excite its acclamations of his illustrious person.

The good folk of Rimini who were scarcely recovered from the excitements of the pageantry of Cesare's State entry into the city were dazzled and dazed again by a spectacle of so much magnificence.

Sinibaldi was housed – and this by the contriving of our friend Capello – in the palace of the Lord Ranieri, a sometime member of the banished Malatesta's council, but none the less one of those who had been loudest in welcoming the conqueror Cesare, acclaiming him in a speech of surpassing eloquence as Rimini's deliverer.

The Duke had not been deluded by these fine phrases. Far from it, he was inspired by them to have a close watch set upon Malatesta's sometime councillor. Neither was he at all deluded by the no less fine phrases of felicitations addressed him on behalf of the Most Serene by her envoy-extraordinary Sinibaldi. He knew too much – for he had received superabundant proof – of Venice's real attitude towards himself. He answered them with words fully as graceful and fully as hollow. And when he learnt that, under himself, Ranieri was to be Sinibaldi's host in Rimini, that both these nimble phrase-makers were to lie under one roof, he bade his secretary Agabito see to it that the vigilance under which that palace was already kept should be increased.

To meet Sinibaldi it must be confessed that Ranieri – a portly, florid gentleman with a bright and jovial blue eye, the very antithesis in appearance to the conspirator of tradition – had assembled an odd company. There was Francesco d'Alviano, a younger brother of that famous soldier, Bartolomeo d'Alviano, than whom it was notorious that the Duke had no more implacable enemy; there was the young Galeazzo Sforza of Catignola, bastard brother to Giovanni Sforza, the divorced husband of Cesare's lovely sister Lucrezia, lately dispossessed by the Duke of his tyranny of Pesaro; and there were four others, three patricians, who are of little account, and lastly Pietro Corvo, that notorious, plebian Forlivese scoundrel who under the name of Corvinus Trismegistus had once to his undoing practised magic. In spite of all that already he suffered by it he could not refrain from thrusting himself into the affairs of the great and seeking to control the destinies of princes.

Now no man knew better than the astute and watchful Duke of Valentinois the art of discovering traitors. He did not wait for them to reveal themselves by their actions – for he knew that by then it might be too late to deal with them. He preferred to unmask their conspiracies whilst they were maturing. And of all the methods that he employed the one to which he trusted most, the one which most often had done his work for him in secrecy and almost independently of himself, was that of the decoy.

Suspecting – and with excellent grounds – that treason was hatching in that gloomy palace of Ranieri's, overlooking the Marecchia, he bade his secretary Agabito put it abroad through his numerous agents that several of the Duke's prominent officers were disaffected towards him. Particular stress was laid upon the disaffection of an ambitious and able young captain named Angelo Graziani, towards whom it was urged that the Duke had behaved with marked injustice, so that this Graziani notoriously but awaited an opportunity to be avenged.

This gossip spread with the speed of all vile rumours. It was culled in the taverns by the Lord Ranieri's spies, who bore it swiftly to their master. With Graziani's name was coupled that of Ramiro de Lorqua, at present the Duke's governor of Cesena, and for a while Ranieri and Sinibaldi hesitated between the two. In the end their choice fell upon Graziani. De Lorqua was the more powerful man and wielded the greater influence. But their needs did not require so much. Graziani was now temporarily in command of the Duke's own patrician bodyguard, and their plans were of such a nature that it was precisely a man in that position who could afford them the opportunity they sought. Moreover, the gossip concerning Graziani was more positive than that which concerned De Lorqua. There was even in the former case some independent evidence to support the tale that was abroad.

The young captain himself was utterly unconscious alike of these rumours and of the test to which his fidelity to the Duke was about to be submitted. Therefore he was amazed when on the last day of October, as Prince Sinibaldi's visit to Rimini was drawing to its close, he found himself suddenly accosted by the Lord Ranieri with a totally unexpected invitation.

Graziani was in the ducal ante-chamber of the Rocca at the time, and Ranieri was departing after a brief audience with his Highness. Our gentleman threaded his way through the courtly throng, straight to the captain's side.

'Captain Graziani,' he said.

The captain, a tall, athletic fellow, whose plain raiment of steel and leather detached him from his silken surroundings, bowed stiffly.

'At your service, my lord,' he replied, addressing Ranieri thus for the first time.

'Prince Sinibaldi, who is my exalted guest, has remarked you,' he said, lowering his voice to a confidential tone. 'He does you the honour to desire your better acquaintance. He has heard of you, and has I think a proposal to make to you that should lead to your rapid advancement.'

Graziani taken thus by surprise flushed with gratified pride.

'But I am the Duke's servant,' he objected.

'A change may commend itself to you when you learn what is offered,' replied Ranieri. 'The prince honours you with the request that you wait upon him at my house at the first hour of night.'

A little dazzled and flustered by the invitation, Graziani was surprised into accepting it. There could be no harm, no disloyalty to his Duke, he reasoned in that brief moment of thought, in hearing what might be this proposal. After all the exchange of service was permissible in a soldier of fortune. He bowed his acknowledgement.

'I will obey,' he said, whereupon with a nod and a smile Ranieri went his ways.

It was only afterwards when Graziani came to consider the matter more closely that suspicion and hesitation were aroused in him. Ranieri had said that the prince had remarked him. How should that have happened since, as he now reflected, he had never been in Sinibaldi's presence? It was odd, he thought; and his thoughts, having started upon such a train as this, made swift progress. He knew enough of the politics of his day to be aware of the feelings entertained for Cesare Borgia by all Venetians; and he was sufficiently equipped with worldly wisdom to know that a man who, like Ranieri, could fawn upon the Duke who had dethroned that Malatesta in whose favour and confidence he had so lately stood, was not a man to be trusted.

Thus you see Graziani's doubts becoming suspicions; and very soon those suspicions grew to certainty. He scented treason in the proposal that Sinibaldi was to make him. If he went, he would most probably walk into a trap from which there might be no withdrawal; for when traitors reveal themselves they cannot for their own lives' sake spare the life of one who, being invited, refuses to become a party to that treason. Already Graziani saw himself in fancy with a hole in his heart, his limp body floating seaward down the Marecchia on the ebbing tide. Ranieri's house, he bethought him, was conveniently situated for such measures.

But if these forebodings urged him to forget his promise to wait upon Prince Sinibaldi, yet ambition whispered to him that after all he might be the loser through perceiving shadows where there was no real substance. Venice was in need of condottieri; the Republic was wealthy and paid her servants well; in her service the chances of promotion might be more rapid than in Cesare Borgia's, since already almost every captain of fortune in Italy was serving under the banner of the Duke. It was possible that in this business there might be no more than the Lord Ranieri had stated. He would go. Only a coward would remain absent out of fears for which grounds were not clearly apparent. But only a fool would neglect to take his measures for retreat or rescue in case his suspicions should be proved by the event well-founded.

Therefore when on the stroke of the first hour of night Captain Graziani presented himself at the Ranieri Palace, he had ambushed a half-score of men about the street under the command of his faithful antient Barbo. To Barbo at parting he had given all the orders necessary.

'If I am in difficulties or in danger I shall contrive to smash a window. Take that for your signal, assemble your men, and break into the house at once. Let one of your knaves go round and watch the windows overlooking the Marecchia, in case I should be forced to give the signal from that side.'

These measures taken he went to meet the Venetian envoy with an easy mind.

ii

The young condottiero's tread was firm and his face calm when one of Sinibaldi's turbaned Moorish slaves, into whose care he had been delivered by the lackey who admitted him, ushered him into the long low room of the mezzanine where the Venetian awaited him.

He had deemed the circumstance of the Moorish slave in itself suspicious; it seemed to argue that in this house of the Lord Ranieri's the prince was something more than guest since his servants did the offices of ushers. And now, as he stood on the threshold blinking in the brilliant light of the chamber, and perceived that in addition to the prince and the Lord Ranieri there were six others present, he conceived it certain that his worst suspicion would be here confirmed.

145

This room into which he now stepped, ran through the entire depth of the house, so that its windows overlooked the street at one end and the River Marecchia, near the Bridge of Augustus, at the other. It had an air at once rich and gloomy; the walls were hung with sombre tapestries, the carpets spread upon the floor of wood mosaics were of a deep purple that was almost black, and amid its sparse furnishings there was a deal of ebony looking the more funereal by virtue of its ivory inlays. It was lighted by an alabaster-globed lamp set high upon the ponderous overmantel and by silver candle-branches on the long table in mid-apartment about which the company was seated when Graziani entered. An enormous fire was roaring on the hearth, for the weather had lately set in raw and cold.

As the door was softly closed behind Graziani, and as he stood adjusting his eyes to the strong light, the Lord Ranieri stepped forward with purring words of welcome, too cordial from one in his lordship's position to one in Graziani's. With these he conducted the captain towards the table. From his seat at the head of it rose a tall and very stately gentleman with a long olive countenance that was rendered the longer by a brown pointed beard, who added a welcome of his own to the welcome which the Lord Ranieri had already uttered.

He was dressed all in black, but with a rare elegance, and upon his breast flashed a medallion of diamonds worth a nobleman's ransom. Graziani did not require to be told that this was Prince Sinibaldi, the envoy-extraordinary of the Most Serene.

The condottiero bowed low, yet with a soldierly stiffness and a certain aloofness in his bearing that he could not quite dissemble. He bowed, indeed, as a swordsman bows to his adversary before engaging, and his countenance remained grave and set.

Ranieri drew up a chair for him to the table at which the other six remained seated, their twelve eyes intent upon the new-comer's face. Graziani gave them back look for look, but of them all the only one whose face he knew was Galeazzo Sforza of Catignola, whom he had seen at Pesaro; for it was this Galeazzo himself who in his brother's stead had surrendered the place to Cesare Borgia. The captain's glance was next arrested by Pietro Corvo, the Forlivese who once had practised magic in Urbino. The fellow detached from this patrician group as he must, for that matter, detach from any group in which he might chance to find himself. His face was as the face of a corpse; it was yellow as wax, and his skin was as a skin of parchment drawn tight across his prominent cheekbones, whence it sagged into the hollow cheeks and fell in wrinkles about the lean sinewy neck. His lank thinning hair had faded to the colour of ashes; his lips were bloodless; indeed no part of his countenance seemed alive save only the eyes, which glittered as if he had the fever. He was repulsive beyond description, and no man who looked on him for the first time could repress a shudder.

One hand only remained him – his left – which was as yellow and gnarled as a hen's foot. Its fellow he had left in Urbino together with his tongue, having been deprived of one and the other by order of Cesare Borgia whom he had defamed. That punishment was calculated to disable him from either writing or uttering further slanders; but he was fast learning to overcome the disabilities to which it had subjected him, and already he was beginning to write with that claw-like left hand that remained to him.

Well had it been for him had he confined himself to the practice of magic under his imposing name of Corvinus Trismegistus. Being a fertile-witted rogue he had thriven exceedingly at that rascally trade, and might have continued to amass a fortune had he not foolishly drawn upon himself by his incautious slanders the attention of the Duke of Valentinois.

Having now no tongue left wherewith to beguile the credulous, nor sufficient magic to grow a fresh one, his trade was ruined, and his hatred of the man who had ruined it was virulent, the more virulent no doubt since his expression of it had been temporarily curtailed.

His fierce, glittering eyes fastened mistrustfully upon Graziani as the young soldier took the chair that was offered him by his host. He parted his bloodless lips to make a horrible croaking sound that reminded Graziani of frogs on a hot night of summer, whilst he accompanied it by gestures to the Venetian which the captain did not attempt to understand.

The Lord Ranieri resumed his seat at the table's foot. At its head the prince remained standing, and he pacified the mute by a nod conveying to him the assurance that he was understood. Then from the breast of his doublet, two buttons of which were unfastened, the Venetian drew a small crucifix beautifully wrought in ivory upon gold. Holding it between his graceful, tapering fingers, he addressed the condottiero solemnly.

'When we shall have made known to you the reason for which we have sought your presence here tonight, Messer Graziani,' said he, 'it shall be yours to determine whether you will join hands with us, and lend us your aid in the undertaking which we have in mind. Should you elect not to do so, be your reason what it may, you shall be free to depart as you have come. But first you must make solemn oath engaging yourself neither by word spoken or written, nor yet by deed, to divulge aught to any man of what may be revealed to you of our designs.'

The prince paused, and stood waiting. Graziani reared his young head, and he could almost have laughed outright at this discovery of how shrewd and just had been the suspicions that had assailed him. He looked about him slowly, finding himself the goal of every eye, and every countenance alive with a mistrust and hostility that nothing could quiet short of that oath demanded of him.

It comforted him in that moment to think of Barbo and his knaves waiting below in case they should be needed. If Graziani knew men at all, he would be likely to need them very soon, he thought.

Sinibaldi leaned forward supporting himself upon his left hand, whilst with his right he gently pushed the crucifix down the table towards the captain.

'First upon that sacred symbol of Our Redeemer...' he was beginning, when Graziani abruptly thrust back his chair and rose.

He knew enough. Here for certain was a conspiracy against the State or against the life of his lord the Duke of Valentinois. It needed no more words to tell him that. He was neither spy nor informer, yet if he heard more and then kept secret he would himself be a party to their treason.

'My lord prince,' he said, 'here surely is some mistake. What you may be about to propose to me I do not know. But I do know – for it is abundantly plain – that it is no such proposal as my Lord Ranieri had led me to expect.'

There was a savage incoherent growl from the mute, but the others remained watchfully silent, waiting for the soldier to proceed, since clearly he had not yet done.

'It is not my way,' he proceeded gravely, 'to thrust myself blindly into any business, and make oath upon matters that are unknown to me. Suffer me therefore to take my leave of you at once. Sirs,' he included the entire company in his bow, 'a happy night.'

He stepped back from the table clearly and firmly resolved upon his feet and every hand was upon a weapon. They were rendered desperate by their realization of the mistake that had been made. That mistake they must repair in the only way that was possible. Ranieri sprang away from the foot of the table, and flung himself between the soldier and the door, barring his exit.

Checked thus, Graziani looked at Sinibaldi, but the smile upon the Venetian's saturnine countenance was not reassuring. It occurred to the captain that the time had come to break a window as a signal to Barbo, and he wondered would they prevent him from reaching one. First, however, he made appeal to Ranieri who stood directly in his way.

'My lord,' he said, and his voice was firm almost to the point of haughtiness, 'I came hither in friendliness, bidden to your house with no knowledge of what might await me. I trust to your honour, my lord, to see that I depart in like case – in friendliness, and with no knowledge of what is here toward.'

'No knowledge?' said Ranieri, and he laughed shortly. His countenance had lost by now every trace of its habitual joviality. 'No knowledge, eh? But suspicions, no doubt, and these suspicions you will voice...'

'Let him take the oath,' cried the clear young voice of Galeazzo Sforza. 'Let him swear to keep silent upon…'

But the steely accents of Sinibaldi cut in sharply upon that speech.

'Do you not see, Galeazzo, that we have misjudged our man? Is not his temper plain?'

Graziani, however, confined his glance and his insistence to Ranieri.

'My lord,' he said again, 'it lies upon your honour that I shall go forth in safety. At your bidding…'

His keen ears caught a stealthy sound behind him, and he whipped round sharply. Even as he turned Pietro Corvo, who had crept as softly, leapt upon him, fierce as a rat, his dagger raised to strike – intending thus to make an end. Before Graziani could move to defend himself the blade had descended full upon his breast. Encountering there the links of the shirt of mail he wore beneath his quilted doublet – for he omitted no precautions – it broke off at the hilt under the force that drove it.

Then Graziani seized that wretched wisp of humanity by the breast of his mean jacket, and dashed him violently across the room. The mute hurtled into Alviano, who stood midway between the table and one of the windows. Alviano, thrown off his balance by the impact, staggered in his turn and reeled against an ebony pedestal surmounted by a marble cupid. The cupid, thus dislodged, went crashing through the casement into the street below.

Now this was more than Graziani had intended, but it was certainly no more than he could have desired. The signal to Barbo had given, and no one present any the wiser. It heartened him. He smiled grimly, whipped out his long sword, swung his cloak upon his left arm, and rushed thus upon Ranieri, forced for the moment to leave his back unguarded.

Ranieri, unprepared for the onslaught, and startled by its suddenness, swung aside, leaving the captain a clear way. But Graziani was not so mad as to attempt to open the door. He knew well that whilst he paused to seize and raise the latch a half-dozen blades would be through his back before the thing could be accomplished. Instead, having reached the door, he swung round, and setting his back to it, faced that murderous company as it swooped down upon him with naked weapons.

Five men confronted him immediately. Behind them stood Sinibaldi, his sword drawn against the need to use it, yet waiting meanwhile, preferring that such work should be done by these underlings of his.

Yet though they were five to one, Graziani's sudden turn to face them, and his poised preparedness, gave them a moment's pause. In that moment he reckoned up his chances. He found them slight but not quite hopeless, since all that was incumbent on him was to ward their blows and gain some instants until Barbo and his men could come to his assistance.

Another moment and they had closed with him, their whirling blades athirst for his life. He made the best defence that a man could make against such an onslaught, and a wonderful defence it was. He was well-trained in arms as in all bodily exercises, supple of joint, quick of movement, long of limb and with muscles that were all steel and whipcord – indeed a very pentathlos.

He warded as much with his cloaked arm as with his sword, but he had no chance, nor for that matter any thought, of taking the offensive in his turn. He knew that a lunge or thrust or cut at any single one of them, even if successful, must leave an opening through which he would be cut down ere he could make recovery. He would attack when Barbo came, and he would see to it then that not one of these cowardly assassins, of these dastardly traitors, was left alive. Meanwhile he must be content to ward, praying God that Barbo did not long delay.

For some moments fortune favoured him, and his shirt of mail proved his best friend. Indeed it was not until Alviano's sword blade was shivered in a powerful lunge that caught Graziani full in the middle of the body, that those gentlemen realized that the condottiero's head was the only part of him that was vulnerable. It was Sinibaldi who told them so, shouting it fiercely as he shouldered aside the now disarmed Alviano, and stepped into the place from which he thrust him. With death in his eyes the prince now led the attack upon that man who made so desperate a defence without chance of breaking ground or lessening the number of his assailants.

Suddenly Sinibaldi's blade licked in and out again with lightning swiftness in a feint that culminated in a second thrust, and Graziani felt his sword arm suddenly benumbed. To realize what had happened and to readjust the matter was with the captain the work of one single thought. He caught his sword in his left hand, that so he might continue his defence, even as Sinibaldi by a turn of the wrist made a cutting stroke at his bare head. Perforce Graziani was slow to the parry; the fraction of a second lost in transferring his sword to the left hand and the further circumstance that his left arm was hampered by the cloak he had wound about it, left too great an advantage with Sinibaldi. Yet Graziani's blade, though too late to put the other's aside, was yet in time to break the force of the blow as it descended. The edge was deflected, but not enough. If it did not open his skull as was intended, at least it dealt him a long slanting scalp-wound.

The condottiero felt the room rock and heave under his feet. Then he dropped his sword, and leaning against the wall, whilst his assailants checked to watch him, he very gently slithered down it and sat huddled in a heap on the floor, the blood from his wound streaming down over his face. Sinibaldi shortened his sword, intent upon making quite sure of his victim by driving the steel through his windpipe. But even as he was in the act of aiming the stroke, he was suddenly arrested by the horrible, vehement outcry of the mute, who had remained at the broken window, and by a thunder of blows that fell simultaneously upon the door below accompanied by a sudden call to open.

That sound smote terror into the conspirators. It aroused them to a sense of what they were doing, and brought to their minds the thought of Cesare Borgia's swift and relentless justice which spared no man, patrician or plebeian. And so they stood limply stricken, at gaze, their ears straining to listen, whilst below the blows upon the door were repeated more vehemently than before.

Ranieri swore thickly and horribly. 'We are trapped, betrayed!'

Uproar followed. The eight plotters looked this way and that, as if seeking a way out, each gave counsels and asked questions in a breath, none heeding none, until at last the mute having compelled their attention by his excited croaks, showed them the road to escape.

He crossed the length of the room at a run, and nimble as a cat, he leapt upon a marble table that stood before the casement overlooking the river, from which the house rose almost sheer. He never so much as paused to open it. The acquaintance he had already made with methods of Borgia justice so quickened his terrors to a frenzy that he hurled himself bodily at the closed window, and shivering it by the force of the impact went through it and down in a shower of broken glass to the black icy waters below.

They followed him as sheep follow their bellwether. One after another they leapt upon the marble table; and thence through the gap he had made they plunged down into the river. Not one of them had the wit in that breathless moment to pause to consider which way the tide might be running. Had it chanced to have been upon the ebb it must have swept them out to sea, and none of them would further have troubled the destinies of Italy. Fortunately for them, however, it was flowing; and so it bore them upwards towards the Bridge of Augustus, where they were able unseen to effect a landing – all save Pietro Corvo, the mute, who was drowned, and Sinibaldi, who remained behind.

Like Graziani, Sinibaldi too wore a shirt of mail beneath his doublet, as a precaution proper in one who engaged in such hazardous methods of underground warfare. It was indeed an almost inveterate habit with him. Less impetuous than those others, he paused to calculate his chances, and bethought him that it was odds this armour would sink him in the flood. So he stayed to doff it first.

Vainly had he called upon the others to wait for him. Ranieri had answered him standing upon the table ready for the leap.

'Wait? Body of God! Are you mad? Is this a time to wait?' Yet he delayed to explain the precise and urgent need to depart. 'We must run no risk of capture. For now more than ever must the thing be done, or we are all dead men – and it must be done tonight as was planned. Excess of preparation has gone near to undoing us. We could have contrived excellently without that fool,' and he jerked a thumb towards Graziani, 'as I told your excellency. And we shall contrive no less excellently without him as it is. But contrive we must, else, I say again, we are dead men – all of us.' And upon that he went through the window and down into the water, after the others, with a thudding splash.

With fingers that haste made clumsy, Sinibaldi tugged at the buttons of his doublet, hampered by having tucked his sword under his arm. But scarcely had Ranieri vanished into the night than the door below was flung inward with a crash. There followed a sound of angry voices, as the servants of the household were thrust roughly aside, and ringing steps came clattering up the stairs.

Sinibaldi, still tugging at the buttons of his doublet, sprang desperately towards the window, and wondered for a moment whether he should take the risk of drowning. But even as he stood poised for the leap, he remembered suddenly the immunity he derived from the office that was his. After all, as the envoy of Venice he was inviolable, a man upon whom no finger was to be laid by any without provoking the resentment of the Republic. He had been over anxious. He had nothing to fear where nothing could be proved against him. Not even Graziani could have said enough to imperil the sacred person of an ambassador, and it was odds that Graziani would never say anything again.

So he sheathed his sword, readjusted his doublet and composed himself. Indeed he actually went the length of opening the door to the invaders, calling to guide them:

'This way! This way!'

They swarmed in, all ten of them, the grizzled antient at their head, so furiously that they bore the prince backwards, and all but trampled on him.

Barbo checked them in mid-chamber, and looked round bewildered, until his eyes alighted upon his fallen, blood-bedabbled captain huddled at the foot of the wall. At the sight he roared like a bull to express his anger, what time his followers closed about the saturnine Venetian.

With as great dignity as was possible to a man at such a disadvantage, Sinibaldi sought to hold them off.

'You touch me at your peril,' he warned them. 'I am Prince Marcantonio Sinibaldi, the Envoy of Venice.'

The antient swung half round to answer him, snarling:

'Were you Prince Lucifer, Envoy of Hell, you should still account for what was doing here and how my captain came by his hurt. Make him fast!'

The men-at-arms obeyed with a very ready will, for Graziani was beloved of all that rode with him. It was in vain that the Venetian stormed and threatened, pleaded and protested. They treated him as if they had never heard tell of the sacredness with which the person of an ambassador is invested. They disarmed him, bound his wrists behind him, like any common malefactor's, and thrust him contumeliously from the room down the stairs and so, without hat or cloak, out into the murky wind-swept street.

Four of them remained above at the antient's bidding, whilst he himself went down upon his knees beside his fallen captain to look to his condition. And at once Graziani began to show signs of life. Indeed he had shown that he was not dead the moment the door had closed after the departing men.

Supported now by Barbo he sat up, and with his left hand smeared away some of the blood that almost blinded him, and looked dully at his antient, who grunted and swore to express the joyous reaction from his despair.

'I am alive, Barbo,' he said, though his voice came feebly. 'But, Body of God! you were no more than in time to find me so. Had you been a minute later you would have been too late for me – aye, and perhaps for the Duke too.' He smiled faintly. 'When I found that valour would no longer avail me I had recourse to craft. It is well to play the fox when you cannot play the lion. With this gash over the head and my face smeared in blood, I pretended to be done for. But

155

I was conscious throughout, and it is a grim thing, Barbo, consciously to take the chance of death without daring to lift a finger to avert it lest thereby you hastened it on. I...' he gulped, and his head hung down, showing that his strength was ebbing. Then he rallied desperately, almost by sheer force of will. There was something he must say, ere everything was blotted out as he felt it would be soon. 'Get you to my Lord Duke, Barbo. Make haste! Tell him that here was some treason plotting...something that is to be done tonight...that will still be done by those who escaped. Bid him look to himself. Hasten, man. Say I...'

'Their names! Their names!' cried the antient urgently, seeing his captain on the point of swooning.

Graziani reared his head again, and slowly opened his dull eyes. But he did not answer. His lids drooped, and his head lolled sideways against his antient's shoulder. It was as if by an effort of sheer will he had but kept a grip of his senses until he could utter that urgent warning. Then, his duty done, he relinquished that painful hold, and allowed himself to slip into the peace and the shadows of unconsciousness, exhausted.

iii

The great need for urgency, the chief reason why 'the thing' must be done that night, as the Lord Ranieri had said before he dived from his window into the river, lay in the circumstance that it was the Duke's last night in the city of Rimini. On the morrow he marched with his army upon Faenza and the Manfredi.

It had therefore seemed proper to the councillors and patricians of Rimini to mark their entire submission to his authority by a banquet in his honour at the Palazzo Pubblico. At this banquet were assembled all Riminese that were noble or notable, and a great number of repatriated patricians, the *fuorusciti* whom upon one pretext or another the hated Malatesta tyrant had driven from his dominions that he might enrich himself by the confiscation of their possessions. Jubilantly came they now with their ladies to do homage to the Duke who had broken the power and delivered the State from the thraldom of the iniquitous Pandolfaccio, assured that his justice would right to the full the wrongs which they had suffered.

Present, too, were the envoys and ambassadors of several Italian powers sent to felicitate Cesare Borgia upon his latest conquest. But it was in vain that the young Duke turned his hazel eyes this way and that in quest of Marcantonio Sinibaldi, the princely envoy-extraordinary of the Most Serene Republic. The envoy-extraordinary was nowhere to be seen in that courtly gathering, and the Duke, who missed nothing and who disliked leaving riddles unsolved – particularly when they concerned a State that was hostile to himself – was vexed to know the reason of this absence.

It was the more remarkable since Prince Sinibaldi's lady, a stately blonde woman, whose stomacher was a flashing cuirass of gems, was seated near Cesare's right hand, between the sober black velvet of the President of the Council and the flaming scarlet of the handsome Cardinal-legate, thus filling the position to which she was entitled by her lofty rank and the respect due to the great Republic which her husband represented.

Another whose absence the Duke might have remarked was, of course, the Lord Ranieri, who had excused himself, indeed, to the president upon a plea of indisposition. But Valentinois was too much concerned with the matter of Sinibaldi's whereabouts. He lounged in his great chair, a long, supple incarnation of youth and vigour, in a tight-fitting doublet of cloth of gold, with jewelled bands at neck and wrists and waist. His pale, beautiful face was thoughtful, and his tapering fingers strayed ever and anon to the tips of his tawny silken beard.

The banquet touched its end, and the floor of the great hall was being cleared by the seneschal to make room for the players sent from Mantua by the beautiful Marchioness Gonzaga who were to perform a comedy for the company's delectation.

It was not comedy, however, but tragedy, all unsuspected, that impended, and the actor who suddenly strode into that hall to speak

157

its prologue, thrusting rudely aside the lackeys who would have hindered him, misliking his wild looks, was Barbo, the antient of Graziani's company.

'My lord,' he cried, panting for breath. 'My lord Duke!' And his hands fiercely cuffed the grooms who still sought to bar his passage. 'Out of my way, oafs! I tell you that I must speak to his highness. Out of my way!'

The company had fallen silent, some startled by this intrusion, others conceiving that it might be the opening of the comedy that was prepared. Into that silence cut the Duke's voice, crisp and metallic:

'Let him approach!'

Instantly the grooms ceased their resistance, glad enough to do so, for Barbo's hands were heavy and he was prodigal in the use of them. Released, he strode up the hall and came to a standstill, stiff and soldierly before the Duke, saluting almost curtly in his eagerness.

'Who are you?' rapped his highness.

'My name is Barbo,' the soldier answered. 'I am an antient in the condotta of Messer Angelo Graziani.'

'Why do you come thus? What brings you?'

'Treason, my lord – that is what brings me,' roared the soldier, setting the company all agog.

Cesare alone showed no sign of excitement. His eyes calmly surveyed this messenger, waiting. Thereupon Barbo plunged headlong into the speech he had prepared. He spoke gustily, abruptly, his voice shaken with the passion he could not quite suppress.

'My Captain, Messer Graziani, lies speechless and senseless with a broken head, else were he here in my place, my lord, and perhaps with a fuller tale. I can but tell what little I know, adding the little that himself he told me ere his senses left him.

'By his command we – ten men of his company and myself – watched a certain house into which he went tonight at the first hour, with orders to break in should we receive a certain signal. That signal we received. Acting instantly upon it we...'

'Wait, man,' the Duke cut in. 'Let us have this tale in order and in plain words. A certain house, you say. What house was that?'

'The Lord Ranieri's palace, my lord.'

A stir of increasing interest rustled through the company, but dominating it, and audible to him because it came from his neighbourhood immediately on his right, the Duke caught a gasp, a faint half-cry of one who has been startled into sudden fear. That sound arrested his attention, and he shot a swift sidelong glance in the direction whence it had come, to discover that the Princess Sinibaldi had sunk back in her chair, her cheeks deadly white, her blue eyes wide with panic. Even as he looked and saw, his swiftly calculating mind had mastered certain facts and had found the probable solution of the riddle that earlier had intrigued him – the riddle of Sinibaldi's absence. He thought that he knew now where the prince had been that evening, though he had yet to learn the nature of this treason of which Barbo spoke, and in which he could not doubt that Sinibaldi was engaged.

Even as this understanding flashed across his mind, the antient was resuming his interrupted narrative.

'At the signal, then, my lord, we broke into…'

'Wait!' the Duke again checked him, raising a hand which instantly imposed silence.

There followed a brief pause, Barbo standing stiffly waiting for leave to continue, impatient of the restraint imposed upon his eagerness. Cesare's glance, calm and so inscrutable as to appear almost unseeing, had passed from the princess to Messer Paolo Capello, the Venetian Orator, seated a little way down the hall on the Duke's left. Cesare noted the man's tense attitude, the look of apprehension on his round white face, and beheld in those signs the confirmation of what already he had conjectured.

So Venice was engaged in this. Those implacable traders of the Rialto were behind this happening at Ranieri's house in which one of the Duke's captains had received a broken head. And the ordinary envoy of Venice was anxiously waiting to learn what might have befallen the envoy-extraordinary, so that he might promptly take his measures.

Cesare knew the craft of the Most Serene and of its ambassadors. He was here on swampy treacherous ground, and he must pick his way with care. Certainly Messer Capello must not hear what this soldier might have to tell, for then – *proemonitus, proemunitus*. In the orator's uncertainty of what had passed might lie Cesare's strength to deal with Venice, perhaps to unmask her.

'We are too public here,' he said to Barbo shortly, and on that he rose.

Out of deference the entire company rose with him – all save one. Sinibaldi's lady, indeed, went so far as to make the effort, but faint as she was with fear, her limbs refused to do their office, and she kept her seat, a circumstance which Cesare did not fail to note.

He waved a hand to the banqueters, smiling urbanely. 'Sirs, and ladies,' he said, 'I pray you keep your seats. It is not my desire that you should be disturbed by this.' Then he turned to the President of the Council. 'If you, sir, will give me leave apart a moment with this fellow...'

'Assuredly, my lord, assuredly!' cried the President nervously, flung into confusion by this deference from one of the Duke's exalted quality. 'This way, Magnificent. This closet here... You will be private.'

Stammering, fluttering, he had stepped down the hall, the Duke following, and Barbo clanking after them. The President opened a door, and drawing aside, he bowed low and waved the Duke into a small ante-chamber.

Cesare passed in with Barbo following. The door closed after them, and a murmur reached them of the babble that broke forth beyond it.

The room was small, but richly furnished, possibly against the chance of its use being desired by his highness. The middle of its tessellated floor was occupied by a table with massively carved supporting cupids, near which stood a great chair upholstered in crimson velvet. The room was lighted by a cluster of wax candles in a candle-branch richly wrought in the shape of a group of scaling titans.

Cesare flung himself into the chair, and turned to Barbo.

'Now your tale,' he said shortly.

Barbo threw wide at last the floodgates of his eagerness, and let his tale flow forth. He related in fullest detail the happenings of that night at Ranieri's palace, repeating faithfully the words that Graziani had uttered, and concluding on the announcement that he had captured at least one of the conspirators – the Prince Marcantonio Sinibaldi.

'I trust that in this I have done well, my lord,' the fellow added with some hesitation. 'It seemed no less than Messer Graziani ordered. Yet his Magnificence spoke of being an ambassador of the Most Serene…'

'The Devil take the Most Serene and her ambassadors,' flashed Cesare, betrayed into it by his inward seething rage. On the instant he suppressed all show of feeling. 'Be content. You have done well,' he said shortly.

He rose, turned his back on the antient, and strode to the uncurtained gleaming windows. There he stood a moment, staring out into the starlit night, fingering his beard, his brow dark with thought. Then he came slowly back, his head bowed, nor did he raise it until he stood again before the antient.

'You have no hint – no suspicion of the nature of this conspiracy? Of what is this thing they were planning and are still to attempt tonight?' he asked.

'None, my lord. I have said all I know.'

'Nor who were the men that escaped?'

'Nor that, my lord, save that one of them would no doubt be the Lord Ranieri.'

'Ah, but the others…and we do not even know how many there were…'

Cesare checked. He had bethought him of the Princess Sinibaldi. This urgently needed information might be wrung from her, or as much of it as lay within her knowledge. That she possessed such knowledge her bearing had proclaimed. He smiled darkly.

'Desire Messer the President of the Council to attend me here together with the Princess Sinibaldi. Then do you await my orders. And see to it that you say no word of this to any.'

Barbo saluted and withdrew upon that errand. Cesare paced slowly back to the window, and waited, his brow against the cool pane, his mind busy until the door re-opened and the President ushered in the Princess.

The President came avid for news. Disappointment awaited him.

'I but desired you, sir, as an escort for this lady.' Cesare informed him. 'If you will give us leave together...'

Stifling his regrets and murmuring his acquiescence, the man effaced himself. When they were alone together Cesare turned to the woman and observed the deathly pallor of her face, the agitated gallop of her bosom. He judged her shrewdly as one whose tongue would soon be loosed by fear.

He bowed to her, and with a smile and the very courtliest and deferential grace he proffered her the great gilt and crimson chair. In silence she sank into it, limply and grateful for its support. She dabbed her lips with a gilt-edged handkerchief, her startled eyes never leaving the Duke's face, as if their glance were held in fascinated subjection.

Standing by the table at which she now sat, Cesare rested his finger-tips upon the edge of it, and leaned slightly across towards her.

'I have sent for you, Madonna,' he said, his tone very soft and gentle, 'to afford you the opportunity of rescuing your husband's neck from the hands of my strangler.'

In itself it was a terrifying announcement, and it was rendered the more terrifying by the gentle, emotionless tones in which it was uttered. It did not fail of its calculated effect.

'O God!' gasped the afflicted woman, and clutched her white bosom with both hands. 'Gesù! I knew it! My heart had told me.'

'Do not alarm yourself, Madonna, I implore you. There is not the cause,' he assured her, and no voice could have been more soothing. 'The Prince Sinibaldi is below, awaiting my pleasure. But I have no pleasure, Princess, that is not your pleasure. Your husband's life is in your own hands. I place it there. He lives or dies as you decree.'

She looked up into his beautiful young face, into those hazel eyes that looked too gentle now, and she cowered abjectly, cringing before him. She was left in doubt of the meaning of his ambiguous words, and his almost wooing manner. And this too he had intended; deliberate in his ambiguity, using it as a flame of fresh terror in which to scorch her will, until it should become pliant as heated metal.

He saw the scarlet flush rise slowly up to stain her neck and face, whilst her eyes remained fixed upon his own.

'My lord!' she panted. 'I know not what you mean. You...' And then her spirit rallied. He saw her body stiffen, and her glance harden and grow defiant. But when she spoke her voice betrayed her by its quaver.

'Prince Sinibaldi is the accredited envoy of the Most Serene. His person is sacred. A hurt to him were as a hurt to the Republic whose representative he is, and the Republic is not slow to avenge her hurts. You dare not touch him.'

He continued to regard her, smiling. 'That I have done already. Have I not said that he is a prisoner now – below here – bound and awaiting my pleasure.' And he repeated his phrase. 'But my pleasure, Madonna, shall be your pleasure.'

Yet all the answer she could return him was a reiteration of her cry:

'You dare not! You dare not!'

The smile perished slowly from his face. He inclined his head to her, though not without a tinge of mockery.

'I will leave you happy, then, in that conviction,' he said on a note at once so sardonic and sinister that it broke her newfound spirit into shards.

As if he accepted the fruitlessness of the interview, and accounted it concluded, he turned and stepped to the door. At this her terror, held in check a moment, swept over her again like a flood. She staggered to her feet, one hand on the table to support her, the other at her breast.

'My lord! My lord! A moment! Pity!'

He paused, and half-turned, his fingers already upon the latch.

'I will have pity, Madonna, if you will teach me pity – if you will show me pity.' He came back to her slowly, very grave now. 'This husband of yours has been taken in treason. If you would not have him strangled this night, if you would ever hold him warm and living in your arms again, it is yours to rescue him from what impends.'

He was looking deep and earnestly into her eyes, and she bore the glance, returned it wildly, in silence for a dozen heart-beats. Then at last, her lids dropped. She bowed her head. Her pallor seemed to deepen until her flesh was as if turned to wax.

'What...what do you require of me?' she breathed in a small, fluttering voice.

There was never a man more versed than he in the uses of ambiguity.

He had employed it now so as to produce in her the maximum of terror – so as to convey to her a suggestion that he asked the maximum price. Thus when he made clear his real meaning, there would be reaction from her worst dread, and in that reaction he would trap her. The great sacrifice he demanded, would be dwarfed in her view by relief, would seem small by comparison with the sacrifice his ambiguity had led her to fancy he required.

So when she asked that faint, piteous question, 'What do you require of me?' he answered swift and sharply with words that he had rendered unexpected:

'All that is known to you of this conspiracy in which he was taken.'

He caught the upward flash of her eyes; their look of amazement, almost of relief, and knew that he had made her malleable. She swayed where she stood. He steadied her with ready hands, and gently pressed her back into her chair.

And now he proceeded to hammer the metal he had softened.

'Come, Madonna, use dispatch, I beg,' he urged her, his voice level but singularly compelling. 'Do not strain a patience that has its roots in mercy. Consider that the information I require of you, and for which I offer you so generous a price, the torture can extract for me from this husband of yours. I will be frank with you as at an Easter shrift. It is true I do not wish to embroil myself with the Most Serene Republic, and that I seek to gain my ends by gentle measures. But, by the Host! if my gentle measures do not prevail with you, why then Prince Sinibaldi shall be squeezed dry upon the rack, and what is left of him flung to the stranglers afterwards – aye, though he were an envoy of the Empire itself. My name,' he ended, almost grimly, 'is Cesare Borgia. You know that repute I enjoy in Venice.'

She stared at him, considering, confused, and voiced the very question that perplexed her.

'You offer me his life – his life and freedom – in exchange for this information?'

'That is what I offer.'

She pressed her hands to her brows, seeking to fathom the mystery of an offer that appeared to hold such extraordinary elements of contradiction.

'But then...' she began, tremulously, and paused for lack of words in which to frame her doubts.

'If you need more assurance, Madonna, you shall have it,' he said. 'You shall have the assurance of my oath. I swear to you by my honour and my hope of Heaven that neither in myself nor through another shall I procure the hurt of so much as a hair of Sinibaldi's head, provided that I know all of the treason that was plotting to be done this night and that thus I may be able to avoid the trap that I believe is set for me.'

That resolved her doubts. She saw the reason of the thing; understood that after all he but offered Sinibaldi's life in exchange for his own safety. Yet even then she hesitated, thinking of her husband.

'He may blame me...' she began, faltering.

Cesare's eyes gleamed. He leaned over her. 'He need never know,' he urged her insidiously.

'You…you pledge your word,' she insisted, as if to convince herself that all would be well.

'Already have I pledged it, Madonna,' he answered, and he could not altogether repress a note of bitterness. For he had pledged it reluctantly, because he conceived that no less would satisfy her. It was a bargain he would have avoided, had there been a way. For he did not lightly forgive, and he did not relish the notion of Sinibaldi's going unpunished. But he had perceived that unless he gave this undertaking he would be without the means to parry the blow that might be struck at any moment.

'I have pledged it, Madonna,' he repeated, 'and I do not forswear myself.'

'You mean that you will not even allow him to know that you know? That you will but use the information I may give you to procure your own safety?'

'That is what I mean,' he assured her, and waited, confident now that he was about to have the thing he desired and for which he had bidden something recklessly.

And at last he got the story – the sum total of her knowledge. Last night Ranieri and Prince Sinibaldi had sat late alone together. Her suspicions had earlier been aroused that her husband was plotting something with this friend of the fallen Malatesta. Driven by these suspicions, jealous perhaps to find herself excluded from her husband's confidence in this matter, she had played the eavesdropper, and she had overheard that it was against Cesare Borgia's life that they conspired.

'The Lord Ranieri,' she said, 'spoke of this banquet at the Palazzo Pubblico, urging that the opportunity it afforded would be a rare one. It was Ranieri, my lord, who was the villain, the tempter in this affair.'

'Yes, yes, no doubt,' said Cesare impatiently. 'It matters not which was the tempter, which the tempted. The story of it!'

'Ranieri knew that you would be returning to sleep at Sigismondo's Castle, and that it was planned to escort you thither in procession by torchlight. At some point on your way – but where I cannot tell you, for this much I did not learn – at some point on your way, then, Ranieri spoke of two crossbow-men that were to be ambushed, to shoot you.'

She paused a moment. But Cesare offered no comment, betrayed no faintest perturbation at the announcement. So she proceeded.

'But there was a difficulty. Ranieri did not account it insuperable, but to make doubly sure he desired it should be removed. He feared that if mounted guards chanced to ride beside you, it might not be easy for the crossbow-men to shoot past them. Foot-guards would not signify, as the men could shoot over their heads. But it was necessary, he held, to make quite sure that none but foot-guards should be immediately about your person, so that riding clear above them you should offer a fair mark. To make sure of this it was that he proposed to seduce one of your captains – I think it would be this man Graziani, whom the soldier told you had been wounded. Ranieri was satisfied that Graziani was disaffected towards your highness, and that he might easily be bought to lend a hand in their enterprise.'

Valentinois smiled slowly, thoughtfully. He knew quite well the source of Ranieri's rash assumption. Then, as he considered further, that smile of his grew faintly cruel, reflecting his mind.

'That is all I overheard, my lord,' she added after an instant's pause.

He stirred at that: threw back his head and laughed shortly.

'Enough, as God lives,' he snorted.

She looked at him, and the sight of his countenance and the blaze of his tawny eyes filled her with fresh terror. She started to her feet, and appealed to him to remember his oath. At that appeal he put aside all trace of wrath, and smiled again.

'Let your fears have rest,' he bade her. 'I have sworn, and by what I have sworn I shall abide. Nor I nor man of mine shall do hurt to Prince Sinibaldi.'

She wanted to pour out her gratitude and her deep sense of his magnanimity. But words failed her for a moment, and ere she had found them, he was urging her to depart.

.

'Madonna, you were best away, I think. You are overwrought. I fear that I have tried you sorely.'

She confessed to her condition, and professed that she would be glad of his leave to return home at once.

'The prince shall follow you,' he promised her, as he conducted her to the door. 'First, however, we shall endeavour to make our peace with him, and I do not doubt but that we shall succeed. Be content,' he added, observing the fresh panic that stared at him from her blue eyes – for she suddenly bethought her of what manner of peace it was Cesare's wont to make with his enemies. 'He shall be treated by me with all honour. I shall endeavour by friendliness to win him from these traitors who have seduced him.'

'It is so – it is so!' she exclaimed, seizing with avidity upon that excuse which he so generously implied for the man who would have contrived his murder. 'It was none of his devising. He was lured to it by the evil counsels of others.'

'How can I doubt it, since you assure me of it?' he replied with an irony so subtle that it escaped her. He bowed, and opened the door.

iv

Following her out into the great hall, where instantly silence fell and a hundred eyes became levelled upon them, he beckoned the President of the Council, who hovered near, awaiting him. Into the President's care he surrendered the princess, desiring him to conduct her thence and to her litter.

Again he bowed to her, profoundly in farewell, and as she passed out of the hall, her hand upon the arm of the President, he stepped up to his place at the board again, and with a light jest and a laugh, invited the return of mirth, as if no thought or care troubled his mind.

He saw that Capello watched him with saucer eyes, and he could imagine the misgivings that filled the Venetian Orator's heart as a result of that long interview which had ended in the withdrawal of

Sinibaldi's lady from the feast. Messer Capello should be abundantly entertained, he thought with grim humour, and when the President had returned from escorting the princess to her litter, Cesare raised a finger and signed to the steel-clad antient who stood waiting as he had been bidden.

Barbo clanked forward, and the talk and laughter rippled down to an expectant hush.

'Bring in the Prince Sinibaldi,' Cesare commanded, and therewith he fetched consternation back into that hall.

The portly, slimy Capello was so wrought upon by his perturbation at this command that he heaved himself to his feet, and made so bold as to go round to Cesare's chair.

'Magnificent,' he muttered fearfully, 'what is this of Prince Sinibaldi?'

The Duke flung at him a glance contemptuously over his shoulder.

'Wait, and you shall see,' he said.

'But, my lord, I implore you to consider that the Most Serene...'

'A little patience, sir,' snapped Cesare, and the glance of his eyes drove back the flabby ambassador like a blow. He hung there behind the Duke's chair, very white, and breathing labouredly. His fleshiness troubled him at such times as these.

The double doors were flung open, and Barbo re-entered. He was followed by four men-at-arms of Graziani's condotta, and in their midst walked Prince Sinibaldi, the envoy-extraordinary of the Most Serene Republic. But his air and condition were rather those of a common malefactor. His wrists were still pinioned behind his back; he was without hat or cloak; his clothes were in some disarray, as a result of his struggles, and his mien was sullen.

The company's amazement deepened, and a murmur ran round the board.

At a sign from the Duke the guards fell back a little from their prisoner, leaving him face to face with Cesare.

'Untie his wrists,' the Duke commanded, and Barbo instantly slashed through the prince's bonds.

Conscious of the eyes upon him, the Venetian rallied his drooping spirits. He flung back his head, drew himself up, a tall figure full now of dignity and scorn, his eyes set boldly upon Cesare's impassive face. Suddenly, unbidden, he broke into a torrent of angry speech.

'Is it by your commands, my lord duke, that these indignities are put upon the inviolable person of an envoy?' he demanded. 'The Most Serene whose mouthpiece I have the honour to be, whose representative I am, is not likely to suffer with patience such dishonour.'

Within the Duke's reach stood an orange that had been injected with rose attar to be used as a perfume ball. He took it up in his long fingers and delicately sniffed it.

'I trust,' said he in that quiet voice which he could render so penetrating and so sweetly sinister, 'that I apprehend you amiss when I apprehend that you threaten. It is not wise to threaten us, excellency – not even for an envoy of the Most Serene.' And he smiled upon the Venetian, but with such a smile that Sinibaldi quailed and lost on the instant much of his fine arrogance – as many another bold fellow had done when face to face with the young Duke of Valentinois.

Capello in the background wrung his hands and with difficulty suppressed a groan.

'I do not threaten, my lord…' began Sinibaldi.

'I am relieved to hear it,' said the Duke.

'I protest,' Sinibaldi concluded. 'protest against the treatment I have received. These ruffianly soldiers…'

'Ah,' said the Duke, and again he sniffed his orange. 'Your protest shall have all attention. Never suppose me capable of overlooking anything that is your due. Continue, then, I beg. Let us hear, my lord, your version of the night's affair. Condescend to explain the error of which you have been the victim, and I promise you the blunderers shall be punished. I will punish them the more gladly since it is in my nature not to like blunderers. You were saying that these ruffianly soldiers…' But continue, pray.'

Sinibaldi did not continue. Instead he began at the beginning of the tale he had prepared during the ample leisure that had been accorded him for the task. And it was a crafty tale, most cunningly conceived, and based as all convincing tales should be upon actualities. It was, in fact, precisely such a tale as Graziani might have told had he been there to speak, and being therefore true – though not true of Sinibaldi – would bear testing and should carry conviction.

'I was bidden, Magnificent, in secret tonight to a meeting held at the house of my Lord Ranieri, whose guest it happens that I have been since my coming to Rimini. I went urged by the promise that a matter of life and death was to be dealt with, which concerned me closely.

'I found a small company assembled there, but before they would reveal to me the real purpose of that gathering, they desired me to make an irrevocable oath that whether or not I became a party to the matters that were to be disclosed to me, I would never divulge a single word of it nor the name of any of those whom I met there.

'Now I am not a fool, Magnificent.'

'Who implies it?' wondered Cesare aloud.

'I am not a fool, and I scented treason instantly, as they knew I must. It is to be assumed that by some misconception they had come to think that I had ends to serve by listening to treason, by becoming a party to it. Therein lay their mistake – a mistake that was near to costing me my life, and has occasioned me this indignity of which I complain. I will not trouble your magnificence with my personal feelings. They matter nothing. I am an envoy, and just as I know and expect what is due to me, so do I know and fulfil – what is due from me. These fools should have considered that more fully. Since they did not...'

'God give us patience!' broke in the Duke. 'Will you go over that again? This is mere oratory, sir. Your take, sir – your take. Let the facts plead for you.'

Sinibaldi inclined his head with dignity.

171

'Indeed, your highness is right – as ever. To my tale then. Where was I? Ah, yes!

'When an oath of that nature was demanded of me I would at once have drawn back. But I perceived that already I had gone too far in thoughtlessly joining that assembly and that they would never suffer me to depart again and spread the alarm of what was doing there. They dared not for their lives' sake. So much was clear. Therefore, for my own life's sake, and in self-defence I took the oath imposed. But having taken it, I announced plainly that I desired to hear no more of any plot. I warned them that they were rash in having set their hands to any secret business, and that if – as I conceived – it had for aim your highness' hurt then they were more than rash since your magnificence has as many eyes as Argus. Upon that I begged them to suffer me to depart since I was sworn to silence.

'But men of their sort are easily fearful of betrayal, and do not lay much store by oaths. They refused to consent to my departure, protesting that I was bent upon denouncing them. From words we passed soon enough to blows. They set upon me, and a fight ensued in which one of them fell to my sword. Then the noise of our brawling brought in a patrol – but for which it is odds I should have left my life there. When these soldiers broke in the plotters flung themselves from a window into the river, whilst I remained, having naught to fear since I was innocent of all evil. It was thus that I alone came to be taken by these fellows who would listen to no assurances I offered them.'

From behind the Duke's chair came a deep sigh of relief uttered by the quaking Capello. He advanced a step.

'You see, my lord, you see...' he was beginning.

'Peace, man!' the Duke bade him sharply. 'Be assured I see as far as any man, and need not borrow your eyes to help me, Ser Capello.' Then turning again to Sinibaldi, and speaking very courteously, 'My lord,' he said, 'it grieves me you should have been mishandled by my soldiery. But I trust to your generosity to see that until we had this explanation, the appearances were against you; and you will acquit us, I am sure, of any discourtesy to the Most Serene. Let me add even that in the case of anyone less accredited than yourself, or representing a power upon whose friendship I did not so implicitly depend as I do upon that of Venice,' (he said it with all the appearance of sincerity and with no slightest trace of irony) 'I might be less ready to accept that explanation, and I might press for the names of the men who, you are satisfied, were engaged in treason.'

'Those names, Magnificent, already I should have afforded you but for the oath that binds me,' answered Sinibaldi.

'That too I understand; and so, my lord, out of deference and to mark my esteem of you and of the Republic you represent, I do not ask a question you might have a difficulty in answering. Let us forget this unhappy incident.'

But at that the antient, who loved Graziani as faithful hound its master, was unable longer to contain himself. Was the Duke mad, to accept so preposterous a tale – to swallow this lying fabrication as smoothly and easily as if it were a sugared egg.

'My lord,' he broke in, 'if what he says is true…'

'If?' cried Cesare. 'Who dares to doubt it? Is he not Prince Sinibaldi and the envoy of the Most Serene? Who will cast a doubt upon his word?'

'I will, my lord,' answered the soldier stoutly.

'By the Host! now here's audacity.'

'My lord, if what he says is true then it follows that Messer Graziani was a traitor – for it was Messer Graziani who was wounded in that brawl, and he would have us believe that the man he wounded was one of those that plotted with his innocence.'

'That, quite clearly, is what he has said,' Cesare replied.

'Why then,' said Barbo, and he plucked the rude buffalo gauntlet from his left hand, 'I say that who says that is a liar, whether he be a prince of Venice or a prince of hell.' And he raised the glove he had plucked from his hand, clearly intending to fling it in Sinibaldi's face.

But the Duke's voice checked the intention.

'Hold!' it bade him sharply; and instantly he paused. The Duke looked at him with narrowing eyes. 'You all but did a thing that might have cost you very dear,' he said. 'Get out of my sight, and take your men with you. But hold yourself at my commands outside. We will talk of this again, perhaps tonight, perhaps tomorrow, Messer Barbo. Go!'

Chilled by tone and glance, Barbo stiffened, saluted, then with a malignant scowl at Sinibaldi, clanked down the hall and out, counting himself as good as hanged, yet more concerned with the foul slander uttered against his captain than with any fate that might lie in store for himself.

Cesare looked at Sinibaldi, and smiled. 'Forgive the lout,' he said. 'Honesty, and fidelity to his captain prompted him. Tomorrow he shall be taught his manners. Meanwhile, of your graciousness forget it with the rest. A place for the Prince Sinibaldi here at my side. Come, my lord, let me play host to you, and make you some amends for the rude handling you have suffered. Never blame the master for the stupidity of his lackeys. The Council whose guest I am have spread a noble entertainment. Here is a wine that is a very unguent for wounded souls – a whole Tuscan summer has been imprisoned in every flagon of it. And there is to be a comedy – delayed too long by these untoward happenings. Sir President, what of these players sent from Mantua? The Prince Sinibaldi is to be amused, that he may forget how he has been vexed.'

You see Prince Sinibaldi, then, limp with amazement, shaken by relief from his long tension, scarcely believing himself out of his terrible position, wondering whether perhaps all this were not a dream. He sank into the chair that was placed for him at the Duke's side, he drank of the wine that at the Duke's bidding was poured for him by one of the scarlet lackeys. And then, even as he drank, he almost choked upon the sudden fresh fear that assailed him with the memory of certain stories of Capello's concerning Cesare's craft in the uses of poisons.

But even as in haste he set down his cup and half-turned, he beheld the lackey pouring wine from the same beaker for the venom-taster who stood behind the Duke's chair, and so he was reassured.

The players followed, and soon the company's attention was engrossed entirely by the plot of the more or less lewd comedy they performed. But Sinibaldi's thoughts were anywhere but with the play. He was considering all that had happened, and most of all his present condition and the honour done him by the Duke as a measure of amends for the indignities he had endured. He was a man of sanguine temperament, and gradually his mistrust was dissipated by the increasing conviction that the Duke behaved thus towards him out of dread of the powerful Republic whose representative he was. Hence was he gradually heartened to the extent of conceiving a certain measure of contempt for this Valentinois of such terrible repute, and a certain assurance even that Ranieri and the others would yet carry out the business that had been concerted.

And meanwhile Cesare, beside him, sitting hunched in his chair, his chin in his hand, his eyes intent upon the players, was conscious of as little of the comedy as was Sinibaldi. Had the company been less engrossed its members might have observed how set remained the Duke's countenance, and how vacant. Like Sinibaldi he, too, was concerned, to the exclusion of all else, with the thing that was to be done that night. He was wondering, too, how far the Most Serene itself might have a hand in this murderous affair, how far Sinibaldi might be an agent sent to do this assassin's work. He bethought him of how at every step in his career, and in every way within her power, Venice had betrayed her implacable hostility; he remembered how she had gone to work with the insidious weapons of intrigue and slander to embroil him now with France, now with Spain, and how by arms and money she had secretly reinforced his enemies against him.

Was Sinibaldi, then, but the hand of the Republic in this matter? Plainly it must be so, since Sinibaldi personally could have no cause to seek his life. Sinibaldi then had all the resources of the Republic behind him. He was a tool that must be broken, both because he had lent himself to this infamous treachery, and because in breaking him would lie Cesare's best answer to the Venetian trader-princes.

Yet although he saw plainly what was to do, the means of doing it were none so plain. He must pick his way carefully through this tangle, lest it should enmesh him and bring him down. Firstly he had pledged his princely word that he would do no hurt to Sinibaldi. If possible he would observe the letter of that promise; as for the spirit of it, it were surely unreasonable to expect him to respect that also. Secondly to destroy Sinibaldi without destroying with him his confederates were to leave the treachery not only alive but quickened into activity by the spur of revenge; in such a case his own danger would persist, and if the arbalest bolt were not loosed at him tonight it might come tomorrow or the next day. Thirdly, in dealing with this pack of Venetian murderers he must so go to work as to leave Venice no case for grievance at the result.

So far as Sinibaldi himself was concerned, it must be remembered that the tale he had told so publicly and circumstantially was impossible of refutation save by Graziani – and Graziani was insensible and might not live to refute it, whilst even if he did, it would be but the word of Graziani – a captain of fortune, one of a class never deemed over scrupulous – against the word of Sinibaldi – a patrician and a prince of Venice.

There you have the nice problem by which Cesare found himself confronted and which he considered whilst with unseeing eyes he watched the antics of the players; and you will agree that the solution of it was matter enough to justify his absorption and to call for all the *ingegno* which Macchiavelli, a connoisseur in the matter, so profoundly admired in the Duke.

Light came to him towards the comedy's conclusion. The grim mask of concentration that he had worn was suddenly relaxed, and for a moment his eyes sparkled with almost wicked humour. He flung himself back in his chair, and listened now to the epilogue spoken by the leader of the company. At its close he led the applause by detaching from his girdle a heavy purse, and flinging it down to the players to mark his own appreciation of their efforts. Then he turned to Sinibaldi to discuss with him a comedy of which neither had much knowledge. He laughed and jested with the Venetian as with an equal, overwhelming him by the courtly charm in which no man of his day could surpass the Duke.

v

Came midnight at last – the hour at which it had been arranged that the torchlight procession should set out from the Palazzo Pubblico to escort the Duke back to the famous Rocca of Sigismondo Malatesta, where he was housed. Valentinois gave the signal for departure by rising, and instantly a regiment of grooms and pages hung about him in attendance.

Sinibaldi, facing him, bowed low to take his leave, to go seek his lady whose withdrawal from the banquet had been occasioned, as he had been informed, by his own adventure. But Cesare would not hear of parting from him yet awhile. He thanked Heaven in his most gracious manner for the new friend it had that night vouchsafed him.

'But for this mischance of yours, excellency, we might never have come to such desirable knowledge of each other. Forgive me, therefore, if I cannot altogether deplore it.'

Overwhelmed by so much honour, Sinibaldi could but bow again, in such humility that you might almost hear him murmuring 'Domine non sum dignus!' almost fancy him beating his secretly armoured breast in self-abasement. And, meanwhile, the oily Capello hovering ever nigh, like some tutelary deity, purred and smirked and rubbed his gross white hands that anon should pen more obscenities in defamation of this gracious Valentinois.

'Come, then, excellency,' the Duke continued. 'You shall ride with me to the citadel, and there pledge our next meeting, which may the gods please shall be soon. And Messer Capello here shall be of the party. I take no denial. I shall account your refusal as the expression of a lingering resentment at what has befallen you through no fault of my own, and to my deep mortification. Come, prince. They are waiting for us. Messer Capello, follow us.'

177

On the word he thrust an arm, lithe and supple as a thing of steel, through that of Sinibaldi, and in this fashion the twain stepped down the hall together, and along the gallery between the files of courtiers gathered there to acclaim the Duke. It almost seemed as if Cesare desired that Sinibaldi should share this honour with him, and Capello following immediately upon their heels puffed himself out with pride and satisfaction to see Valentinois doing homage to the Most Serene Republic in so marked a manner through the person of her envoy-extraordinary.

Thus they came out upon the courtyard into the ruddy glare of a hundred flaming torches that turned to orange the yellowing old walls of the Palazzo. Here was great press and bustle of grooms about the cavaliers who were getting to horse and still more about the ladies who were climbing to their litters.

It was here that Cesare and Sinibaldi were met by a pair of the Duke's vermilion pages bearing his cloak and cap.

Now it happened that the cloak, which was fashioned from the skin of a tiger, heavily laced with gold and reversed with yellow satin, was as conspicuous as it was rare and costly. It was a present that the Sultan Bajazet had sent the Borgia out of Turkey, and Cesare had affected it since the cold weather had set in, not only out of his inherent love of splendour, but also for the sake of the great warmth which it afforded.

As the stripling stood before him now presenting that very gorgeous mantle, the Duke swung suddenly upon Sinibaldi, standing at his elbow.

'You have no cloak, my lord!' he cried in deep concern. 'No cloak, and it is a bitter night.'

'A groom shall find me one, Magnificent,' the Venetian answered, and half turned aside to desire Capello give the order for him.

'Ah, wait,' said Cesare. He took the lovely tiger skin from the hands of his page. 'Since not only in these my new dominions, but actually out of loyalty to myself it was that you lost your cloak, suffer me to replace it with this, and at the same time offer you an all unworthy token of the esteem in which I hold your excellency and the Serene Republic which you represent.'

Sinibaldi fell back a single step, and one of the pages told afterwards that on his face was stamped the look of one in sudden fear. He looked deep into the Duke's smiling eyes and perhaps he saw there some faint trace of the mockery which he had fancied that he detected in his smooth words.

Now Sinibaldi, as you will have seen by the promptitude and thoroughness with which he adapted to himself the story of Graziani's misadventure, was a crafty subtle-witted gentleman, quick to draw inferences where once a clue was afforded him.

As he met now that so faintly significant smile of Cesare's, as he pondered the faintly significant tone in which the Duke had spoken, and as he considered the noble gift that was being proffered him, understanding came to him swift, sudden and startling as a flash of lightning in the night.

The Duke had never been deceived by his specious story; the Duke knew the truth; the Duke's almost fawning friendliness – which he, like a fool, had for a while fancied to be due to the Duke's fear of Venice – had been so much make-believe, so much mockery, the play of cat with mouse, the prelude to destruction.

All this he understood now, and saw that he was trapped – and trapped, moreover, with a cunning and a subtlety that made it impossible for him so much as to utter a single word to defend his life. For what could he say? How, short of an open avowal which would be equally destructive to himself, short of declaring that the wearing of that cloak would place him in mortal peril, could he decline the proffered honour?

It came to him in his despair to refuse the gift peremptorily. But then gifts from princes such as the Duke of Valentinois and Romagna are not refused by ambassadors-extraordinary without putting an affront upon the donor, and that not only in their own personal quality but also in a sense, on behalf of the State they represent.

Whichever way he turned there was no outlet. And the Duke smiling ever stood before him, holding out the cloak which to Sinibaldi was the very mantle of death.

And as if this had not been enough, the ineffable Capello must shuffle forward, smirking and rubbing his hands in satisfaction at this supremely gratifying subjection of the Duke to a proper respect for the Most Serene Republic.

'A noble gift, highness!' he purred, 'a noble gift; worthy of your potency's munificence.' Then, with a shaft of malice, he added, that the Duke might know how fully his ulterior motives were perceived and no doubt despised: 'And the honour to Prince Sinibaldi will be held by the Most Serene as an honour to herself.'

'It is my desire to honour both in the exact measure of their due,' laughed Cesare, and Sinibaldi alone, his senses rendered superacute by fear, caught the faintly sinister note in that laugh, read the sinister meaning of those amiable words.

He trembled in the heart of him, cursing Capello for a fool. Then, since he must submit, he took heart of grace. He found courage in hope. He bethought him that after all that had happened that night, it would be more than likely that the conspirators would hold their hands at present, that they would postpone to a more opportune season the thing that was to be done. If so, then all would be well, and Cesare should be confounded yet.

Upon that hope he fastened tenaciously, desperately. He assured himself that he had gone too fast in his conclusions. After all, Cesare could have no positive knowledge; with positive knowledge the Duke would unhesitatingly have proceeded to more definite measures. It was impossible that he should harbour more than suspicions, and all his present intent would be to put those suspicions to the test. If, as Sinibaldi now hoped, Ranieri and his friends held their hands that night, Cesare must conclude that those suspicions had been unfounded.

With such reasonings did the Prince Sinibaldi hearten himself, knowing little of Borgia ways and nothing of Cesare's sworn promise to the princess. He recovered quickly his assurance. Indeed, his vacillation had been but momentary. Meeting dissimulation with dissimulation, he murmured some graceful words of deep gratification, submitted to have the cloak thrust upon him, and even the velvet cap with its bordure of miniver that was also Cesare's own, and which was pressed upon him on the same pretext that had served for the cloak.

Thereafter he allowed himself to drift with the tide of things, like a swimmer who, realizing that the current is too strong for him, ceases to torture himself by the effort of stemming it, and abandons himself, hoping that in its course that current will bring him safe to shore. In this spirit he mounted the splendid Barbary charger with its sweeping velvet trappings which also was Cesare's own, and which became now a further token of his princely munificence.

Yet that fool Capello, looking on, perceived nothing but what was put before his eyes. He licked his faintly sneering lips over this further proof of Cesare's servility to the Republic, and began in his mind to shape the phrases in which he would rejoice the hearts of the Ten with a description of it all.

The prince was mounted, and by his stirrup stood the Duke like any equerry. He looked up at the Venetian.

'That is a lively horse, my lord,' he said at parting, 'a fiery and impulsive child of the desert. But I will bid my footmen hang close upon your flanks, so that they will be at hand in case it should grow restive.' And again Sinibaldi understood the true meaning of those solicitous words, and conceived that he was meant to realize how futile it would be in him to attempt to escape the test to which he was to be submitted.

He bowed his acknowledgement of the warning and the provision, and the Duke stepped back, took a plain black cloak and a black hat from a page who had fetched them in answer to his bidding, and mounted a very simply equipped horse which a groom surrendered to him.

Thus that splendid company rode out into the streets of the town, which were still thronged, for the people of Rimini had waited for the spectacle of this torchlight procession that was to escort the

Duke's potency back to the Rocca of Sigismondo. To gratify the people, the cavalcade went forward at a walking pace, flanked on either side by a file of footmen bearing torches.

Acclamations greeted them, ringing and sincere, for the conquest of Rimini by Cesare Borgia held for the people the promise of liberation from the cruel yoke under which the tyrant Pandolfaccio Malatesta had oppressed them. They knew the wisdom and liberality of his rule elsewhere, and they hailed him now as their deliverer.

'Duca! Duca! Valentino!' rang the cry, and Sinibaldi was perhaps the only one in the cavalcade who remarked that the cry arose in a measure as he himself came into view, that it was at himself – travestied in Cesare's barbaric splendour – that the people looked as they shouted and waved their caps. And so it was, for there were few indeed in those lines of sightseers who perceived that the tall man in the tiger-skin mantle and scarlet and miniver bonnet riding that sumptuously caparisoned horse – the most splendid figure in all that splendid cavalcade – was not the Duke of Valentinois whom they acclaimed; fewer still were there to pay much heed to the man in the black cloak and heavy hat who came next, a few paces behind, riding beside the Orator of Venice, who bestrode a white mule.

Thus the procession made its way across the wide square of the Palazzo Pubblico, and down a narrow street into the main way that runs east and west almost straight across the city from the Bridge of Augustus to the Porta Romana.

At the corner of the Via della Rocca, such was the clamour of the sightseers that none heard the twice repeated twang of an arbalest-cord. Indeed the first intimation the Duke received that the thing he expected had come to pass was when the cavalier in the tiger-skin cloak was suddenly seen to crumple forward upon the neck of his charger.

Instantly the grooms sprang to seize the bridle and support the limp figure of its rider. Those following Cesare – Capello foremost amongst them – reined in upon the instant; and a sudden awe-stricken silence fell upon the assembled crowd, when, notwithstanding the efforts of the grooms, the man whom they imagined to be Cesare Borgia rolled sideways from the saddle into the arms of those below, an arbalest bolt through his brain.

That moment of silent panic was succeeded by an awful cry, a wail which in itself expressed the public fear of the awful vengeance that might follow upon the city:

'The Duke is dead!'

And then in answer to that cry, by some unaccountable magic – as it seemed to the people – there in his stirrups stood the Duke himself, his head bare, his tawny hair glowing ruddily in the torch-light, his brazen voice dominating the din and confusion.

'It is murder!' he proclaimed, and added fiercely the question, 'Who has done this foul deed?' Then he flung an arm towards the corner house on his right. 'In there!' he shouted to his halberdiers who came thrusting towards him through the crowd. 'In, I say, and on your lives see that not a man escapes you. It is the Envoy of Venice whom they have murdered, and they shall pay for it with their necks, whoever they may be.'

In a moment the house was surrounded by Cesare's men-at-arms. The door crashed inwards under the fierce blows of halberds, and the soldiers went in to take the assassins, whilst Cesare pushed on towards the open square before the citadel, all pouring after him, courtiers, grooms and people, in a vociferous disorder.

Before the citadel Cesare drew rein, and his halberdiers cleared a space, and with their long pikes held horizontally formed a barrier against the surging human tide. Other men-at-arms coming presently down the street clove through the press, flinging the mob in waves on either side of them. In their midst these pikemen brought five prisoners taken in that house from which death had been launched upon Prince Sinibaldi.

The captives were dragged forward, amid the furious execrations of the people, into that open space which the halberdiers had cleared, and so brought before the Duke, who stood there waiting to deal out summary justice. Beside him on his mule, bewildered, pale and flabby, was Messer Capello, retained by Cesare, since as the only

183

remaining representative of Venice it concerned him to witness this matter to its end.

He was a dull fellow, this Orator, and it is to be doubted whether he had any explanation of the truth until he had looked into the faces of those five wretches whom the men-at-arms now thrust forward into the Duke's awful presence. It was now, at last, I think, that he understood that Sinibaldi had been mistaken for the Duke and had received in his treacherous brain the bolt intended for Valentinois. Swift upon that realization followed an obvious suspicion. Had the Duke so intended it? Had Cesare Borgia deliberately planned that there should be this mistake? Was it to this end that he had arrayed Sinibaldi in the tiger-skin cloak and ducal cap and set him to ride upon his own charger?

Conviction settled upon Messer Capello; conviction and rage at the manner in which the Duke had fooled them and turned the tables upon Sinibaldi. But there was yet the Most Serene to be reckoned with, and the Most Serene would know how to avenge the death of her envoy; heavy indeed should be the reckoning the Republic would present.

In his rage Messer Capello swung round, threats already on his lips, his arm flung out to give them emphasis. But ere he could speak Cesare had caught by the wrist that out-flung arm of his and held it as in a vice.

'Look,' he bade the envoy. 'Look, Messer Capello! Look at those prisoners. There is my Lord Ranieri, who was the prince's host and announced himself his friend – Ranieri of all men to have done so foul a thing! And those other two, both of them professed friends of Sinibaldi's, too.'

Capello looked as he was bidden, an incipient bewilderment thrusting aside his sudden anger.

'And consider me yet those other two,' the Duke persisted, his voice swelling with passion. 'Both of them in the prince's own livery – his own familiars, his own servants whom no doubt he trusted. Belike their treachery has been bought by these others, these patrician assassins. To what black depths of villainy can man descend!'

Capello stared at the Duke, almost beginning to believe him sincere, so fervidly had he spoken. But, dull fellow though he was, he was not so dull as to be hoodwinked now, nor did the Duke intend it. Cesare desired him to know the truth, yet to know it unuttered.

The Orator saw clear at last. And, seeing clear, he no longer dared to speak the words that had been on his lips, lest by implication they should convict the dead Sinibaldi, and so bring Capello himself under the wrath of the Ten of Venice. He saw it crystal clear that to proclaim that Sinibaldi had been slain in Cesare's place were to proclaim that it was Sinibaldi – and so, presumably, the Most Serene itself – that had planned the murder, since all those taken were Sinibaldi's friends and servants.

Capello, looking into the Duke's eyes, understood at last that the Duke mocked him. He writhed in a boiling wrath that he must for his own sake repress. But that was not all. He was forced to drain to its very dregs the poisonous cup that Cesare had thrust upon him. He was forced to play the dupe; to pretend that he saw in this affair no more than Cesare intended that the world at large should see; to pretend to agree that Sinibaldi had been basely murdered by his friends and servants, and to leave it there.

Swallowing as best he could his rage, he hung his head.

'My lord,' he cried so that all might hear him, 'I appeal to you for justice against these murderers in the name of Venice!'

Thus through the lips of her ambassador, Venice herself was forced to disown these friends of hers – Ranieri and his fellows – and demand their death at the hands of the man whom she had hired them to slay. The tragic irony of it stabbed the Orator through and through, the rage begotten of it almost suffocated him, and was ever afterwards with him all his life to inform his pen when he wrote aught that concerned the House of Borgia.

And Cesare, appreciating the irony no less, smiled terribly into the eyes of the ineffable Capello, as he made answer:

185

'Trust me to avenge this offence against the Most Serene as fully as though it were an offence against myself.'

My Lord Ranieri thereupon shook himself out of the stupor that had numbed his wits when he found Capello deserting and disowning him.

'Magnificent!' he cried, straining forward in the hands that held him, his face distorted with rage at Capello and Venice, whose abandoned cat's-paw he now conceived himself. 'There is more in this that you do not know. Hear me! Hear me first!'

Cesare advanced his horse a pace or two, so that he was directly over the Lord Ranieri. Leaning slightly from his saddle, he looked into the patrician's eyes much as he had looked into Capello's.

'There is no need to hear you,' he said. 'You can tell me nothing that I do not know. Go get you shriven. I will send the hangman for you at dawn.'

He wheeled about, summoned his cavaliers and ladies, his grooms and his guards, and so rode ahead of that procession over the drawbridge into the great Citadel of Sigismondo.

The first citizens about the streets of Rimini upon the morrow beheld in the pale wintry light of that 2 November – appropriately the Day of the Dead – five bodies dangling limply from the balcony of the house whence the bolts had been shot – the justice of the Duke of Valentinois upon the murderers of Prince Sinibaldi!

Cesare Borgia himself paused to survey those bodies a little later, when he passed by with his armed multitudes, quitting Rimini in all the panoply of war to march against the Manfredi of Faenza. The subtlety of his vengeance pleased him. It was lightened by a vein of grim humour that he savoured with relish, thinking of the consternation and discomfiture of the Ten when they should come to hear of it, as hear of it they would in detail from their Orator.

But the cream of the jest was yet to come. It followed a week later at Forli, where the Duke had paused to assemble his condotte for the investment of Faenza.

Thither came Capello, seeking audience on behalf of the Council of Ten. He was the bearer of a letter in which the Most Serene

Republic expressed to the Duke's magnificence her thanks for the summary justice he had measured out to the murderers of their beloved Prince Sinibaldi.

That pleased Valentinois, and it pleased him no less to reflect that he had faithfully kept the letter of his promise to Sinibaldi's lady, and that neither he nor any man of his had so much as laid a finger upon Sinibaldi to avenge the latter's plotting against himself. There was humour in that, too.

Rafael Sabatini

Captain Blood

Captain Blood is the much-loved story of a physician and gentleman turned pirate.

Peter Blood, wrongfully accused and sentenced to death, narrowly escapes his fate and finds himself in the company of buccaneers. Embarking on his new life with remarkable skill and bravery, Blood becomes the 'Robin Hood' of the Spanish seas. This is swashbuckling adventure at its best.

The Gates of Doom

'Depend above all on Pauncefort', announced King James, 'his loyalty is dependable as steel. He is with us body and soul and to the last penny of his fortune.' So when Pauncefort does indeed face bankruptcy after the collapse of the South Sea Company, the king's supreme confidence now seems rather foolish. And as Pauncefort's thoughts turn to gambling, moneylenders and even marriage to recover his debts, will he be able to remain true to the end? And what part will his friend and confidante, Captain Gaynor, play in his destiny?

'A clever story, well and amusingly told' – *The Times*

Rafael Sabatini

The Lost King

The Lost King tells the story of Louis XVII – the French royal who officially died at the age of ten but, as legend has it, escaped to foreign lands where he lived to an old age. Sabatini breathes life into these age-old myths, creating a story of passion, revenge and betrayal. He tells of how the young child escaped to Switzerland from where he plotted his triumphant return to claim the throne of France.

'…the hypnotic spell of a novel which for sheer suspense, deserves to be ranked with Sabatini's best' – *New York Times*

Scaramouche

When a young cleric is wrongfully killed, his friend, Andre Louis, vows to avenge his death. Louis' mission takes him to the very heart of the French Revolution where he finds the only way to survive is to assume a new identity. And so is born Scaramouche – a brave and remarkable hero of the finest order and a classic and much-loved tale of the greatest swashbuckling tradition.

'Mr Sabatini's novel of the French Revolution has all the colour and lively incident which we expect in his work' – *Observer*

Rafael Sabatini

The Sea Hawk

Sir Oliver, a typical English gentleman, is accused of murder, kidnapped off the Cornish coast, and dragged into life as a Barbary corsair. However Sir Oliver rises to the challenge and proves a worthy hero for this much-admired novel. Religious conflict, melodrama, romance and intrigue combine to create a masterly and highly successful story, perhaps best known for its many film adaptations.

The Shame of Motley

The Court of Pesaro has a certain fool – one Lazzaro Biancomonte of Biancomonte. *The Shame of Motley* is Lazzaro's story, presented with all the vivid colour and dramatic characterisation that has become Sabatini's hallmark.

'Mr Sabatini could not be conventional or commonplace if he tried'
 – Standard

TITLES BY RAFAEL SABATINI AVAILABLE DIRECT
FROM HOUSE OF STRATUS

Quantity	£	$(US)	$(CAN)	€
FICTION				
ANTHONY WILDING	6.99	11.50	15.99	11.50
BARDLEYS THE MAGNIFICENT	6.99	11.50	15.99	11.50
BELLARION	6.99	11.50	15.99	11.50
CAPTAIN BLOOD	6.99	11.50	15.99	11.50
THE CAROLINIAN	6.99	11.50	15.99	11.50
CHIVALRY	6.99	11.50	15.99	11.50
THE CHRONICLES OF CAPTAIN BLOOD	6.99	11.50	15.99	11.50
COLUMBUS	6.99	11.50	15.99	11.50
FORTUNE'S FOOL	6.99	11.50	15.99	11.50
THE FORTUNES OF CAPTAIN BLOOD	6.99	11.50	15.99	11.50
THE GAMESTER	6.99	11.50	15.99	11.50
THE GATES OF DOOM	6.99	11.50	15.99	11.50
THE HOUNDS OF GOD	6.99	11.50	15.99	11.50
THE JUSTICE OF THE DUKE	6.99	11.50	15.99	11.50
THE LION'S SKIN	6.99	11.50	15.99	11.50
THE LOST KING	6.99	11.50	15.99	11.50
LOVE AT ARMS	6.99	11.50	15.99	11.50
THE MARQUIS OF CARABAS	6.99	11.50	15.99	11.50
THE MINION	6.99	11.50	15.99	11.50
THE NUPTIALS OF CORBAL	6.99	11.50	15.99	11.50
THE ROMANTIC PRINCE	6.99	11.50	15.99	11.50
SCARAMOUCHE	6.99	11.50	15.99	11.50

ALL HOUSE OF STRATUS BOOKS ARE AVAILABLE FROM GOOD BOOKSHOPS OR
DIRECT FROM THE PUBLISHER:

Internet: **www.houseofstratus.com** including author interviews, reviews, features.

Email: **sales@houseofstratus.com** please quote author, title and credit card details.

TITLES BY RAFAEL SABATINI AVAILABLE DIRECT
FROM HOUSE OF STRATUS

Quantity	£	$(US)	$(CAN)	€
FICTION				
☐ SCARAMOUCHE THE KING-MAKER	6.99	11.50	15.99	11.50
☐ THE SEA HAWK	6.99	11.50	15.99	11.50
☐ THE SHAME OF MOTLEY	6.99	11.50	15.99	11.50
☐ THE SNARE	6.99	11.50	15.99	11.50
☐ ST MARTIN'S SUMMER	6.99	11.50	15.99	11.50
☐ THE STALKING-HORSE	6.99	11.50	15.99	11.50
☐ THE STROLLING SAINT	6.99	11.50	15.99	11.50
☐ THE SWORD OF ISLAM	6.99	11.50	15.99	11.50
☐ THE TAVERN KNIGHT	6.99	11.50	15.99	11.50
☐ THE TRAMPLING OF THE LILIES	6.99	11.50	15.99	11.50
☐ TURBULENT TALES	6.99	11.50	15.99	11.50
☐ VENETIAN MASQUE	6.99	11.50	15.99	11.50
NON-FICTION				
☐ HEROIC LIVES	6.99	11.50	15.99	11.50
☐ THE HISTORICAL NIGHTS' ENTERTAINMENT	6.99	11.50	15.99	11.50
☐ KING IN PRUSSIA	6.99	11.50	15.99	11.50
☐ THE LIFE OF CESARE BORGIA	6.99	11.50	15.99	11.50
☐ TORQUEMADA AND THE SPANISH INQUISITION	6.99	11.50	15.99	11.50

ALL HOUSE OF STRATUS BOOKS ARE AVAILABLE FROM GOOD BOOKSHOPS OR
DIRECT FROM THE PUBLISHER:

Hotline: UK ONLY: 0800 169 1780, please quote author, title and credit card details.
INTERNATIONAL: +44 (0) 20 7494 6400, please quote author, title, and
credit card details.

Send to: House of Stratus Sales Department
24c Old Burlington Street
London
W1X 1RL
UK

Please allow for postage costs charged per order plus an amount per book as set out in the tables below:

	£(Sterling)	$(US)	$(CAN)	€(Euros)
Cost per order				
UK	2.00	3.00	4.50	3.30
Europe	3.00	4.50	6.75	5.00
North America	3.00	4.50	6.75	5.00
Rest of World	3.00	4.50	6.75	5.00
Additional cost per book				
UK	0.50	0.75	1.15	0.85
Europe	1.00	1.50	2.30	1.70
North America	2.00	3.00	4.60	3.40
Rest of World	2.50	3.75	5.75	4.25

PLEASE SEND CHEQUE, POSTAL ORDER (STERLING ONLY), EUROCHEQUE, OR INTERNATIONAL MONEY ORDER (PLEASE CIRCLE METHOD OF PAYMENT YOU WISH TO USE)
MAKE PAYABLE TO: STRATUS HOLDINGS plc

Cost of book(s): _____ Example: 3 x books at £6.99 each: £20.97

Cost of order: _____ Example: £2.00 (Delivery to UK address)

Additional cost per book: _____ Example: 3 x £0.50: £1.50

Order total including postage: _____ Example: £24.47

Please tick currency you wish to use and add total amount of order:

☐ £ (Sterling)   ☐ $ (US)   ☐ $ (CAN)   ☐ € (EUROS)

VISA, MASTERCARD, SWITCH, AMEX, SOLO, JCB:

☐☐☐☐☐☐☐☐☐☐☐☐☐☐☐☐☐☐☐☐

Issue number (Switch only):

☐☐☐

Start Date: **Expiry Date:**

☐☐ / ☐☐   ☐☐ / ☐☐

Signature: _____

NAME: _____

ADDRESS: _____

_____

POSTCODE: _____

Please allow 28 days for delivery.

Prices subject to change without notice.
Please tick box if you do not wish to receive any additional information. ☐

House of Stratus publishes many other titles in this genre; please check our website (**www.houseofstratus.com**) for more details.